FUGITIVE OF FAITH

ENDORSEMENTS

As the voice of Conservative Christian politics in Kansas, I am constantly in the bull's-eye of today's Godless cancel culture. Author David Mathews, through his artistic gift *Fugitive of Faith*, teaches me that I rest comfortably in God's hands. I know this brilliant book will be an incredible gift to you as well. Simply put, *Fugitive of Faith* is a glorious journey through the perils of our progressive society and an honor to read.

STATE SENATOR MARK B. STEFFEN, M.D.

Since all but a handful of states have hate crimes laws on the books, this fictional look at how a Bible-believing pastor might deal with being accused of violating the law and face both criminal charges and devastating real world effects is especially relevant. As recent events in Canada clearly illustrate, a day of reckoning for members of the clergy may not be as far away as some Christians believe it to be. This work will serve as a catalyst for soul searching and spark spirited discussion for Christians in all walks of life!

COURTNEY MONTGOMERY
Political blogger at The Cerebral Conservative

BOOKS BY DAVID MATHEWS

A Future and A Hope
Fugitive of Faith

FUGITIVE OF FAITH

Ambassador International
GREENVILLE, SOUTH CAROLINA & BELFAST, NORTHERN IRELAND

www.ambassador-international.com

Fugitive of Faith

©2021 by David Mathews
All rights reserved

ISBN: 978-1-64960-127-8
eISBN: 978-1-64960-177-3
Library of Congress Control Number: 2021941826

Cover design by Hannah Linder Designs
Interior typesetting by Dentelle Design
Digital edition by Anna Riebe Raats

This is a work of fiction. Names, characters, and incidents are all products of the author's imagination or are used for fictional purposes. Any resemblance to actual events or persons, living or dead, is entirely coincidental. Any mentioned brand names, places, and trademarks remain the property of their respective owners, bear no association with the author or the publisher, and are used for fictional purposes only.

Unless otherwise noted, all Scripture quotations are from the ESV® Bible (The Holy Bible, English Standard Version®), copyright © 2001 by Crossway, a publishing ministry of Good News Publishers. Used by permission. All rights reserved.

Scripture marked KJV taken from King James Version. Public Domain.

Quote from the movie *Sheffey* (Bob Jones University, Unusual Films, Greenville, SC 29614, Sheffey.org), used by permission. All rights reserved.

Unknown. "I Have Decided." Public Domain.

AMBASSADOR INTERNATIONAL
Emerald House
411 University Ridge, Suite B14
Greenville, SC 29601
United States
www.ambassador-international.com

AMBASSADOR BOOKS
The Mount
2 Woodstock Link
Belfast, BT6 8DD
Northern Ireland, United Kingdom
www.ambassadormedia.co.uk

The colophon is a trademark of Ambassador, a Christian publishing company.

DEDICATION

To all those believers who have gone on before and remained
faithful to the end, no matter the cost.

ACKNOWLEDGMENTS

A special thanks to my wife's friend, Sharon Baltzer, for her quote that has come to mean so much to me since I first heard it: *"Step out of the physical into the spiritual; then you will see the eternal, and that will make all the difference!"*

I appreciate my wonderful daughter, Karin, whose military experiences contributed to the development of the main character in this story. Whether you like it or not, sweetheart, you are still one of my heroes.

I would be remiss if I failed to mention the love, encouragement, and support of my precious wife, Donna, who, upon completion of my first book, thought she had endured the last of this writing nonsense.

I am eternally grateful to my Lord and Savior Jesus Christ, Whose daily mercy and steadfast love allow me to be used by Him in spite of my many failures.

"And they all forsook Him, and fled."

Mark 14:50 (KJV)

CONTENTS

CHAPTER ONE
THE "INTERROGATION"

PETE HOLLOWAY HAD ALWAYS CONSIDERED himself a brave man. He had the reputation of being a straight shooter who faced difficulties and challenges head on, a person with a keen sense of right and wrong who displayed solid integrity and moral fortitude, one who always, at least in his own mind, stood up for what he believed to be just and equitable.

After all, he'd earned that reputation, hadn't he? Enlisting in the Army following high school, he'd served four years with the 101st Airborne. Then after college, on the heels of the tragic events of 9/11, he'd voluntarily re-enlisted and was deployed during the Iraq War, earning a Purple Heart for being wounded by shrapnel from an IED. He'd survived a faith crisis at age thirty and had beaten testicular cancer at age thirty-two while in seminary. Yes, for all intents and purposes, Pete Holloway was a brave man.

Then why were his palms so sweaty? He tightly gripped the wheel of his well-maintained, late model sedan as he drove through heavy traffic along Alemany Boulevard. Rush hour had nothing to do with the nausea he was feeling. Having lived in the heart of San Francisco most of his life, he was used to navigating the vehicle-choked arteries that crisscrossed the city without giving it a second thought. Then what could be causing these unwanted manifestations of nerves? His thoughts accelerated past his feelings and arrived at his destination, the Ingleside Station of the San Francisco Police Department.

"We'd like you to come down to the station and answer a few questions, that's all," a Detective Branch had told him over the phone. He'd been intentionally vague when asked what the questions were about. "No need to worry," the officer had assured him, "we'd like to get some information from you, that's all. Just a matter of routine." But Pete had detected a somewhat artificial casualness in the man's tone.

He eased his car into a parking space in front of the station and killed the engine. It was then that he noticed his heart beating a little more rapidly than normal. Shame and anger flooded his mind for showing such weakness.

"There's nothing to be concerned about," he said out loud, trying to convince himself. "I'll just go in, answer their questions as truthfully as possible, and that will be that. Just like the man said." He'd done nothing wrong, certainly nothing to warrant the case of nerves he was experiencing at the moment. He was merely overreacting, that's all. But even that thought troubled him. He was usually not one to overreact. This was not like him. He needed to get a grip.

After stating his name to the desk sergeant, he was ushered into a small room. He'd seen a thousand rooms like this in the movies and on TV: an eight-foot cube containing three chairs and a small desk, nothing more. He glanced up at the corner of the ceiling and was not surprised to see the camera staring back at him. After what seemed like an eternity, a man in his late thirties with slicked-back hair and wearing a sport shirt and khaki pants entered the room with a manila file folder in one hand.

"Mr. Holloway?"

"Yes?"

The man closed the door behind him. "I'm Detective John Branch," he announced, flashing his badge as evidence.

Pete stood up and shook the officer's hand. "Pete Holloway."

"Sit down, please." His tone was familiarly cordial. Both men sat facing each other across the desk.

Feeling the need to regain some of his confidence, Pete initiated the conversation. "I thought you had to have *two* detectives present when interrogating a suspect."

The detective studied him briefly, then laughed lightly. "We usually do, but this isn't an interrogation. And you're not a suspect. I just have a few questions I'd like for you to answer, that's all."

"Well, I mean to cooperate any way I can," Pete affirmed, "but you were rather vague on the phone. I'm not sure why I'm here."

Detective Branch offered no explanation. Instead, he folded his hands across his stomach, leaned back as far as he could in his chair, and led with his first question. "You're a minister, is that correct?"

Pete blinked in surprise. "Um . . . yes, I'm the pastor of Diamond Heights Baptist Church on East Addison Avenue."

"And how long have you held that title in that particular church?"

"For the past thirteen years."

"Am I right to assume that the primary responsibility of a man in your position is conducting the public meetings? Giving speeches to those in attendance and that sort of thing?"

"I preach a sermon during our gatherings, yes." Something told him not to expound on that answer.

"And can you tell me what resource materials you use for your speeches? Your, um . . . sermons?"

Pete shifted uneasily in his seat and cleared his throat. "Mr. Branch, can you tell me why SFPD needs that information?"

The detective bristled noticeably. "I'll ask the questions for the time being, if you don't mind, Mr. Holloway. Now, about your resource materials . . ."

Pete chose his words carefully. "Well, my primary source is the Bible, of course. I believe God's Word is our sole and final authority for all matters of faith and practice. But I also use commentaries, concordances, lexicons, and books by other authors and theologians as support material." He gave a nervous little laugh. "I don't see what this line of questioning could possibly have to do with police business."

Detective Branch stared hard at him for a moment. "Well then, let me shed some light on that for you." He opened the folder lying on the desk in front of him and shuffled through the papers inside. "Have you heard about the Hate Speech Reparation and Elimination Act?"

Pete stared at the folder on the desk and tensed noticeably. His pulse quickened and his face flushed. So that was what this was all about! Forcing himself to return the detective's unwavering gaze, he prayed his true feelings wouldn't betray the confident tone of his reply. "Of course, I've heard about it. I received the official letter like every other member of the clergy in this state."

"Then you're familiar with the contents of that letter, as well as the full intent of the law."

"Well, yes, I believe so. As much as I can recall, anyway."

"Then allow me to refresh your memory." The detective held out a paper. "Would you mind reading the highlighted section for me? Just so we're both on the same page." He offered what appeared to be an insincere smile.

Pete took the paper from him and began reading. "'The purpose of HB231 is to eradicate all forms of hate speech in the public domain by mandating reeducation, community service, and/or penalties ranging from fines to incarceration for those convicted of this heinous crime. "Hate speech" is defined as any speech that attacks or disparages a person or group on the basis of race, religion, ethnic origin, national origin, sex, disability, sexual orientation, or gender identity. An "attack" may be defined as any statement, either verbal or written, that reflects intolerance toward or denunciation of any individual or group listed above. This includes, but is not limited to, any religious expression that is in conflict with this bill.'"

He glanced up at Detective Branch. The man sat there smugly silent; his lips tightly pressed together. Finally, the officer posed his next question. "Mr. Holloway, are your church services open to the general public?"

Pete felt a tingling sensation shoot down his spine. He nodded. "Yes, of course. We welcome all those who attend our services. We don't turn anyone away." His voice intensified. "And we don't discriminate against anyone seeking to visit our church, if that's what you're driving at."

Ignoring Pete's last comment, the detective made his point. "Then based on that fact, anything you say or preach in those meetings is considered part of the public domain, and therefore falls under the jurisdiction of this bill, does it not?"

Pete hesitated. "That depends on your definition of 'public domain'. Preaching in a church building to a voluntary gathering isn't the same as preaching out on a street corner, or in a public park, or at some civic event where people are forced to listen to what you have to say against their will."

The officer was unfazed. "According to the terminology in the bill, doesn't the public domain include church services that are open to the general public?"

Pete was still reluctant to agree. "Um . . . according to the terminology in the bill, I'd have to say . . . yes." A sudden sharpness creased his voice. "But I can tell you that I don't agree with it!"

Detective Branch shot him a thinly veiled look of amusement. "Your opinion is irrelevant as far as the state is concerned. I'm sure you're aware that the governor signed HB231 into law last October."

"I'm well aware of that. But I still don't see what this has to do with me."

"Then I'll get right to the heart of the matter, Mr. Holloway." The officer pulled a report from the stack of papers in front of him. "An official complaint has been filed with this station by someone accusing you of making certain statements in one of your recent public meetings. Statements that, according to this law, are classified as hate speech."

Stunned, Pete sat frozen in his chair. "I've been accused of hate speech? You've got to be kidding! I've never preached hate, or anything that even comes close to that." He squared his shoulders and frowned at the man sitting across from him. "What exactly am I accused of saying? And when was I to have made these . . . these alleged illegal statements?"

The detective glanced at the report in his hand. "Two weeks ago, on March twenty-third, during your Sunday morning service."

Pete's mind flashed back over the past few weeks. What did he say that might remotely have been considered hateful? And who could possibly have taken offense to it? He remembered greeting several visitors in the congregation recently. A middle-aged married couple had even come back two weeks in a row. But they didn't strike him as the type who would want to get him into trouble.

"Mind telling me who filed those charges? I have the legal right to confront my accuser, don't I?"

The officer dismissed the question with a wave of his hand. "This isn't a court of law, Mr. Holloway, just an interview. Anyway, didn't you read the whistle blower provision?"

"Whistle blower provision?" Pete fought but failed to suppress his irritation. "Please, do refresh my memory!"

Ignoring the comment, Detective Branch read from a paper in the folder. "Anyone filing a complaint under HB231 is granted full immunity and anonymity to avoid harassment and retribution by the accused." He returned to the business at hand. "Do you recall what you preached on the morning in question?"

"Offhand, yes. But I can't quote myself verbatim. I'd have to listen to the tape of the message to be sure."

The detective looked as pleased as a hound dog that had just treed a raccoon. "Well, apparently someone in your audience had the same idea." He paused to let that statement sink in. Then he pulled a small recording device from the drawer and set it on the desk between them. "Do you want to hear what you said?"

Pete felt set up and used. His face flushed with anger. "Of course I want to hear it!" he snapped. "I'm dying to know what I said that someone found so offensive." With a slight smirk, the officer pushed the play button. Pete leaned forward, eager to catch every one of his own words.

"Turn in your Bibles, if you will, to Romans chapter one. Romans chapter one. Last week we began our journey through the Apostle Paul's letter to the church in Rome by covering verses one through seventeen. If you recall, that section concluded with the statement that through the gospel, God's righteousness is revealed to those who believe. In today's passage, Paul shifts his focus from the *righteousness* of God to the *wrath* of God, which is revealed from heaven against all ungodliness. What follows is a clear and unmistakable description of the lifestyles of those who suppress the truth and exchange it for a lie. Follow along as I read verses eighteen through thirty-two."

Detective Branch hit the pause button. "I won't make you listen to your whole sermon. I'll just replay the most disturbing parts."

"Yes, please do!" Pete replied tersely, not bothering to hide the sarcasm. The man pushed "play" again.

"God has clearly revealed Himself to the ungodly so that they are without excuse. He calls them fools. Three times Paul uses the phrase *'God gave them up.'* In verse twenty-four He gave them up to the lusts of their impure hearts; in verse twenty-six He gave them up to dishonorable passions; and in verse twenty-eight He gave them up to a debased mind. But it is not only God who does the giving up. Those who reject Him also give up something as well. In verse twenty-five they give up the truth for a lie. And in verses twenty-six and seven they give up natural sexual desires for those contrary to nature. But their rebellion against God doesn't stop there. Verses twenty-nine and thirty say '*They were filled with all manner of unrighteousness, evil, covetousness, malice. They are full of envy, murder, strife, deceit, maliciousness. They are gossips, slanderers, haters of God, insolent, haughty, boastful, inventors of evil, disobedient to parents, foolish, faithless, heartless, ruthless.*' That's quite an extensive list, isn't it? The downward spiral starts with the rejection of God's truth for Satan's lie. But the rebellion of the ungodly degenerates quickly as God gives them over to many debased, sinful desires of the flesh. It culminates with their own destruction. Verse thirty-two states, and I quote, '*those who practice such things deserve to die.*'"

The detective stopped the recording and leaned back in his chair. "Well? What do you have to say to that?"

"I didn't say anything that could be classified as hate speech, certainly not toward any individual or group," Pete responded defensively. "I merely preached what the Bible says. Nothing more, nothing less."

Detective Branch raised his eyebrows and his voice. "In your own words you attacked those who don't believe like you. You called them fools, dishonorable, debased, unnatural, evil. And you even said these people deserve to *die*! If that isn't hate speech, I don't know what is."

Pete shook his head. "Those aren't my words. Those statements didn't originate with me. I read what God thinks about sin. If I may be so bold as to say it, Mr. Branch, your beef isn't with me. It's with God and His Word."

The officer glowered at him before responding. "Then perhaps the Bible itself should be banned as hate speech." Pete started to reply but thought better of it. "Let me play another segment of your sermon for you." He pushed "play" again.

"Paul addresses this topic in his letter to the Corinthian church as well. In First Corinthians six he unequivocally states, ' . . . *do you not know that the unrighteous will not inherit the kingdom of God? Do not be deceived: neither the sexually immoral, nor idolaters, nor adulterers, nor men who practice homosexuality, nor thieves, nor the greedy, nor drunkards, nor revilers, nor swindlers will inherit the kingdom of God.'*"

Pete spoke up before his interviewer could comment. "Again, that's a passage straight out of Scripture. Those words are the Apostle Paul's, not mine."

"If you want to believe that rhetoric yourself, fine," the detective retorted. "If you want to share it in a closed meeting, fine. The state doesn't have a problem with that. That falls under your right to free speech. But when you preach those ideals publicly, that's an entirely different matter. Then it falls under the state's jurisdiction. What you said publicly is nothing short of hateful and offensive."

"I'll admit that some people might take offense to the words of the Bible, there's no denying that," Pete replied. "Paul also said in First Corinthians, '*the word of the cross is folly to those who are perishing, but to us who are being saved it is the power of God.'*"

"So, you're saying those who don't believe like you or who are offended by your words are going straight to hell?"

"Disagreeing with me doesn't send anyone to hell. Rejecting Christ does. Those who rebel against God will be offended by His Truth. Those are not my words, Mr. Branch, they're Paul's."

The detective cocked his head to one side. "Then maybe you should be more careful who you quote in public from now on.

And maybe you should choose your sermon passages a little more wisely."

"I don't believe I'm hearing this!" Pete was incredulous. He pursed his lips and shook his head. "Sir, I can't do what you're suggesting. The entire Bible is God's Word. We're told that *all* Scripture is breathed out by God, and therefore profitable for teaching, reproof, correction, and training in righteousness."

"I never said you couldn't preach about things that are 'profitable'. But there is nothing profitable, or positive, or even, to use your own terminology, *'righteous'* about calling individuals or groups 'ungodly people who deserve to die and go to hell' simply because their lifestyles, beliefs, or standards differ from yours. You're singling them out and disparaging them. Some might even say your words are inciting violence against them. That's hate speech in anybody's book."

Pete fought to control his voice. "God alone has the authority to define what is righteous and what is not."

"*Whose* God, Mr. Holloway? Yours, perhaps. But I'm quite sure the Muslims, Hindus, Buddhists, the LGBTQ community, and anyone else who doesn't hold to the same religious and moral standards as you would be highly offended by your words. And rightfully so. Besides, how can you be so callous as to include those who are suffering from alcoholism in your judgmental list of evil people? Alcoholism is an unfortunate disease, for goodness' sake. They can't help it. Can't you see the obvious intolerance, bigotry, and hatefulness in your words?"

"Mr. Branch, if you would just listen to the rest of the sermon, you'd know that I also said there is *hope* for the ungodly," Pete pleaded his case. "Yes, God condemns all sinners because we're all without excuse. But He offers His salvation as the only way to avoid

His wrath and judgment. Then Paul goes on to say, "*And such were some of you. But you were washed, you were sanctified, you were justified in the name of the Lord Jesus.*" It's true that sin brings judgment, and sinners deserve death, but Christ offers the only way to complete forgiveness, eternal life, and true righteousness. That's not hate at all. If anything, that's *hope!*"

The detective leaned his elbows on the desk and replied forcefully. "Mr. Holloway, I'm not here to debate theology with you. I'm here to see that you comply with the law." His demeanor gradually softened, and a slight smile crossed his face. "But if you must know, I *did* listen to the rest of your sermon. Every word of it. Several times, in fact." He cleared his throat. "Look, you're obviously a man of conviction and character. I'm sure your statements, however flawed, were made with the best of intentions. And I seriously doubt you meant to offend anyone, much less break the law." He leaned back in his chair. "I'll tell you what I'm going to do. Since this is the first offense that I'm aware of, I'm going to be lenient with you. The state believes in giving people who unintentionally break the law a second chance."

"Well, it's certainly good to know at least *one* of us has some tolerance!" Pete blurted out sarcastically, before chastising himself for letting the cutting remark slip past his lips and out into the public domain.

Detective Branch shot him an amused grin. Then he withdrew a paper from the file and slid it toward the pastor. "We're willing to give you the benefit of the doubt and overlook this unfortunate incident if you're willing to sign this Voluntary Compliance Agreement."

Pete picked up the one-page form and eyed it warily. "What is this exactly?"

"It simply states that you voluntarily agree to abide by the laws of the state of California in this matter." The man flashed a disarming smile. "If my memory serves me correctly, doesn't your Bible also tell you to obey those who have authority over you?"

"Sure, as long as that obedience doesn't conflict with the rest of God's Word."

"Then you should have no problem signing that agreement. It's really just a formality, that's all."

Pete silently scanned the document for a few minutes. Then he glanced up at the detective. "And if I elect *not* to sign this, what then?"

"You're under no obligation to sign anything, Mr. Holloway. In fact, you can get up and walk out of here any time you choose. But I'd strongly advise against that if I were you," he cautioned, shaking his head. "The state is committed to taking a hard line with those who refuse to comply with this law. If you won't sign that agreement, let's just say, ah . . . things will *not* go well for you."

"And just what do you mean by that cryptic threat?" Pete demanded sharply.

The officer held up both palms. "No threat intended. I was merely stating the facts. If you choose not to sign the agreement, then you would be looking at some rather stiff fines and mandatory participation in the state's reeducation program. Additionally, it's possible that you could be required to submit all future sermons to the Public Speech Compliance Council for pre-approval."

Pete stared at him in disbelief. "You've got to be kidding! You'd force me to have my sermons censored by the state? Mr. Branch, this isn't Communist China, or the Cold War Soviet Union we live in. This is America, the land of the free. Last time I checked, that included free speech."

Detective Branch nodded. "I totally understand your frustration, Mr. Holloway. But I don't make the laws. I just enforce them."

"What if I refuse to submit my sermons to the state and continue preaching the Scriptures according to my conscience?"

"Depending on the frequency and severity of future offenses, you could be looking at serving time as well as the possible confiscation of your church property." He paused to let the full weight of his statement sink in.

Pete ran his hand through his hair and let the air slowly escape his lungs. The detective studied him briefly, and then softened his tone again.

"Mr. Holloway, I know you don't want the current situation to escalate into something more serious than it already is. And to be honest with you, neither do I. But my hands are tied. I'm sworn to uphold the law. I'm sure you can understand the position I'm in here. However, you should know that the state *does* offer leniency toward those who have a signed copy of that agreement in their files. You wouldn't have to look over your shoulder all the time."

Pete stared at the paper in his hands. He did not want to sign it. If he did, wouldn't that be the same as admitting he agreed with the law? Wouldn't he be setting himself up for more serious charges? On the other hand, he didn't relish the thought of being in the crosshairs of the state.

Apparently aware of the internal struggle going on in front of him, Detective Branch added, "And I can promise you, as long as it's on file, you will not have to submit your sermons for pre-approval, nor will your church be targeted for compliance." He paused for emphasis. "Your word is good enough for us."

He certainly wasn't going to let the state sensor his sermons! But he also didn't want to put the church under the microscope of further scrutiny. That would be detrimental to the ministry he'd worked so hard to establish over the past thirteen years. Besides, those fines would not be a good stewardship of the Lord's money. He carefully read through the agreement while the detective waited silently. This would allow him to continue preaching without further government interference. Wasn't that better than not having a church to preach in at all?

Sighing heavily, he reluctantly accepted the pen offered him, and with a slight tremble in his hand signed his signature to the bottom of the agreement.

Feeling like an inmate released from a claustrophobic prison cell, Pete walked out of the Ingleside police station and deeply inhaled the late afternoon air. He rubbed his neck to relieve the physical tension. Then he got in his car and drove home. But something deep within his spirit told him he'd just made a very grave mistake.

CHAPTER TWO
WAITING FOR THE
OTHER SHOE TO DROP

AS PETE ENTERED THE KITCHEN of his modest Diamond Heights home from the attached garage, the tantalizing aroma of baked chicken and fresh, hot cornbread welcomed him. His wife, Angela, wearing two quilted oven mitts, was in the process of removing a glass baking dish from the oven.

"Hi, babe!" she said, tossing him a warm smile. "You're just in time for dinner." She gave him a light peck on the cheek before she disappeared into the adjacent dining room, transporting the hot dish as delicately as if it were a golden crown sitting on a red velvet pillow. He headed upstairs to change shirts and wash up, stopping briefly in front of his daughter's open bedroom door. She was sitting at her desk doing homework.

"Dinner's ready, pumpkin," he announced.

Twelve-year-old Brienna glanced up from her schoolbooks. "Oh, hi, Daddy! I'll be right there."

"Would you mind calling your brother?" Pete asked, as he headed into his bedroom.

"Okay."

After washing his hands, Pete entered the hallway just as Brienna pounded on her older sibling's door.

"Drew!" she yelled. "Dinner!"

Not bothering to wait for a reply, she opened the door and popped her head into his room. Pete watched silently from the hallway. His seventeen-year-old son was lying on his side on the bed, back to the door, tapping a pencil on an open textbook in time with the music that escaped from his headphones.

"Drew!" she yelled again, but he didn't miss a beat. Brienna looked around and grabbed one of his tennis shoes lying near the door. She tossed it at him, hitting him squarely in the back.

"Ow!" Drew jerked around, yanked off his headphones, and glared at his sister. "Cut it out, will ya?"

"Dinner is ready," she informed him, in a syrupy-sweet voice. "We are having chicken casserole and cornbread, just in case you are wondering."

"I can smell for myself, thank you very much," he shot back sarcastically. "I don't need your help."

Brienna picked up her brother's other shoe, sniffed it, and made a sour face. "You sure don't. You smell bad enough all by yourself!" She burst into peals of laughter. Pete couldn't help chuckling.

Drew threw his other shoe back at her, but she ducked, and it bounced harmlessly off the door. He leaped off the bed and made a beeline for his sister. Laughing and squealing simultaneously, she fled past her father into the hallway with her brother close behind. Pete watched his two offspring go thumping down the stairs and heard them race into the living room. Their laughter informed him that his intervention was not needed this time.

He followed his children downstairs and took a seat at the dining room table just as Angela entered from the kitchen with a steaming plate of cornbread. As she set it on the table, Brienna skipped into the room and hopped into a chair, her tied-back hair swishing like a horse's tail in deer fly season.

"Chicken casserole. Yesssss!"

"Did you wash your hands?" her mother asked, as if she already knew the answer.

"Oops, sorry." The gangly seventh grader hopped out of her chair and skipped into the kitchen.

A few minutes later, the four Holloways were seated around the dinner table, holding hands as Pete offered the blessing. "Lord, we thank You for Your love, and grace, and abundant provision. Thank You for our family, our friends, and our church. You have given us so much. We're truly grateful for every good gift that comes from above. Bless this food to our bodies and us in Your service. In Jesus' name, amen."

Angela served up the casserole and cornbread to her hungry children, then to her husband and herself. The usual mealtime chatter followed. Familiar topics such as school, homework, sports, and friends were all thoroughly discussed. Pete did his best to stay engaged, but his mind was elsewhere. He picked halfheartedly at his food. During a lull in the conversation, Angela glanced across the table at her husband, who was silently staring down at his plate and toying with his meal.

She watched him for a minute. "Are you all right, babe?" Her concern revealed itself in her tone and face. "You haven't said much tonight. You look tired."

Pete jerked his head up and returned to the present. "Tired? Yeah, I guess I do feel pretty wiped out."

"Stressful day at the church?"

"You might say that."

"Aren't you hungry? You usually love my chicken casserole."

"Your casserole's fine, Ange, as usual." He forced a smile. "Nothing wrong with the meal. I . . . I've just got something on my mind, that's all." He drew a deep breath. "I was going to share it with you later tonight, but I might as well tell you now. I was studying for Sunday's message this morning in the office when a call came into the church from SFPD. They asked if I would come down to the Ingleside Station this afternoon to answer a few questions. That's why I was a little late getting home."

Drew's eyes widened. "The cops hauled you in for questioning?"

Pete arched an eyebrow and then faked a frown. "Um . . . they *called* me in for questioning, Drew, not *hauled* me in. Big difference!"

Drew grinned. "So what did you do, Dad? Witness a murder? Or steal from the offering plate last week?"

Pete managed to keep a straight face. "Son, you've got me there. I have to confess—it was the offering plate. But when I told them it was to pay for all those expensive basketball shoes you keep growing out of, they said they completely understood and let me off with a warning this time." His confession elicited laughter from his two children.

"What kind of questions?" Angela pressed. "What did they want?"

Pete thought about whitewashing his narrative of the "interview" but decided to be forthright. They'd always discussed things as a family, and this was definitely an issue that would very likely affect them all. "Well, they asked me about my pastoral responsibilities and wanted to know how I come up with my sermons."

His wife shook her head. "Why in the world would they want to know about that?"

"Um . . . it has something to do with that bill that was signed into law last year. You know, the one intending to clamp down on hate speech."

"What?" Angela scrunched up her nose. "*That* horrible bill?" Then she frowned. "I don't get it. What does that have to do with your sermons?" Her face suddenly turned ashen. "No way! Pete, someone didn't turn you in for preaching hate speech, did they?"

Pete glanced around the table at his family. "I'm afraid so," he admitted reluctantly.

Brienna broke into the conversation with a shaky voice. "Daddy, are you in trouble? Are they going to arrest you?" Worry lines creased her usually cheerful face.

He smiled to ease her fear. "No, pumpkin, they're not going to arrest me." He tried to lighten the mood. Leaning back in his chair, he pointed both thumbs at his chest. "Does your old man look like a criminal to you?"

Brienna laughed and shook her head vigorously, sending her ponytail smacking across her face.

Drew leaned forward on his elbows. "What bill are you talking about, Dad?"

"It's called the Hate Speech Reparation and Elimination Act. It's supposed to deter hate speech in the public domain by imposing strong penalties on whoever the state considers to be guilty."

Drew shrugged his shoulders. "Well, that doesn't sound like a bad thing to me. I mean, stopping hate speech is a good thing, right?" He turned to his mother. "So why did you call it a horrible bill?"

His mother replied with conviction. "Because the wording in that bill is far overreaching. It defines hate speech in such broad terms that it infringes on people's religious freedom and right to free speech. And it allows the state to determine what churches can and can't preach from their pulpits."

"Well, *that's* not good," Drew acknowledged. He turned to his father. "But I've never heard you preach hate speech from the pulpit before. Why'd they call you in?"

"Drew, this bill defines hate speech as any attack on a person or group based on their race, religion, gender, sexual orientation, etc. You know, all the usual classifications. But the problem lies with the broad power the state has given itself to define an 'attack'. Anything disparaging or negative written or spoken in public, which now includes church services, is considered public hate speech against anyone in those protected groups. For example, if I state from the pulpit that God defines marriage as a union between a man and a woman, or quote Scriptures that say homosexuality is unnatural and those who practice such things will not inherit the kingdom of God, that's an attack against the LGBTQ community. If I call abortion murder, that's an attack against women and women's rights. And if I preach passages that say Jesus is the only way or the door, and anyone seeking to enter heaven by any other means is a thief and a robber, that's an attack against all other religions." He paused to take a breath. "Get the picture?"

Drew nodded as he digested his father's words.

Brienna spoke up. "Seems to me they left out a group on their list."

"What group is that, Brie?"

"Christians, Daddy. Why aren't attacks against Christians protected by that law?"

Pete glanced at his wife and raised his eyebrows before replying to his daughter. "The law is supposed to apply to *all* religions, honey. But you may have a point there. Much of the enforcement seems to be disproportionately aimed at *Christianity*, doesn't it? A Christian quotes the Bible and is accused of hate speech, while some other religions deny women their basic rights or call for the annihilation of entire people groups and seem to get away with it."

Brienna scrunched up her face. "That's not fair!"

"I'm glad you see that, Brie," her mother chimed in. "But we have to remember one thing. Those who don't know Jesus don't know Truth. It doesn't make sense to them yet. And they might be offended by what they don't understand."

For a brief moment, Pete was back in the interview room. "*The word of the cross is folly to those who are perishing, but to us who are being saved it is the power of God.*" Then he was back in the dining room again. How wonderful it was to be on the side of Truth and know the power of God. He gazed appreciatively at his spouse. And how wonderful it was to have a wife who was on the same side!

"I am really glad you brought that up at the table," Angela praised him, as she squeezed a dab of mint-flavored toothpaste onto her toothbrush.

Standing in front of his side of the double vanity, Pete attempted to floss while replying. "I debated waiting . . . until now to tell you, but . . . I . . . decided it was best that the family . . . know what's going on."

"Well, I think it was the right decision. Plus, it was a great learning opportunity for Drew and Brie. They need to be aware of what's going on in the world, aware of the challenges we're facing in our country, and in our own state." She ran her toothbrush under the faucet and began brushing her teeth.

"I agree," Pete mumbled. He finished flossing and stared at himself in the mirror for a while. "But somehow I get the impression there are going to be more 'learning opportunities' coming our way. Maybe sooner than we think."

Angela turned to him, foaming green and white at the mouth. "What do you mean by that? Don't you think they'll leave us alone like they promised?"

"To be honest, no I don't," Pete replied firmly. "All I have is one detective's promise. Not that having it in writing would make much difference, mind you. The state has the law on its side and intends to enforce it to the fullest extent."

After completing their nighttime ritual, the couple climbed into bed and turned out the light. They lay quietly in the dark for several minutes before Pete addressed the ceiling. "I think I may have made a mistake signing that compliance agreement!"

Angela turned on her bedside lamp and rolled onto her side to face her husband. "You did what you thought was best at the time. What else could you do?" She placed her hand on his chest. "Let's not worry about it for now, okay, babe? Maybe nothing will come of it.

You'd think the police would have more important things to do than monitor every single preacher in the state."

Pete pulled his wife close, grateful for her support. "Yeah, you're probably right. For all I know, it might have been a bluff anyway. Just a scare tactic to get me to comply." He planted a kiss on her forehead. "Besides, what would they want with me, anyway? What am I to SFPD? Small potatoes, that's all. One little flea on a mongrel." He suddenly chuckled.

"What's so funny?" Angela wondered, looking up into his face.

"I just thought of what David said when King Saul was chasing him."

"What's that?"

"He said, 'Who has the King of Israel come out against? Who are you pursuing? A dead dog. A single flea!'" Pete chuckled again. "I'm just one insignificant flea on a dead dog!" They shared a hearty laugh together. After the day he'd had, laughing felt really, really good. Angela kissed him, then reached over and turned out the lamp. For a full minute they lay on their backs, holding hands.

Suddenly her voice pierced the darkness. "Babe, I may not know what's going to happen tomorrow, but right now I do know one thing for sure."

"What's that?"

She gave his hand a squeeze. "You're the *hottest* flea on that dog!"

In the days and weeks that followed the Ingleside interview, Pete went about his church business: studying for upcoming sermons, conducting worship services, chairing deacons' meetings, and visiting sick church members. He preached a funeral service for an elderly woman who'd been in a care facility for many years and met several times with a young couple interested in premarital counseling. But while his schedule was filled with the usual responsibilities, a new uneasiness hovered over him like a gray cloud on an otherwise sunny day. After his meeting with Detective Branch, Pete had informed his deacons about the situation, but the lively and lengthy discussion that followed concluded with the consensus that there was nothing more to be done about it for the time being.

He sat in the sanctuary of his office one Tuesday morning, thinking. To date he'd not uncovered the identity of the person responsible for the complaint against him. How would he go about making inquiries of that nature? As a pastor, he just couldn't come right out and publicly ask his congregation if they had an idea who the culprit might have been. And he couldn't very well ask individuals privately, either. That would certainly precipitate all kinds of rumors and gossip and finger pointing which might culminate in an ugly and unwanted church split. Then where would that leave his ministry?

Although he loathed himself for it, he'd grown suspicious of visitors in the services. Were they genuinely interested in the church, or were they police informants checking on his compliance with the law? He'd resolved to continue preaching the truth of God's Word without apology or alteration, so if anyone were there for nefarious reasons, it would be only a matter of time before he received another phone call or a letter requesting his presence down at the police station again, maybe even demanding it this time. There was a big difference between calling him in for questioning and hauling him in for noncompliance! This waiting for the other shoe to drop was growing wearisome.

For encouragement and inspiration, Pete opened his big study Bible on the desk and flipped through its thin pages, stopping at the sixth chapter of Daniel. He began reading aloud:

> "It pleased Darius to set over the kingdom 120 satraps, to be throughout the whole kingdom; and over them three high officials, of whom Daniel was one, to whom these satraps should give account, so that the king might suffer no loss. Then this Daniel became distinguished above all the other high officials and satraps, because an excellent spirit was in him. And the king planned to set him over the whole kingdom. Then the high officials and the satraps sought to find a ground for complaint against Daniel with regard to the kingdom, but they could find no ground for complaint or any fault, because he was faithful, and no error or fault was found in him. Then these men said, 'We shall not find any ground for complaint against this Daniel unless we find it in connection with the law of his God.'

> "Then these high officials and satraps came by agreement to the king and said to him, 'O King Darius, live forever! All the high officials of the kingdom, the prefects and the satraps, the counselors and the governors are agreed that the king should establish an ordinance and enforce an injunction, that whoever makes petition to any god or man for thirty days, except to you, O king, shall be cast into the den of lions. Now, O king, establish the injunction and sign the document, so that it cannot be changed, according to the law of the Medes and the Persians, which cannot be revoked.' Therefore King Darius signed the document and injunction.

> "When Daniel knew that the document had been signed, he went to his house where he had windows in his upper chamber open toward Jerusalem. He got down on his knees three times a day and prayed and gave thanks before his God, as he had done previously."

Pete stared at the words of Scripture in front of him for the longest time, contemplating Daniel's predicament. Here was this faithful and faultless servant of the one true God, and King Darius, yet pressured to comply with a law that went contrary to God's commands and his own convictions. But even though the penalty for breaking the law was death, his decision had already been made. His faith in God overruled his fear of man, and he stayed the course. Stayed the course *publicly*!

Pete opened his desk drawer and took out a pen. Then he underlined the last phrase of the passage in his Bible: *"as he had done previously."*

The buzzer echoed loudly throughout the gymnasium, informing even those few who were not paying attention that the game had ended. A sea of ecstatic red-and-white-clad Warriors fans poured from the bleachers, inundating the hardwood like a tsunami. Pete glanced up at the scoreboard clock, which showed 00:00 time remaining. The final score read: Emmanuel Christian 59, Daly City Christian 52. He located his son near the eye of the storm and made visual contact. Drew, grinning broadly, waved briefly to his father and mother before disappearing under a billow of teammates and fans. It had been a close championship game, closer than the final score indicated. Neither team had led by more than four points throughout the contest, and it wasn't until the final two minutes that the Warriors had taken the lead for good, outscoring their archrivals 8-2 down the home stretch.

Pete and Angela remained in the stands, chatting with other parents and friends about the game and random subjects. Following the trophy presentation, they located Brienna, and the trio made their way to the car to wait for Drew. About twenty minutes later he emerged from the building, crossed the parking lot toward the family sedan, and eased his six-foot-two-inch frame into the back seat next to his sister.

Angela twisted in her seat. "Congratulations, Drew! That was a very exciting game."

"Thanks, Mom. I can't believe we won! Daly City was favored by at least ten points, I think. And when Ryan sprained his ankle, I thought it was all over."

Pete glanced at his son in the rear-view mirror as he pulled out of the parking space. "I couldn't make out what Coach Nelson said in the huddle during the injury timeout, but whatever it was sure worked. You guys came out on fire! How many points did you end up with, anyway? Twenty-two? Or was it twenty-four? I lost count in all the excitement."

"Twenty-four. And I scored six of our last eight points."

"Is that the most you've ever scored in a game?" Brienna asked her brother.

"I had thirty-six in the preseason game against Grandview. But that doesn't really count. Besides, the guys kept feeding me the ball to see if I could beat the school record, which I didn't."

"Pacific Coast Christian Conference Champions. How does that title grab you?" Pete tossed the question to his son sitting behind him.

"Sounds mighty good to me, Dad. It took three long years for the team to reach this goal, but we finally did it."

"Yes, I'm mighty proud of you, son. We all are. And you did it the right way, too. This goes to show that discipline, hard work, and sacrifice pay off in the long run." He glanced in the mirror again and grinned. "I guess this makes buying all those shoes worthwhile after all!"

"Dad, I need to ask you something." Drew addressed him as they sat at dinner a few nights later. Brienna was away at a friend's house for the evening.

Pete wiped his mouth with his napkin and placed it on the table. "Okay, ask away."

"On the way home from the game the other night you said something that got me thinking. You said we won by doing it the right way, remember?"

"I seem to recall saying something like that," Pete replied. "I've always believed that if you're going to do something, you need to do it right. Whether it's sports, schoolwork, building relationships, or serving God, you can't take shortcuts or the easy road and expect to honor Him. He's interested not only in *what* we do, but *how* we do it."

Drew leaned forward. "Yeah, like that line from your 'Arrive Alive' speech you gave me when I got my first speeding ticket: 'The drive is just as important as the destination.'"

Angela cut in on the conversation. "Your *first* speeding ticket?" She glanced briefly at her husband, then squinted at her son. "Drew, is there something more you'd like to tell us?"

Drew gave her a wry look. "My one and only speeding ticket," he clarified, before turning back to his father. He spoke tersely. "Dad, you've always preached that compromising the truth is a shortcut, haven't you? A journey leading down the wrong road?"

"Yes, I have. And I still believe that." Pete shifted in his chair. "What are you getting at, Drew?"

Drew's brow furrowed, and he took a deep breath. His terseness grew into irritation. "You say you still believe that, but I don't see you living it. You weren't willing to compromise so I could achieve *my* dream, but now you're perfectly willing to compromise to hold on to *yours!*"

Pete stared at his son, then calmly replied, "Go on, I'm listening."

Bitterness crept into Drew's voice. "Remember all those discussions we had about where I should go to high school? I wanted to play basketball at South Central so I could have the best chance of being noticed by Division One recruiters. But no, you guys thought I might be tempted to compromise my faith, so you sent me to Emmanuel Christian instead."

"But you just won the PCCC championship," his mother interjected again. "You were celebrating just a few days ago. You certainly didn't seem unhappy about it then."

Drew threw his mother a barely concealed look of disdain. "Of course, I'm happy we won the conference. But it would have meant a whole lot more if I'd been playing for South Central." He scowled deeply. "No college recruiter is gonna waste his time looking at a player in a small, insignificant Christian school league."

Pete crafted his reply carefully. "Look, son, I know we've never seen eye-to-eye on that one, and I'm really sorry it still bothers you. We had to make a tough decision based on what we thought was best for you in the long run. But that was three years ago." He rubbed his chin thoughtfully. "What dream of mine do you think *I've* been willing to compromise for?"

Drew responded immediately. "Your church, Dad, your church! You've worked hard for thirteen years to build your dream ministry. You've reached your goal. But now you go and sign that agreement with the state just to protect your investment."

Pete thoughtfully stared out the dining room window before replying. "And you think that by signing the Compliance Agreement I've compromised my faith?"

"Well, haven't you? You weren't willing to compromise with *my* dream. You didn't trust God to take care of me in a public school. But now, because it's *your* dream, you're willing to compromise to protect it. Signing that agreement shows you don't trust God to take care of your own church! I think you've taken the shortcut, the easy way out."

Pete fought to keep his voice under control. "Drew, I can assure you my decision to sign that paper was not an easy one. And I'll be honest with you, sometimes I wonder if it was the right decision. But considering the options, I think it was the best choice under the circumstances. How is that compromising?"

"Because you violated your own Christian principles when you signed it. You never intended to comply with that agreement, did you?" Drew's volume increased a few decibels. "You only signed it to get the state off your back and out of your church. That's the same as lying, isn't it? Only you did it in writing. You signed a written promise you never meant to keep!"

Pete grew defensive. "What was I supposed to do, Drew? I explained to you what the consequences would be if I refused to sign. Would you rather I allowed the state to censor what I preach from the pulpit, just to comply with a non-biblical law? Now *that* would be compromising!"

Drew angrily threw his napkin at his plate and stood up. "I'd rather you practice what you preach! If you're so serious about honoring God, then why don't you let *Him* deal with the consequences? Or are you afraid you'll lose your dream? Like I lost mine!" He stormed out of the room and into the hall, shouting over his shoulder, "You've always preached that it's His church, anyway. It's not yours at all!"

Pete's shoulders sagged. He stared at his wife, who was close to tears. Together they listened in stunned silence as Drew stomped up the stairs and down the hall to his room. The dishes on the sideboard rattled as their son slammed his bedroom door.

"What have I done?" Pete moaned, his voice barely audible. He crossed the living room carpet to where Angela sat reading on the sofa and slumped into the brown faux-leather recliner. He stared vacantly at the slowly revolving ceiling fan above him, his eyes deep pools of pain. The two of them were alone. Shortly after his outburst, Drew had stomped downstairs and stormed out of the house into the night.

Angela stared at him for a minute, then laid her open book face down. Getting up from the sofa, she walked around behind her husband's favorite chair and began massaging his tight neck and shoulder muscles with firm fingers. "I know it was a difficult decision," she answered gently, "but you did what you had to do."

Pete twisted his head to look up at her. "Do you think I compromised my faith by signing that agreement?" he asked, the anguish evident in his eyes.

"Babe, you can't go on beating yourself up over this," she replied firmly. "You've made the decision, and we'll all face it together."

"But we're *not* all facing this together, Ange. Not as a family anyway. I understand Drew's anger. He had a point about me agreeing to something I had no real intention of doing. And about me not being willing to risk his future or the church's."

"At least you were attempting to be consistent," Angela responded, trying to sound encouraging. "You made those decisions because you care deeply about Drew and about your ministry. You were trying to be a good father to your son and a good shepherd to your church."

Pete wasn't convinced. "But what about his accusation that I lied by signing it? Do you think that violated my Christian principles?"

"What does your heart tell you?" Angela suggested.

Pete took a long time before answering. "I agreed not to preach hate speech in the public domain, as those terms are defined by the state. But the state doesn't have the right to define those terms, at least in this case. The truth is, what I'm preaching is God's Word, not hate speech. And where I'm preaching it is in a church that belongs to Him, not the state. I've been trying to console myself with that technicality for the past three weeks." His face fell. "But maybe I'm only trying to justify my decision."

Angela squeezed his shoulders firmly enough to make him wince. "Well, you made the decision and I'll support you, come what may."

"What about Drew?" Pete wanted to know, still shaken by his son's explosion of pent-up feelings.

She leaned down and kissed the top of his head. "Give him time, Pete. You know he's a good kid. He's given us static before from time to time, but he's gotten over it. Like when we wouldn't let him go on that unsupervised camping trip with some of his friends last summer. Or when we didn't approve of that Richardson girl he wanted to go out with. I know he's angry and doesn't agree with us right now. Maybe he'll *never* agree with us on this issue." She continued working the muscles of his taut shoulders with her fingers. "But sooner or later he has to see that we're just trying to be consistent."

"I hope you're right." Pete sighed deeply. "Anyway, thanks for the encouragement." He looked up at her again. "You really are a 'messenger from God', Ange." He managed an appreciative smile. "And you give the best neck massages I've ever had."

Angela playfully swatted the back of his head like a kitten batting a ball of yarn. "The *best* neck massages?" She leaned across his shoulder and gave him the eye. "Babe, is there something more you'd like to tell me? As far as I know, I give the *only* neck massages you've ever had!"

She laughed to lighten the mood. But this time, Pete didn't feel like laughing.

CHAPTER THREE
I'M UNDER ARREST?

THREE DAYS LATER, PETE SAT in his church office putting the finishing touches on next Sunday's sermon when a knock sounded on the door and the church secretary stuck her head into the room.

"Pastor Pete, mail's here," the graying, middle-aged woman announced. She crossed to his desk and handed him a couple of envelopes. "Not much today. Only these two and the electric bill."

"Thanks, Marilyn," he replied with a smile. "Are you heading out to lunch now?"

"Yes, but I'll be back around one."

"Good." He held up his handwritten sermon notes. "I should have these ready to type up by then. Enjoy your lunch."

"Thanks, I will." She reached the open door, then turned around. "Oh, FYI, the bulletin insert is almost finished. You can proofread it when I get back."

Pete nodded and the secretary left the room. He glanced at the two business-size envelopes in his hand. The first was addressed to the church. Using the letter opener on his desk, he tore open the envelope and pulled out the stationary inside. The letterhead informed him it was from a church in Sacramento led by Jim Sutherland, an old friend of his from seminary. He scanned the contents of the letter. It was an invitation to attend a ministerial conference scheduled later that fall. The main topic of the conference was "The unchanging role of the church in an ever-changing world." Jim was inviting him to speak in one of the sessions. Pete opened his electronic day planner to check his schedule and was pleased to see that nothing conflicted with the dates of the conference. He made a note to send his acceptance and set the letter to one side.

He shifted his attention to the second envelope, which was addressed to him personally. As he glanced at the return logo, his heart skipped a beat. It was from the San Francisco Police Department! His mind began to spin like a clothes dryer gone berserk.

Why would they be contacting me by mail? Are they wanting me to come in for more questioning? Is my wait for the other shoe to drop finally over?

His hand trembled as he tore open the envelope and extracted the single sheet of paper inside. With his heart pounding in his ears, he anxiously unfolded it and read the short letter.

Mr. Pete Holloway
Diamond Heights Baptist Church
1476 East Addison Avenue
San Francisco, CA 94131

Dear Mr. Holloway:

I wanted to personally thank you for agreeing to come in and answer my questions on the third of this month. My apologies for keeping you in the dark prior to our meeting, but due to the sensitive nature of the subject matter, I'm sure you understand.

Although you don't see eye-to-eye with the state on everything that was discussed, your willingness to sign the Voluntary Compliance Agreement is greatly appreciated. Your continued cooperation with the state concerning the Hate Speech Reparation and Elimination Act is vital to achieving our mutual goal. By working together, we can eradicate all forms of hate speech, and make the state of California a safer and better place in which to live.

If you have any further questions, or if I can be of any assistance, please don't hesitate to call me.

Sincerely,
Det. John Branch, SFPD
Ingleside Station

Pete re-read the letter twice. It seemed straight forward enough, no between-the-lines hidden messages. He leaned back in his chair and gave himself permission to relax. It was almost four weeks since the interview, and in that span of time, he'd preached three more Sunday morning sermons in his series on the book of Romans. And even though there had been visitors in the services, he'd purposefully held nothing back. Like Daniel, he was determined to continue preaching as he had done previously.

He'd certainly given them additional opportunities to get him in trouble if they wanted to. But since they hadn't called him in again, Detective Branch must be honoring his promise to keep the state out of his church. This letter seemed to confirm that.

He allowed himself a congratulatory moment. Apparently signing the Voluntary Compliance Agreement was the right thing to do after all.

After taking a lunch break, Pete returned to the church. By mid-afternoon, his sermon notes were complete and in the hands of his competent secretary. He placed a call to Jim Sutherland in Sacramento, informing his pastor friend that he would be honored to accept the speaking engagement at the conference. The two chatted for about half an hour.

He was anxious to get home tonight and share the details of both letters with the family. Since the conference was open to pastors and their wives, Angela would be glad to hear about it. She enjoyed events like this which allowed her not only to get away from home for a while but also to fellowship with other women involved in ministry. And he was sure the good news in the SFPD letter could be used as an opportunity to open dialog with Drew, and hopefully help mend the rift in their fractured relationship.

Pete's desk phone buzzed once. He pushed a red button and picked up the receiver. "Yes?"

It was his secretary in the next room. "Maria Gonzalez is on line one. She says it's urgent."

"Maria Gonzalez? Okay, I'll take it. Send her through."

"Um, Pastor Pete," the secretary spoke hesitantly, "she sounds like she's been crying."

"Crying? Did she tell you why?"

"No. Just that it's very urgent and she needs to speak with you immediately."

"All right. Thanks, Marilyn." He took a deep breath, then pushed the button for line one. "Maria? This is Pete. What can I do for you?"

he asked the wife of his good friend. There was silence on the other end, then muffled sobbing, as if she was crying into a towel or handkerchief. "Maria? What's wrong? What's going on?"

Her heavy Hispanic accent finally reached across the connection. The anguish in her voice was palpable. "Oh, Pastor Pete, I need your help! I . . . I do not know what to do. They have just arrested Jorge!"

Stunned, Pete sat frozen in his chair. Then the questions began swirling in his head. "Jorge's been arrested? What in the world for?"

"Two men from the San Francisco police showed up at the apartment a few minutes ago with a warrant. When he asked why they were arresting him, they told him he had violated the hate speech law. Then they handcuffed him and took him away." Maria broke down and began sobbing again.

"Do you know where they took him?"

"The Mission Station, I think." Maria's tone turned to pleading. "Pastor Pete, my husband did not do anything wrong. He did not preach anything hateful. You know Jorge. He is a kind and gentle man, full of love, not hate."

"Yes, yes he is. I don't know anyone more compassionate than Jorge. Maria, where are you calling from? Are you at home?"

"Yes, I am home with the children. They are very upset about what just happened."

"I can only imagine. Listen, would you like Angie to come over and stay with you for a while? At least until the kids calm down?"

"I am sure that would be very helpful. If it is not too much trouble."

"No trouble at all," Pete assured her. "I'll give her a call as soon as we hang up. I'm sure she'll want to come right over."

"Thank you so much, Pastor Pete." The gratefulness in her voice was unmistakable. "You and Angela are a true brother and sister in Christ."

"And don't worry about Jorge. I'll make a few phone calls and drive up to the Mission Station to see if there's anything I can do." Pete heard her sigh with relief. "You are so kind, Brother Pete!"

With his friend's family taken care of, Pete sought some additional information from her. "Maria, when the police were at your apartment, did they say anything else you can remember? Think carefully. It might be important."

There was a brief pause on the other end. "They said that his name was on a list of people they were looking for. People who are in trouble for hateful things they have said in public. I think they called it a sweep. But I do not know exactly what that means."

A low groan slipped past Pete's lips. "It means the authorities are serious about clamping down on public hate speech throughout the entire city. They're simultaneously and systematically going through each district rounding up everyone on their list. They must be trying to send a message."

"What message is that?"

"That they will not tolerate anyone who preaches what they determine to be hate speech." He heard Maria sniffle and blow her nose. "Maria, did SFPD question Jorge about this recently?"

"Yes, last month, on the fifteenth or sixteenth, maybe the seventeenth. I do not know the exact date."

Pete felt compelled to ask the next question, perhaps for personal reasons. "Do you know if your husband signed the Voluntary Compliance Agreement when he was there?"

"What is that?"

"It's a document that says the signer promises not to speak or write anything the state classifies as hate speech in the public domain, which now includes church services."

"I do not know for sure," she answered. "He did not tell me about it. But I do not think he would have signed such a document. When the apostles were told by the chief priests not to teach in the name of Jesus, their answer was, 'We must obey God rather than men.'" She paused. "Jorge is very much like the apostles, I think."

He must have refused to sign the agreement and now he's under arrest. I signed it and I'm not under arrest. For a split second he felt a splash of relief. Then a wave of guilt crashed down hard on him.

Pete phoned his wife just as soon as his call with Maria Gonzalez ended and told her the bad news. Angela agreed to go straight over to the apartment to stay with their friend and her children. After praying together about the situation over the phone, he placed another call to SFPD's Mission Station to check on the status of his fellow pastor. But the receptionist said she had no information on a Jorge Gonzalez and speculated that he might not have been booked and processed yet. She suggested Pete call back in a couple of hours.

Pete leaned back in his desk chair and closed his eyes. He felt numb. *What now?* How long would they hold him? Would he get out on bail? What would his consequences be for not signing the cooperation agreement? At minimum he was facing some stiff fines and mandatory participation in the state's reeducation program. That's what Detective Branch said would happen. Or could Jorge be looking at doing time? Might the state even confiscate his church over this? What if the penalties for noncompliance were far worse than the detective was willing to let on to?

Pete rose and walked down the carpeted hallway to the church kitchen. His mouth was dry as dust. He grabbed a bottled water from the refrigerator and returned to his office. After shutting the door, he twisted off the plastic cap and took a long swig. Then he walked over to the two bookcases containing his pastoral library and stared at the volumes of commentaries, Bible dictionaries, lexicons, and sermon collections of well-known and not-so-well-known preachers and scholars. Running his hand over the spines of his treasured books, he retraced the events in his life leading up to his call to the ministry.

He'd never planned on becoming a pastor, never gave it so much as a thought growing up. He'd asked Christ to save him when he was ten years old, but he'd always wanted to be a soldier for as long as he could remember. After postponing college to serve a four-year hitch in the Army, he'd enrolled at San Jose State and earned his bachelor's degree in Management. He'd met Angela there, and they'd married in the summer of 2000 following graduation.

Then, on the heels of 9/11, he'd voluntarily re-enlisted with a ground support battalion of the 101st Airborne Division. When Drew was only six months old his unit had been deployed to Iraq in early 2003, and he'd seen action in the "shock and awe" bombing of Baghdad in March of that year. While in theater, he'd been wounded by IED shrapnel and had been awarded the Purple Heart.

Upon his return home he'd suffered a serious faith crisis, doubting his salvation and even the goodness of God. But at a revival meeting Angela had dragged him to, he'd surrendered his life and will to the Lord, and soon after that had answered God's call to the ministry. While in seminary, he'd survived a battle with testicular cancer, as hard-fought as any in the military. But he'd conquered that and had graduated with his M-Div. and had become pastor of Diamond Heights Bible Church in late 2007. A year later Brienna had been born. That was twelve years ago.

Pete stepped in front of the two diplomas and the Purple Heart medallion hanging on the wall, all framed and under glass. He stared at his achievements for a while, wondering why this current skirmish with the state was so difficult, considering all the battles he'd faced in the past. Maybe Drew was right for accusing him of taking the easy road. He suddenly felt ashamed for his lack of courage, and envious of Jorge for his display of it.

The ring tone of his cell phone jarred him loose from his troubled thoughts. He fished the vibrating device out of his pocket and checked the caller ID. It was the number of his golf partner, Carter Joseph.

"C.J.! Nice of you to call. Wah gwaan?"

A loud Jamaican voice cheerfully returned his greeting. "Wah gwaan yuhself, Pasta Pete!"

The upbeat tone of his large Caribbean friend sent his spirits soaring. "Always good to hear your voice. It's been a while. Want to get together for another round of golf? Or have you been avoiding me because I beat you by three strokes last time?"

The hulk on the other end guffawed loudly. "Ha, that's a good one!" Pete held his phone away from his ear to avoid further pain. "Mi dead wid laugh! You jus' lucky, that's all. I been to the driving range since then. Nex' time will be diff'rent. Ya mon!"

Pete laughed heartily. "Maybe it will and maybe it won't," he teased the likable giant. "I have some free time in a couple of weeks. Want to schedule a round then?"

"Perhaps, Pasta Pete. I will check my schedule and let you know." There was a pause, after which Carter's tone took on a somberness Pete had never heard before. "Uh . . . I did not call, my friend, to, how do you say it, 'shoot the breeze'. I called to warn you of trouble headin' your way."

"Trouble? What kind of trouble, C.J.?"

"The wors' kind, Pasta Pete. You know the department moved me from fingerprints to documents three months ago, right? Well, I jus' delivered a stack of warrants to Judge Connelly's office this afternoon. All that is needed for them to be executed is his signature."

Pete filled in the gaps quickly. "They wouldn't have anything to do with that sweep SFPD is conducting right now, would they?"

"How do you know 'bout *that*?" Carter asked suspiciously.

"Remember my pastor friend, Jorge Gonzalez? He subbed for Mike Sutton that time we played a foursome at Lincoln Park. He was picked up earlier this afternoon at his home."

"Bad lucky! I am very sorry to hear that," his friend replied sympathetically.

Pete sighed. "Yeah, I expect I'll hear about more friends and acquaintances who've gotten caught up in the dragnet as time goes on."

"Uh . . . Pasta Pete, I hate to tell you this, but it is the reason why I called. One of those warrants I delivered to the judge has *your* name on it."

A lightning bolt shot through Pete's body and brain, rendering him incapable of movement or thought.

"Pasta Pete? Mi parri, you okay?"

Pete fought through his paralysis to force a reply. "You . . . you *sure* about that, C.J.?"

"I checked the address on the warrant. It is your home address, all right. No doubt 'bout it, mon."

The blood began flowing to Pete's brain again. He reacted in disbelief. "But I *signed* the Voluntary Compliance Agreement about a month ago! It's on file with SFPD. You can check it out. I signed it at the Ingleside Station in the presence of a Detective John Branch, and I have a copy at home."

"Perhaps maybe you violated the terms of the agreement?"

Pete hesitated, knowing that he had, but not wanting to admit it to a member of SFPD over the phone, even if it *was* Carter Joseph. Instead of answering his friend's question, he turned the tables. "C.J., why are you tipping me off about this? Can't you get in trouble for what you're doing?"

"For sure, Pasta Pete, I could lose my job for this. Maybe go to jail." He chuckled, as if trying to ease the tension. "But you know how much of a blabba mout I am! Anyway, I think to myself, how can I know 'bout this and not warn mi parri? I could never forgive myself."

Pete shook his head. "You're taking a mighty big risk, my friend. I can't begin to tell you how much I appreciate this." A chilling thought crossed his mind. "How long before those warrants get served? Do you have any idea?"

"The judge usually signs them within a few hours, depending on the time of day and what his schedule looks like. It may be tomorrow before he gets 'round to it. Or . . . " he hesitated, as if trying not to sound alarming, " . . . or he might have already signed them. I do not know."

Pete shuddered. "And how long after that before they come knocking at my front door?"

"I know the department is busy with the current warrants now. Yours is part of the nex' round. That is the good news, if there is any to be had. You prob'ly will not be served for at leas' twenty-four hours, maybe forty-eight. What are you gwaan do, mi parri?"

C.J. had never referred to him as 'my friend' so often before. Obviously, he was very concerned about Pete's welfare. "I'm not sure. But I'm going to go home and talk it over with Angie." Another thought came to him. "Do you think it might go better for me if I were to surrender at the station before they come looking for me?"

"No! No, Pasta Pete, do not do that!" C.J.'s panic forced him to hold the phone away from his ear again. "Then they will know that someone informed you 'bout the warrant." He began to plead. "Please do not do that, mi parri. I would lose my job for sure."

"Of course, you would. I'm sorry, C.J., forgive me. I wasn't thinking at all."

"No problem, I understand. Bad business, this hate speech thing." C.J. slipped into his native dialect again. "Dis whole t'ing be sick inna head, if yuh ask mi, mon!"

Pete sat lifeless on the edge of the sofa with his head in his hands. He heard the door from the garage open and someone enter the kitchen.

"Babe, I'm back," his wife called out, but the words barely registered in his mind. He heard her toss her keys onto the counter and kick off her shoes, something she always did when coming into the house. A moment later she passed by the living room. Then she reappeared in the doorway with a look of puzzlement on her face. She paused and took a step into the room.

"Pete?" He didn't respond. "Pete, are you all right?" She walked across the room and stopped in front of him. "Babe, what's the matter?"

He looked up at her, strain creasing his face. Angela sat down next to him and took his hand in hers. "Pete, what's going on? What's happened?" Before he could reply, a spark of fear flashed in her eyes. "Are the children all right?"

Pete snapped out of his funk. "Yes, the children are fine, Ange. They're both up in their rooms." His shoulders slumped. "I got a call from . . . from a very reliable source a while ago, not long after Maria's. He saw an arrest warrant at the police department with my name on it."

"What? An arrest warrant! You've got to be—" She cut herself off. He was clearly not kidding.

"It's true, Ange. I'm part of the same sweep that got Jorge this afternoon." He laid out the details of his conversation with C. J., being careful to not mention him by name.

"What are you going to do, Pete? I mean, what can you do? Maybe you should contact Mr. Murdock down at the law office."

"I did that, Ange, right after the call. But he said if there's already a warrant sworn out for me, his hands are tied until I'm arrested and booked. Then he'll see about getting me out on bail."

"Then I guess that's all we can do for now," Angela conceded, squeezing her husband's hand.

Pete stared out the window for the longest time. "Well, not exactly. I've been mulling over something else."

"What's that?" she asked cautiously.

A spark flashed in his former lifeless eyes. He stood up and began pacing back and forth in front of her. "If SFPD arrests me, I'll be facing some heavy fines and be forced to participate in that politically correct brainwashing program they want to shove down my throat, right? Maybe more. Obviously, someone's reported that I haven't kept my end of the agreement I signed. Who knows, I could be looking at jail this time. And the way the city is cracking down, there's even the chance we could lose the church. Mr. Murdock said the law was crafted to give the state sweeping powers to arrest, convict, and punish anyone who they decide has violated the law. They pretty much have carte blanche this time: Judge, jury, and executioner!"

Angela's eyes widened. "But it's your first offense. Surely you don't think they'd go that far, do you?"

"I wouldn't put it past them!" he replied forcefully. He suddenly stopped pacing and looked intently at her. "But I'm not going to give them the satisfaction."

Angela stared at him. "Just . . . what do you have in mind?"

Fire flared up in Pete's eyes. He clenched his fists resolutely. "I'm not going to be here when they come to arrest me, *that's* what!"

CHAPTER FOUR
MAN ON THE RUN

"ARE YOU SURE I CAN'T give you a hand with something?" Angela asked her husband as she watched him scurry back and forth between the dresser and his suitcase. She glanced at the luggage lying open on the bed beside her. "At least let me pack some food and canned goods for you."

"No!" Pete replied, perhaps a little too forcefully. He stopped and stared at his wife. Then he sat down on the bed and put an arm around her shoulders. His tone softened. "I'm sorry, hon. But like I told you downstairs, I have to do this myself. That way, if the police ask, you can honestly say you didn't assist me. It's for your protection, so you can't be charged as an accessory."

Angela grabbed his hand in hers and squeezed it tightly. "Are you *sure* you're making the right decision?" she asked for the third time.

"No, I'm *not* sure," Pete replied for the third time. He returned her squeeze and forced a grin. "Not one hundred percent, anyway." He arose from the bed and resumed his packing. "But I still think it's the best option at the moment. What I really need is time, time to think this all through, time to sort things out." He stepped into the closet and grabbed a couple of belts. "But what I don't have right now is time. If I stay here, the decision will be made for me." He paused long enough to catch her eye. "And it won't be a good one." He ducked into the master bath and began collecting items from the counter.

Angela rose off the bed and followed him to the doorway. She watched him stuff his electric shaver, toothbrush, and other toiletries into his travel pouch. "Babe, you can't keep *everything* from me. I need to know where you'll be staying. Can't you at least give me a hint?" she pleaded, as pain and sadness flooded her eyes.

Pete glanced at her as he closed the large hard-shell suitcase. "Not now, Ange. Wait until you're sure the police are done questioning you. Then call me and I'll let you know where I am. But whatever you do, don't text, okay? Just in case they check your phone." Angela nodded. "Anyway, I'm not sure which direction I'm going or where I'll end up. The more random my decisions the better chance I'll have of buying the time needed to figure out my next move." He dragged the heavy suitcase off the bed and extended its handle. Then he slung a bulging gym bag over his shoulder and headed downstairs.

Twenty minutes later, once the sedan was fully loaded, Pete called a family meeting in the living room. As he sat facing his wife and kids, his heart was heavy. *This may be the last family meeting we have for a while.*

He explained as much as he could to the children without burdening them with too much information. Plus, should the police question them as well, he wanted to spare them the knowledge. Drew was uncharacteristically subdued but agreed to be the man of the house in his father's absence. Brienna clung to her father and cried in his arms. Then they all held hands and prayed together as a family.

Pete made one final sweep of the house to make sure he had everything he needed. After checking the master bedroom one last time, he headed toward the hall, but stopped in the doorway. Returning to the closet, he flipped on the light and reached for a small metal box tucked away on the top shelf. He pulled it down, opened the lid, and stared at the flat black handgun nestled in the molded foam liner. He started to put it back, but hesitated. Then he picked up the Taurus PT111 and stuffed it in his pocket. He replaced the box and grabbed a handful of cartridges from his nightstand.

In the driveway, he hugged his children one last time, and shared a long embrace and kiss with his wife. Then he climbed into the car and drove off into the night.

Pete merged onto Interstate 280 heading east toward the bay, keeping in the right-hand lane and staying five miles below the speed limit to avoid drawing attention to himself. He needed to get out of the San Francisco city limits as quickly and safely as possible. His plan was to take Highway 101 South to San Jose, spend the night there, and then make his way down to Los Angeles, where it would be easier to disappear into the teeming masses. But when he reached the on-ramp to Highway 101, he made the last-second decision to go north instead. Maybe he should cross the Golden Gate Bridge and drive up to San Rafael or Petaluma. But he made another random decision and merged onto I-80. It wasn't until he'd crossed the Bay Bridge that he decided to drive all the way to Sacramento. He set the cruise control at 65 miles per hour and stretched his right leg. Although those random directional changes probably meant nothing at all, for some reason they gave him a sense of security. He felt a bit like a fleeing outlaw who had just given the pursuing posse the slip.

Ninety minutes later, Pete pulled into a hotel on the outskirts of Sacramento and secured a room for the night. Once inside, he tossed his suitcase on the table, drew the heavy curtains, and cranked up the air conditioner. He flopped onto the bed and slowly purged the air from his lungs. It was only then that he realized how tense he still was. *I could sure use one of Ange's massages about now.*

He'd been gone only two hours, and he already missed her. It seemed as though she were on the other side of the world. A glance at the bedside clock informed him of the late hour. Next to the clock lay a metal box with a round dial in the center. A vibrating bed timer! Pete eagerly set the device for the maximum time and lay back onto the pillow, allowing the bed's undulations to drain away the stresses of the day. *Not as good as Ange's fingers, but definitely better than nothing!*

Pete blinked open his eyes and surveyed the semi-dark room. A shaft of sunlight squeezed between the two halves of the heavy curtain and cast a bright, narrow stripe across the bed. Yawning, he rolled over and checked the time: It was 8:44 a.m. His stomach reminded him that in all the previous day's excitement, he'd forgotten to eat anything since lunch. He threw on a clean shirt, ran a comb through his hair, and headed down to the lobby before the continental breakfast bar closed.

Most of the hotel guests had already eaten and gone, but thankfully there was still some food left. He grabbed a paper plate and piled on as much as it would hold. Then he sat down at one of the small tables and began watching the TV mounted to the wall, hoping to catch the news. But all that was on were the morning talk shows. When he finished eating, he returned to his room and jumped into the shower. The hot streams of water rejuvenated his body and refreshed his mind.

What should I do now? Where should I go next?

He had no set schedule, no plan of attack, and no real mission for the day ahead. He hated how utterly lost that made him feel. He'd had that lost feeling before, and things hadn't turned out well at all.

Suddenly, he was back inside an armored Humvee, dressed in full BDU, his M16 rifle in hand and Beretta M9 strapped to his side. Three other soldiers, two of whom he'd gone through basic with, were packed like sardines into the stifling interior. He adjusted his helmet and wiped the stinging sweat from his eyes. The taste of dust was inside his mouth, and the grit from it was inside his uniform. The lead vehicle of the small convoy turned down another side street, desperately seeking an escape from the impossible maze, but all the streets in the Al Yarmuk section looked alike. They had no idea where in Baghdad they were. The Humvee came to an intersection and stopped, then turned left onto a wider avenue that looked as if it might take them in the direction of their base. They hadn't traversed 300 yards before everything exploded around them.

When he came to, his ears were ringing, and it felt as if a two-hundred-pound weight was pressing squarely against his chest. Fighting to catch his breath, he choked on dust and sand, and the noxious fumes of diesel fuel made him nauseated. He sensed that his helmet was gone, and he felt a warmth flowing down his temple. Instinctively he raised his hand and touched the side of his head. When he pulled it away, his fingers were wet with a mixture of sand and blood.

Pete took a step back and frantically wiped his face with both hands. His eyes gradually focused on the faucet handle in front of him, then on the shower head above him, and the gentle streams of warm water emanating from it. His body suddenly shuddered involuntarily. *No, I definitely do not like that lost feeling!*

He shut off the faucet and reached for a towel.

Once he had dressed, Pete retrieved his Bible from the gym bag and sat down at the small desk. He flicked on the lamp, turned to the book of Romans, and began reading the text of what was to have been his sermon for this coming Sunday's morning service, Romans 5:1-5.

> *"Therefore, since we have been justified by faith, we have peace with God through our Lord Jesus Christ. Through Him we have also obtained access by faith into this grace in which we stand, and we rejoice in hope of the glory of God. Not only that, but we rejoice in our sufferings, knowing that suffering produces endurance, and endurance produces character, and character produces hope, and hope does not put us to shame, because God's love has been poured into our hearts through the Holy Spirit Who has been given to us."*

He was grateful that God had declared Pete Holloway justified when he had placed his trust in Jesus Christ at the age of ten. And he was thankful for the peace *with* God, the grace *of* God, and the hope *in* God that were his as a result. But at the moment, he didn't feel quite so appreciative of the suffering *for* God he was experiencing. Of course, suffering was meant to produce character and hope, but then why did he feel so lost, so unsure of himself, so . . . alone? He reread the passage, then bowed his head.

"Father, thank You for justifying me by declaring me righteous through the blood of Your Son, Jesus. Ever since You gave me the assurance of my salvation after I came home from Iraq, I've never doubted that I belong to You. And I know that You're always with me because of the Holy Spirit indwelling me. But right now, You seem so far away. I've tried my best to remain Your true and faithful servant, but I admit I'm unsure about some of the decisions I've made recently. And I don't know what to do going forward. What should I do next, Lord? Show me the way. Please, show me the way!"

Pete got up and opened the curtains. He gazed out across the city at the Sierra Nevada foothills rising to the east some thirty miles away. They loomed in the distance, majestic and peaceful against the brilliant azure sky. As he drank in the view, enjoying its grandeur, a verse from Psalm 121 came to mind:

> *"I lift up my eyes to the hills.*
> *From where does my help come?*
> *My help comes from the Lord,*
> *Who made heaven and earth."*

Pete felt a sense of peace wash over him. "My help comes from You, Lord," he whispered out loud, "the Creator of all this. You are *my* Creator, *my* Lord, and *my* God."

He turned away from the spectacular view and went into the bathroom to shave and brush his teeth. Standing in front of the mirror, he recalled the letter from Jim Sutherland, inviting him to speak at the pastors and wives conference in November. Jim's church was here in Sacramento, not more than half an hour away. Maybe he should stop in and surprise his old seminary friend. A visit with Jim might just ease the burden he was carrying all by himself.

He could sure use someone to talk to right now.

On the way out of the hotel, Pete stopped by the front desk and paid for another night's lodging. Then he got into his car, entered the address of Jim's church into the navigation system, and pulled out of the parking lot. About thirty minutes later, he saw the sign on the left: "Highland Hills Bible Church." He turned onto the driveway and parked near the front entrance.

Once inside the vestibule, he entered the church office and identified himself to the secretary, explaining his relationship to Jim Sutherland. She had him take a seat while she buzzed the pastor in his study. A minute later, the heavy oak door at the far end of the room opened and the former seminarian walked through. As soon as Jim saw Pete, he broke into a broad smile.

"Well, well, this is an unexpected pleasure!" Bypassing the perfunctory handshake, the two embraced warmly. Jim stepped back. "It's good to see you, Pete. I didn't know you were coming out this way. You didn't mention it on the phone yesterday afternoon."

Pete forced himself to return Jim's smile. "I didn't know I'd be in Sacramento myself until late last night. It's always a pleasure when I get a chance to see my old friend from seminary. But this time you might say I'm here on business." His smile quickly disappeared. "Rather serious business, if you ask me, Jim."

Jim frowned. "Oh?" He studied Pete's face for a moment, then placed an arm around Pete's shoulders. "Why don't we go into my study where we can talk in private." He turned to his secretary. "Judy, would you mind holding my calls, please?" She gave him an understanding nod as the two men entered Jim's office. The pastor closed the door behind them and offered a seat to his visitor. They sat facing each other across the large desk.

"I sensed something was troubling you, Pete. Perhaps we should postpone the usual small talk. We can always catch up on the personal stuff later," Jim suggested with a warm smile. He settled back in his chair. "Now, what's on your mind, my friend?"

Pete took a deep breath as he formulated where to begin. "Well, I don't think I'm going to be able to speak at the November conference after all. In fact, I may not even be in a position to attend."

Jim cocked his head. "Oh?" He shot Pete a wry grin. "And you drove all the way from San Francisco just to tell me that?"

Pete couldn't help but return the grin. "Well, not exactly." He launched into his narrative of the events leading up to his visit, holding nothing back. It was wonderful being able to pour out his heart to someone he could trust, someone who would understand, someone who knew all about the weighty burdens associated with shepherding God's flock. Jim listened intently, occasionally nodding in agreement. When Pete finished, he rubbed his chin thoughtfully.

"Pete, I had no idea the state was going to enforce the hate speech law so quickly, or with such an iron fist. This is the first I've heard about multiple, city-wide arrests. There have been a few here and there, of course, but nothing of this magnitude. Maybe San Francisco is the test case for this law. But I must say, I'm not at all surprised. I've been researching this issue for some time now, even before it became law, along with several other area pastors. We're greatly alarmed that the state has given itself such broad authority over churches and their exercise of free speech. We've contacted the Alliance Defending Freedom and the CLS and asked them to get involved. To date, several motions have been filed seeking to exempt California churches from complying with the law."

Pete stared down at the carpet. "I'm afraid I haven't gotten involved in this as much as you have, Jim. I've thought of it as more of a political issue than a spiritual one." He paused. "At least until now. I've always believed that the First Amendment was enough to protect our freedom to preach God's Word in this country, that it would be the barrier needed to maintain the separation of church and state." He shook his head. "Apparently that's not true anymore."

Jim opened a desk drawer and pulled out a paper. "Interesting that you should mention the separation of church and state. Thomas Jefferson used that phrase in a letter he wrote to the Danbury Baptist Association of Connecticut in 1802. It was even published in a Massachusetts newspaper. I happen to have an excerpt from that letter right here." He grinned. "Part of my research on this subject." He read from the paper.

> "Believing with you that religion is a matter which lies solely between Man & his God, that he owes account to none other for his faith or his worship, that the legitimate powers of government reach actions only, & not opinions, I contemplate with sovereign reverence that act of the whole American people which declared that their legislature should 'make no law respecting an establishment of religion, or prohibiting the free exercise thereof,' thus building a wall of separation between Church & State."

Pete responded with conviction. "The government says the church has no business inserting itself into the political arena, but it certainly has no trouble inserting itself into the church! Apparently free speech has now become a one-way street, with the government deciding which direction traffic can flow."

Jim leaned forward. "It does seem that way, doesn't it? Pete, you and I both know that hate speech is wrong and we'd never condone it. The Bible condemns hate in any form. But that's not the issue here. What's so dangerous about this law is that it exempts hate speech from First Amendment protection and gives the state the right to set its own definitions and determine its own punishments. It's given itself way too much power."

"Like the old saying, 'Absolute power corrupts absolutely'?" Pete added.

"Exactly. There are no safeguards built into this law as far as I've been able to determine. The state can enforce it however it chooses."

"Remember the official state letter sent to all of us in the clergy?" Pete asked. Jim grimaced and nodded his head. "It stated that non-compliance would result in fines and mandatory reeducation. But when I was questioned by SFPD, the detective said the state also has the right to enforce incarceration and confiscate church property if need be."

Jim scowled again. "I'd heard that as well. In fact, did you know that when HB231 was in committee, one of our illustrious congressmen had the audacity to suggest that *Alcatraz* be refurbished to house prisoners labeled as 'incorrigible haters', so as to make them an example and discourage others from breaking the law?"

"You've got to be kidding!" Pete blurted out in disbelief. "Alcatraz? You mean they'd be willing to forego the tourism income that place generates just to make a statement? Wow, there must be some real haters of free speech among our elected officials to go that far."

"Thankfully, the suggestion was never given serious consideration," Jim replied, "but it does make you wonder, doesn't it?"

"Think of the irony if that had become reality," Pete said. "The same prison that once housed inmates who *took* human life would now be housing inmates who tell of the One Who *gives* eternal life!"

"We've come a long way, haven't we?" Jim bemoaned. "Just not in the right direction, I'm afraid. But we have to keep in mind that the Truth sounds like hate to those who hate the Truth." He smiled. "And it's our job to keep proclaiming that Truth and trust God to change hearts and minds."

"Amen, preach it!" Pete responded vigorously, raising both hands in the air.

Jim laughed at his outburst. "So, Brother, if I may ask, what was it that prompted you to make the decision to . . . to avoid being arrested?"

There had been enough time since leaving home for Pete to justify his decision. "Jim, I'm fully aware that not everyone might agree with me. I have another pastor friend in San Fran who refused to sign the Voluntary Compliance Agreement, and now he's sitting in jail. I made the decision to sign it, hoping to get the state off my back and out of my church. But I drew the line at compromising my preaching. You know I won't do that. I left because I thought it might put some distance between me and my church. I mean figuratively, not just literally. If the state is pursuing *me*, then maybe they'll leave my church and my family alone." He ruefully stared out the office window. "I don't know. To be honest with you, there wasn't much time to think it through. Had I stayed any longer though, I wouldn't have had *any* options."

Jim spoke gently to his fellow pastor. "Pete, by avoiding arrest, what options do you think that gives you now?"

Pete pondered his friend's question. "Well, at least it buys me some more time." He studied Jim's face for any sign of agreement.

Finding none, he posed a question of his own he'd been wanting to ask since first thinking of Jim in the hotel room. "Jim, you're a good friend and a brother in Christ. Over the years we've seen eye-to-eye on most subjects, haven't we?" He allowed himself a slight smirk. "Except when it comes to the Warriors and the Kings." Jim couldn't help laughing. Pete grew serious again. "I highly value your perspective and wisdom. What do you think I should do? Do you think I made the right decision?"

Jim took his time answering. "Like you, I was offered the chance to sign the compliance agreement, but I chose not to. As a result, I've been issued some heavy fines, and I'll be starting my 'reeducation' in two weeks. But I can tell you this much: if the Sacramento police came knocking on that door right now, I'd go with them peacefully. After all, they're not the enemy. And neither is the state. This battle we're in is not against flesh and blood as Ephesians six tells us. It's in the spiritual realm, *'against the rulers, against the authorities, against the cosmic powers over this present darkness, against the spiritual forces of evil in the heavenly places.'* It's between righteousness and unrighteousness, light and darkness, good and evil." He hesitated, noticing the inner guilt and conflict reflecting in Pete's eyes. "But that was my personal decision. Dear brother, I can't tell you what you should have done, or what you should do now. That's between you and God. But this much I do know: *'Commit your way to the Lord, trust in Him, and He will act.'* I know you well enough to know that you want the Lord's will in this matter. Just keep trusting Him. He will make your paths straight."

"I know He will," Pete replied, with firm conviction. "I still believe that. It's just that I've never been in a situation quite like this before. Not even in the military."

"This is new territory for all of us in America who desire to fully obey God," Jim acknowledged. "The freedoms we've enjoyed for over two hundred and forty years are rapidly eroding. But we need to be prepared and ready to face it. The time for sticking our heads in the sand or looking the other way is over. And I don't think it's going to get any better in the near future."

Pete's shoulders slumped. "I think you're absolutely spot-on about that, Jim."

Jim pushed his chair back from the desk and changed the subject. "Where are you staying tonight?" he inquired.

"At the Holiday Inn on the west side of town. At least for the time being, anyway."

"Why don't you come stay at my house?" Jim offered. "Sarah and I have a guest room with a private bath. You're welcome to stay with us for as long as you need."

Pete hesitated. "That's very kind of you, Jim, really it is. I'd love to take you up on that. But I don't think I should accept your offer. By now SFPD has already tried to serve my warrant, and if that's the case, then they know that I'm avoiding them. That makes me a marked man. I wouldn't want to put you and Sarah in a compromising position. It's entirely possible they could charge you with harboring a fugitive."

"Hmm," Jim frowned deeply, "I see what you mean. Well, how about this, then. If you plan on staying around for a few days, why not join us here for worship Sunday morning? It would be good for you to be with other believers at a time like this. And nobody needs to know anything. I won't even tell Sarah about our conversation."

Pete thought about the invitation, then nodded in agreement. "Yeah, I think I can do that." He smiled weakly. "I have no other plans at the moment."

Pete spent the rest of Friday and much of Saturday in his hotel room, sitting at the desk reading his Bible or kneeling beside the bed praying. He prayed for his wife and children, and his church and ministry. And he prayed that God would show him what to do. Several times he was tempted to call Angela to check on her and the kids, but he resisted the urge.

She'll be calling me as soon as it's safe anyway.

Before leaving home, he'd had the foresight to turn over the leadership of his church to the head of the deacon board, so he knew his ministry was in solid hands for the interim. But how long that interim would last was anyone's guess at this point.

It all depended on what choices he made from now on.

Later that evening he went out for dinner at a nearby restaurant, then returned to his hotel room and flipped on the TV. Relaxing on a pile of pillows, he channel-surfed for a while before settling on a couple of *The Andy Griffith Show* reruns, enjoying the simplistic levity they afforded him. Then it was time for the ten o'clock news.

"Good evening, and welcome to WSLN Channel 6 News at ten," the anchor began. "I'm Cody Simmons, and here are tonight's top headlines. We begin with breaking news. The Sacramento Police Department conducted a metro-area sweep this morning. Armed with over two dozen warrants, officers went door-to-door in an attempt to round up violators of the state's hate speech law, which went into effect last October."

Pete sprang from his reclining position and sat on the end of the bed. He turned up the volume.

"For the latest details, we go to our street reporter, Brandi Benton." The newscast cut to a live shot of a reporter standing on a dark residential street somewhere in the city.

"I'm standing in front of a house in the fourteen-hundred block of Foothills Drive," the reporter began, "where earlier today SPD arrested an occupant on charges of promoting hate speech in a public park. According to spokesperson Toni Harrison, warrants were served across the metro area and nineteen persons in all were arrested, making this the largest operation of its kind to date in the city. In addition to the arrests, police seized personal computers, hate speech pamphlets, and several firearms. I spoke with Ms. Harrison regarding the objective of the sweep."

The TV station played a segment of a previously recorded interview:

"The Sacramento Police Department is committed to enforcing the Hate Speech Reparation and Elimination Act with all the resources available to it," the police spokesperson stated. "SPD is responsible for seeing that our streets and parks and public areas remain safe and free from any hateful rhetoric that might lead to inciting violent or illegal actions against any person or group protected under the law. In cooperation with the Stop the Violence Alliance of greater Sacramento, we urge the public to report anyone suspected of being involved in the promotion or dissemination of hate speech of any kind. By working together with law enforcement, we can put an end to this threat in our communities."

Pete stared blankly at the screen as the TV anchor moved on to other local news. *So, San Francisco isn't the only city rounding up people under the hate speech ban. I wonder if this is a coordinated statewide effort. If that's true, then no one is safe in any urban jurisdiction. This is going to get ugly real fast!*

CHAPTER FIVE
A SYMPATHETIC EAR

AFTER EATING BREAKFAST IN THE hotel lobby, Pete left the Holiday Inn around 9:45 Sunday morning and drove across Sacramento to Jim's church. By the time he arrived at Highland Hills Bible Church the parking lot was nearly full. But there were several parking spaces reserved for visitors near the main entrance, and two were still unoccupied, so he laid claim to one of them.

He entered the vestibule of the church building. It was full of people, some delivering kids to their classrooms, some moving into the sanctuary, some standing around talking. Pete picked up on a few conversations as he walked by a couple of groups. They were discussing yesterday's police sweep. As he entered the sanctuary, he was greeted by several friendly people, and an usher handed him a program. He took a seat near the back of the room and waited for the service to start. When the worship leader got up to lead the congregation in a hymn, Jim wasn't on the platform yet. Perhaps he was still backstage getting miked up. Pete recalled his own Sunday morning battles with faulty electronics and dead microphone batteries.

Following the announcements and offering, a man he didn't recognize got up and approached the pulpit. *Jim didn't say anything about having a guest preacher.*

"For those of you who don't know me, I'm Pastor Mark Miller," the man began. "I'm the associate pastor here at Highland Hills. I know most of you were expecting Pastor Sutherland to continue his series from the gospels this morning, but due to unforeseen circumstances, he is unable to be with us." A murmur of whispers rippled through the audience. Pastor Miller continued. "Many of you may have heard or read about the city-wide round-up our police department conducted yesterday morning. Well, I hate to be the bearer of bad tidings, but for nothing more than proclaiming the truth of God's Word to this congregation, our own dear pastor was caught up in that sweep!"

Loud gasps and cries of "Oh no!" filled the auditorium. People looked at one another in shock and disbelief. A few sobbed in their seats.

No, not Jim! Why would they arrest him? He was cooperating with the authorities. He'd agreed to pay the state's fines and complete their reeducation program.

Anger welled up inside Pete. The state had no right to treat men like Jim, and Jorge, and himself with such cold-hearted callousness. They were dedicated men of God, whose only crime was the preaching of Truth to those who would listen. They were actually making a positive difference in their communities, not a negative one. He sat fuming in the pew.

Why doesn't the state put as much effort into rounding up the real criminals?

Pastor Miller spent the next ten to fifteen minutes explaining the situation facing the church. He invited several men onto the platform to pray for their lead pastor and those who arrested him. Then he preached the message that Pastor Jim was to have delivered.

Following the service, Pete made his way through the maze of people who were milling about the sanctuary and vestibule, animatedly discussing the heinous arrest of their pastor and the ramifications of the horrible hate speech law. As he passed a trio of men on his way to the door, their conversation caught his attention.

"I say we all show up at the rally in droves," a tall man in a three-piece suit was saying, quite heatedly. "There's no way they can arrest all of us at once. We'd overwhelm them for sure!" The others laughed and voiced their agreement.

"We need to make a loud statement, send a clear message," the dark-haired man to his right said. "Let the state know that there are more than just a handful of its citizens who think this law is unconstitutional."

"Not to mention despicable and immoral," the short, stocky one chimed in. The tall man responded with a firm "Amen!"

Pete stopped and approached the circle. "Excuse me, but I couldn't help overhearing your conversation. What rally are you talking about?" There was an awkward silence as the men eyed him suspiciously.

Then the man in the three-piece suit spoke up. "I don't believe I've had the pleasure of meeting you." He held out his hand. "I'm Richard. And you are . . . ?"

Pete hesitated. He couldn't risk them finding out why he was here. But he did insert himself into their conversation. He shook the man's hand and introduced himself only as "Pete."

"Is this your first time at Highland Hills, Pete?" Richard asked.

"No, I've been here several times before," he admitted. "But not since last year."

The three men glanced at each other. "What brings you to our services today?" the dark-haired man asked. Their inquiries reminded him of his interview with Detective Branch. But the questions seemed innocuous enough, and the men appeared to be on Pastor Jim's side, which probably meant they were on his side, too. Pete took a chance.

"I'm here on business," he replied. "Pastor Sutherland is a friend of mine. Actually, we were in seminary together. He invited me to speak at the pastor's conference you're hosting here in November. I met with him in his study Friday afternoon, but I had no idea he'd been arrested until I heard about it in the service."

The men let down their guard, and the other two introduced themselves as Vince and Colin. Richard told him about the rally. "It was organized by the California Free Speech Alliance to protest the hate speech law. It's scheduled for noon tomorrow at State Capital Park. There will be hundreds if not thousands of people there from all over the state and beyond, congressmen, ministers, free-speech advocates, you name it."

"And the police," Colin added. The other two chuckled.

"I'm surprised the city granted a permit for the event," Pete remarked, "with the blitzkrieg going on this weekend." The men laughed heartily at his analogy.

"We think that's why they conducted the raid on Saturday," Vince explained. "It was meant to send a message to the organizers, as well as scare away some of the crowd."

Richard put his hand on Pete's shoulder. "Listen, Pete, if you're still in town tomorrow, why don't you join us at the rally? Seeing as how you've got a personal interest in the subject."

A sudden jolt shot up and down Pete's spine. "Uh . . . what do you mean by that?"

"Just that I thought you'd want to be there, with Pastor Jim being arrested yesterday, and you being old seminary friends and everything."

Pete surreptitiously heaved a sigh of relief. He glanced at the three men awaiting his answer. "Yeah, sure," he replied, as casually as he could. "I think my schedule tomorrow will allow me to attend."

Pete drove his car around the block several times until a parking space became available. He parallel parked and fed four quarters into the meter. Not wanting to risk being caught by a simple parking violation, he added two more. Then he walked to the corner, crossed at the light, and headed down L Street in the direction of the capital building. He could have gotten closer, but he'd chosen a quiet side street six blocks away, in case the police decided to run license plates on vehicles parked near the rally.

A large number of people, many with homemade signs and posters, were already gathered on the lawn in front of the statehouse by the time he reached State Capital Park. A temporary platform with folding chairs and a podium had been set up facing the open space. Two large speakers mounted on tripods flanked the stage. Television news trucks lined 15th Avenue, and local and network reporters mingled with the crowd, interviewing random attendees. Not wanting to risk being buttonholed, he kept his distance from the handheld cameras. All he needed was for his face to be plastered across the evening news.

He made note of the large police presence, and every time a uniformed officer passed by, he avoided eye contact.

Make yourself as inconspicuous as possible, Pete. And just keep breathing!

Pete located the large oak tree near the park's entrance where the men had agreed to meet. The others were already there waiting for him. As the speakers for the rally climbed the steps and took their seats, he observed the heaviest concentration of police patrols was nearest the stage and was relieved when his group stationed itself in the back half of the crowd.

The rally went off without incident. First, the president of the California Free Speech Alliance welcomed the crowd and briefly summarized the problems inherent with the hate speech law. Then he introduced three speakers. The first was a state senator who had opposed the bill from its inception. He vowed he and his conservative compatriots would keep fighting to have the law repealed. His speech was routinely interrupted by heavy applause. The next speaker was a prominent Sacramento lawyer and a member of the Christian Legal Society. He informed the attendees his organization was challenging the constitutionality of the law and promised to defend those unjustly arrested in the recent sweep. The final speaker, the head of the local ministerial association, used his allotted time to urge the public to pray for those arrested, and for the legislators responsible for passing the law, and the police officers charged with enforcing it. He encouraged peaceful resistance and asked that the attendees contact their representatives and let their voices be heard at the ballot box. Then he pronounced the benediction and led the crowd in singing "God Bless America."

As the crowd dispersed, the four men walked back to the park entrance. Richard invited Pete to join them for lunch at a nearby restaurant. Having carried the burden of being alone the past two days, and sensing a common bond with the other men, he accepted the invitation. The quartet had walked about a block and a half when

Vince suddenly stopped in his tracks, causing Pete, who was walking directly behind him, to step on his heels.

"My car!" Vince exclaimed, staring wide-eyed at an empty parking space next to the curb. "Somebody stole my car!" He placed his hands on his head and paced back and forth in disbelief.

"Are you sure this is where you parked?" Colin, the shorter man, asked.

"Yes, I'm sure this is the space. I remember that trash can with the dent in it. And that pole." He shook his head in disbelief and repeated himself. "Somebody stole my car." He threw his hands in the air. "Now that's public safety for you. Half the metro police force is here making sure nobody misbehaves at the rally, and somebody goes and steals my car from right under their noses!" He snorted in disgust.

Richard pointed to a cardboard sign stapled to the pole. "I don't think your car was stolen, Vince. I think it's been towed." Pete read the temporary notice: "NO PARKING TODAY." Beneath that in a smaller font were the words, "By order of the Sacramento Police Department. Violators will be towed." Richard grinned and patted Vince on the back. "Tough break, pal. The police didn't haul away anyone at the rally, they just hauled away your car!" Colin threw back his head and guffawed. Pete couldn't help but chuckle.

"That sign wasn't up there when I parked the car," Vince protested vehemently. "I'd swear to that. It wasn't there! They must have posted it sometime after eleven fifteen."

"Well, the sign's there now," Colin pointed out, "and your car's not. I guess that means you'll be making a trip to the impound lot fairly soon."

Vince glowered at him. "Thanks for the reminder, C.B."

"Let's go eat anyway," Richard suggested. "I'm starved. You can call the impound lot after lunch."

"Oh, all right," Vince grumbled, shaking his head. The group turned the corner and headed toward the restaurant at the far end of the block. Suddenly Richard stopped. It was his turn to stare.

"They got *my* car, too!" Beside the empty parking space was a lamp post, with the same cardboard sign attached to it. "Can you believe this? They targeted my car, too!"

Pete could identify with their frustration at being targeted by the police. "Did any of you notice that those were the only two signs posted along both streets?" he asked. "And no other vehicles appear to have been towed but yours. Don't you find that odd? Is there anything about your cars that might have drawn the attention of the police? Like any similarities, for example?"

Vince and Richard looked at him, then at each other. "I don't think so." Vince shrugged. "They're completely different makes and models, and the colors aren't even close. I can't think of any similarities at all."

Richard snapped his fingers. "The bumper stickers! We both have the same bumper sticker on the back, remember?"

"The CFSA sticker!" Vince blurted out. "The one that says, 'YOU WILL NEVER SHUT ME UP!'"

"Well how do you like that!" Richard growled, through clenched teeth. "They targeted our cars just because we support the Free Speech Alliance."

"Come on, would they really do that?" Colin asked skeptically. "I mean, that seems rather underhanded to me."

"You mean *heavy*-handed, don't you?" Vince retorted. "I wouldn't put it past them. Did you notice the photographers mingling with the crowd? Those weren't news photographers; those were state police photographers! I caught a glimpse of one guy's badge clipped on his belt. They were taking pictures of everyone at the rally. I'd say that's more than being underhanded."

Pete cringed. He hadn't noticed them at all. *If they captured my face in one of their photos, I could be in real trouble.*

Vince turned to Richard, who appeared to be stewing inside. "What are you thinking, Rich?" Pete could almost see the smoke coming out of his ears.

Richard was staring at the spot where his car used to be. "I think it's high time we *did* something about this!" he said, spitting venom.

The four men sat at the round table in the crowded downtown restaurant, discussing the rally as they awaited their lunch orders.

"I agree with most of what the speakers said, but I have a problem with the 'peaceful resistance' the minister called for," Richard confessed, still upset about his car being towed.

"Why's that?" Colin spoke up. "It sounds a lot like the civil disobedience Dr. Martin Luther King championed. Are you saying we have the right to resist the law *beyond* that point?"

"I'm not advocating violence, per se," Richard acknowledged, "I'm just saying that there comes a time when all the petitions and protests and rallies don't seem to make much of a difference. There's got to be more we can do to change things. We can't afford to sit around on our hands watching our country go down the drain."

"Yeah," Vince agreed, "who was it who said, 'The only thing necessary for the triumph of evil is that good men should do nothing'?"

"I don't know, but I'll tell you in a jiff." Colin grinned and did a quick search on his smartphone. "Aha! It's attributed to the Irish-born statesman Edmund Burke. And the context was prohibition. The rest of the quote says, 'Leave the Drink Trade alone and it will throttle all that is good in a nation's life. Let it alone, that is all that is required. Cowardice will suffice for its triumph. Courage will suffice for its overthrow.'"

Richard resolutely crossed his arms. "You could substitute 'Hate Speech Law' for 'Drink Trade,' and it would mean the exact same thing. Doing nothing is cowardly. Taking action is courageous."

"Here's another one of his quotes," Colin announced to the group. "'Nobody made a greater mistake than he who did nothing because he could do only a little.'"

"My point exactly!" Richard exclaimed, smacking the table for emphasis. "Even if we think we can do only a little, we don't have the option of doing nothing. Don't you see? If enough people did little things, it would soon add up to something very big. I've read how the POW's attempted to sabotage the Japanese and German war efforts by removing railroad spikes from the tracks while on work details, or by putting plaster and other toxic things in the guards' food to make them sick. We have no idea how much those little acts of resistance contributed to the outcome of World War Two. We need to take action and resist wherever we can, too."

Pete spoke up for the first time. "What kind of action are you suggesting? Legal or illegal?"

Richard stared at him. "If we can't stop evil through legal means, then I think we have the right to use other means. More than a right, an obligation!"

"I agree," Vince affirmed. "It's no longer a matter of legality but of morality. A bad law is immoral, and as Christians, we can't obey an immoral law. We need to resist. Fight back."

"You say resist," Pete challenged him, "but what about *desist?* Shouldn't we simply refuse to obey an ungodly law and seek to overturn it through legal channels rather than use unethical or compromising methods?"

Drew's voice suddenly echoed in his conscience. *"You violated your own Christian principles! You never intended to comply with that agreement, did you? You signed it only to get the state off your back and out of your church. That's the same as lying, isn't it?"*

Vince squinted at him. "I didn't figure you for a pacifist."

"Pacifist? I'm not a pacifist!" Pete squared his shoulders. "I believe in standing up for my rights. I'm a veteran of the Iraq War, 101st Airborne. I've done my share of defending our country and freedoms. But the fight we're talking about can't be won using unlawful methods or force."

"Why not?" Richard asked bluntly.

"Because I don't believe this is a legislative, or legal, or even moral battle we're in. It's a spiritual one." He told the men what Jim had shared from the Ephesians six passage with him on Friday. Then he added, "The question really isn't *how* we should resist, but *whom* we should resist. We're commanded to resist the devil, not men." Pete paused, feeling a twinge in his conscience. *Isn't resisting arrest the same as resisting men?*

"What are you, a preacher or something?" Vince grinned knowingly, breaking the tension.

Pete chuckled along with the others. Then Richard resumed his argument. "Pete, I get what you're saying, but do you remember what Jesus instructed His disciples to take with them the second time He sent them out? He said, '*Let the one who has no sword sell his cloak and buy one.*' If that doesn't give us the right to take up arms, I don't know what does!"

"I believe that was for self-defense, not for overthrowing the Romans," Pete parried. "And what about what Jesus said the night He was betrayed, when Peter drew his sword to fight back? He said, '*No more of this! Put your sword back into its place. For all who take the sword will perish by the sword.*'"

"Yeah, but that was in context of the moment," Richard deftly thrust back. "The disciples didn't understand that God's plan was for Jesus to be arrested, tried, and crucified. By stopping that, they would have ruined mankind's only hope of redemption. That's not what we're fighting against today. We're fighting against corruption and evil in high places."

"But who would you have us fight against?" Pete countered intently. "The police? The legislators? Those who hate what we stand for? They're not the real enemy, just pawns on a chessboard."

"Then I guess that would make Vince the knight," Colin quipped light-heartedly. The men laughed. "Vince owns several horses," he explained to Pete.

Richard patted Pete on the back. "And that would make Pete here the bishop!" Pete searched for sarcasm in the remark but found none.

"Then who's the king?" Vince wondered, "The governor?" The men laughed again.

Richard raised both hands and bowed mockingly. "Long live the governor! Hail Caesar!" This time his words were dripping with sarcasm.

The waitress came with their food order. As they began eating, Richard continued pressing his point to the group. "Look, I understand that we are in a spiritual battle. I get that. We still need to practice our faith and pray that God will change the hearts of men and all that. But when I became a citizen of heaven, I didn't surrender my citizenship in the United States. I have a responsibility to both. And I need to do what I can for both. Take today's speakers, for example. Senator Heinrich is doing what he can by trying to repeal a bad law. And the lawyers are doing their part by challenging its constitutionality."

"But what can average Joe citizens like us do to combat the evil encroaching on our freedoms?" Colin posed. "I mean, besides voting, and protesting, and such."

"We can desist, like Pete said. That's a start," Richard acknowledged. "But I think we should also resist."

"I'm not sure I agree with you on that," Pete interjected. "Paul said in the first two verses of Romans chapter thirteen that whoever resists the powers that be resists the ordinance of God Himself."

Richard squinted at him for a moment before replying. "Pete, you're right about that, of course. But I've made a study of that passage, too. And the next verse says, *'For rulers are not a terror to good works, but to the evil.'* Can you honestly sit there and tell me that what our leaders are doing is not a terror to good works? You can't! They aren't fulfilling their God-given role as ministers of good. In fact, they're the ones resisting God! Therefore, I believe we have the right to resist them because of the evil they're doing."

"But how do we resist?" Colin pressed, reiterating his previous question.

Richard gestured toward the front window of the restaurant. "Take our cars for example. The cops impounded them illegally, right? Just to make a statement. They don't have any right to hold them. I say that gives us the right to take them back, by any means necessary. We need to make a statement of our own!"

"Why not just pay the towing and impound fees?" Pete argued. "Wouldn't you get your cars back just the same?"

Vince leaned forward before Richard could respond. "I agree with Rich on this one. That would only encourage more of the same kind of behavior. The government means to wear us down until we comply without putting up any resistance at all."

"I remember when my daughter was nine or ten," Colin mused. "She had a neighbor friend who came over to play dolls with her, and a lot of her doll clothes began to disappear. Then one day she was at her friend's house and discovered all the missing items among the other girl's things. So, she simply stole them back. I don't think the other girl ever knew what she'd done. But Evelyn got back what was rightfully hers."

Vince sat up straight in his chair. "Yeah, my son Josiah did the same thing."

Richard eyed him warily. "I didn't know your son played with dolls, Vince!" The men burst into laughter.

Vince scowled. "Not dolls, Rich, his bike! It was stolen from the front stoop one day. We searched the neighborhood for a week before we found it in a back yard three blocks away. We knew it was his because he'd wrecked it once and there were identifying scratches on the frame. So he simply grabbed it and rode it back home."

Pete turned to Richard. "And you think you should do the same with your cars?"

"And why not?" Richard retorted defiantly. "I think we should fight fire with fire. If enough of us push back, they'll think twice before pulling that stunt again. They won't be able to do anything about it because the sheer magnitude of the resistance will wear *them* down for a change!" Richard leaned forward and dropped his voice to almost a whisper. "Listen, guys, Vince and I have been involved in some clandestine meetings for several months now. A number of us are trying to mobilize an organized resistance that would overwhelm the corrupt system and allow us to take back our inherent rights in this state, including our right to free speech."

"You mean like a grass roots-type movement?" Colin queried.

Richard glanced around the room before replying. "More like an *underground* movement! A band of outlaw citizens committed to resisting a corrupt government that has illegally taken away their rights and freedoms."

"Sounds more like a Clint Eastwood movie to me," Colin replied with a nervous laugh.

Richard held up both palms in a show of innocence. "Hey, I'm not advocating the use of violence or anything like that. No gunslinger showdowns or shootouts in the Wild, Wild West. And not like those radical left-wing activist groups do, rampaging through the streets tearing down statues and looting and setting fire to public property. I'm just advocating for working outside of a bad law to restore what's rightfully ours."

"So, how do you propose we go about getting our cars back?" Vince asked, between bites of his sandwich.

Richard glanced around again before replying. "I have a cousin who works at the police impound lot. You remember Charlie don't you, Vince?" Vince nodded. "He's on board with this whole underground resistance thing. I'm pretty sure I can persuade him to help us get our cars off the lot. All we'd need is for someone to drive us there after dark." He looked at Colin. "Can you lend us a hand, C.B.?"

Colin hesitated. "Uh, when are you thinking of doing it?" He didn't look at all sure about it.

"Tomorrow night. Wednesday night, maybe. What do you say?"

"Well, I have to fly down to LA tomorrow afternoon for some high-level business meetings. I won't be back until sometime Saturday evening."

Richard frowned. "We can't wait that long. We've got to act now." He turned to Vince. "What about Darryl? Think he might be willing to take us there?"

"I'm sure he'd be willing, but he's in Denver right now. I don't know when he's coming back."

Richard was silent for a moment. Then he threw a look Pete's way. "Pete, how long are you going to be in town? Do you think you could help us out here? All you'd have to do is drive to the impound lot and drop us off. We'll handle the rest of the details."

Alarms went off in Pete's head. *Don't do it, Pete. You don't want to get involved in this.*

But there was a part of him that did. Wasn't he already involved in the resistance, in his own small way? Perhaps Richard was right. Maybe there was more that he could do to aid in this noble cause seeking to restore the rights and freedoms which the state had stolen from its citizens, even if was just a small thing. He recalled Jim's words from three days ago. *"The time for sticking our heads in the sand or looking the other way is over."*

Pete glanced around the table. The three men were staring at him, awaiting his answer. "I'll be around for a few more days," he replied hesitantly. Then he smacked his palm on the edge of the table and nodded resolutely. "All right, gentlemen, count me in!"

CHAPTER SIX
JOINING THE UNDERGROUND RESISTANCE

PETE LEFT THE HOLIDAY INN at one o'clock Thursday morning and drove to the 24-hour convenience store where he had agreed to pick up Richard and Vince. As he pulled into the nearly empty parking lot, two men dressed in dark clothing from head to foot emerged from a car parked beside the building and hurried toward him. Richard climbed into the front and Vince got into the back.

His front seat passenger turned to him with a scowl. "You're ten minutes late! I was beginning to think you'd backed out on us."

Pete shot him a sideways glance. "I'm not familiar with this area," he explained. "It took a little longer to get here than I expected."

"No problem," Richard said, with a disarming smile. "Go left out of the parking lot."

Pete turned onto the street and began driving. He glanced at Vince in the rear-view mirror. "So how do you guys figure on getting into the lot? I'd imagine there are alarms and security cameras everywhere."

Richard was the one who answered cryptically. "Leave that to me. I've got it all taken care of."

Pete drove in silence for a few blocks. "Aren't they going to know who took the cars if yours are the only two missing?"

There was an edge to Richard's reply. "Look, Pete, I think it's best if you don't ask questions. The fewer details you know the better. All you need to do is drive us there and wait until you see us drive out, that's all."

Pete turned to his passenger. "What do you mean, 'wait until you drive out'? You didn't say anything about wanting me to wait around. All you said was that you needed someone to drop you off!"

"Yeah, that's all you need to do," Richard repeated himself. "But just in case we aren't able to get our cars out, we'll need a ride back, won't we? It shouldn't take more than seven or eight minutes tops."

Vince grabbed the back of the seat and pulled himself forward. "You won't even have to drive onto police property," he promised. "You'll just be letting us out across the street."

"Turn right at the next intersection," Richard instructed him tersely.

Pete turned the corner. He sensed the nervous tension in his two passengers, and it only added to the anxiety he already felt. As they drove in silence, he studied the two men. Alarm bells triggered in his head.

"Uh . . . are you guys expecting trouble?"

Richard stared at him with narrowed eyes. "Of course not. Why would you ask that?"

"Well, if this has all been worked out like you say, then why are you both packing heat?"

Richard stiffened and zipped up his jacket to conceal the shoulder holster.

From the back seat, Vince offered a wordy explanation. "Of course we don't expect trouble. But we *always* carry. It's just habit, that's all. Rich and I both have CCW permits. We never go anywhere without them. Truth is, crime is so bad around here, you never know when you might have to defend yourself."

"Will you relax, Pete?" Richard chided him. "You have nothing to worry about. My cousin has seen to it that we can safely get in and out in a few minutes. That's all you need to know."

"Besides, if there's any risk, *we're* the ones taking it, not you," Vince added persuasively.

Twenty minutes later, Richard told Pete to pull the car off the road onto the gravel shoulder, directly opposite the main gate. The impound lot itself was set back from the road about two hundred and fifty feet and was surrounded by a ten-foot-high chain link fence topped with barbed wire. A couple of mercury vapor lights were mounted on a tall wooden pole in the center of the lot, casting light and shadows across the whole area. To the far right of the rows of cars was a low, wooden office building.

Richard pointed ahead to a copse of trees adjacent to the road. "Park under those trees," he instructed him. "It's dark enough there that nobody will pay attention to you if they happen to drive by." Pete pulled forward into the shadows and shut off the engine. The two men got out and came around the front of the car.

Richard approached the driver's side window. "This won't take long. Keep all the lights off, and duck down if anyone drives past, okay?" Pete nodded. "When I come out, I'll flash my headlights to let you know when it's okay to take off." The two men donned ski masks and pulled small, military-style flashlights from their pockets. "One

more thing. Stay in the car! No matter what, stay in the car, got it?"
Pete nodded again; quite sure he did not want to be here. Richard and
Vince crossed the road and scurried along the fence, disappearing
into the shadows around the right side of the impound lot.

"What did I get myself into?" Pete muttered under his breath. He
glanced into his rear-view mirror to make sure the road was clear. He
had a bad feeling about this.

He checked his watch. It was 1:56 a.m. Leaning back against the
headrest, he began counting the minutes. Time crawled. Five minutes,
six minutes, seven minutes went by. They should be coming out any
moment now. He stared intently at the impound lot across the street
but detected no lights or movement whatsoever. Eight minutes, nine
minutes, ten minutes.

Where were they? *Hurry it up, will ya?*

Suddenly, a dim light flickered from inside the office building.
At first, he thought he'd imagined it. But no, there it was again. What
were they doing inside the office? They should be driving out by now.
Eleven minutes, twelve minutes. Pete pounded the steering wheel
impatiently. "C'mon, guys, c'mon!" he growled under his breath.
"We've gotta get out of here!"

Then he saw a flash of car headlights. Finally, they were on their
way out. *'Bout time!* He reached for the starter button but froze. The
lights hadn't come from inside the compound, but from his rear-view
mirror. A pair of headlights was rapidly approaching from behind.
No, make that two pairs of headlights! He ducked down and waited
for the cars to pass. Two streaks of light flashed across the headliner.
After counting to ten, he cautiously lifted his head and looked
through the windshield. The road ahead was dark. He glanced out

his side window toward the lot and nearly had a heart attack. Two marked police cars had turned into the gravel drive and were silently pulling to a stop in front of the main gate. The doors of the cruisers flew open and four uniformed officers jumped out, drawing their sidearms in one synchronous motion. One of them ran to the control box off to the side and punched in the code.

C'mon, guys, get out! Get out now!

With a metallic scraping sound, the gate began to move. Four armed policemen slipped through the widening crack and melted into the shadows created by the rows of vehicles.

Pete sat motionless in his seat. What should he do? It was too late to warn Richard and Vince now. He'd have to leave without them. They were on their own. Besides, more cops were probably on the way! He hit the starter button on the dash and the engine came to life.

Pop! Pop! Pop! His head jerked upward at the sound of the muffled gunfire. Specialist Pete Holloway of the 586th Forward Support Battalion instinctively sprang into full military mode. With adrenaline pumping, he jumped from his Humvee and took cover behind it. Cautiously peering over the hood at the enemy compound, he detected movement inside. Suddenly two soldiers burst through the open gate on the dead run.

"SPD! Get on the ground!" An enemy fighter emerged from the shadows in full pursuit, then another. "Get on the ground *now!*" The taller soldier stopped fleeing and spun around to engage the pursuing fighter. Pete saw an object in his right hand.

POP! POP! POP! POP! The soldier turned and took a few staggering steps toward him before crumpling to the ground. The shorter one stopped running and raised both hands in the air, then lay down on the gravel, arms extended from his sides. When the pursuers caught up to the men lying prone on the driveway, one of them kicked the gun out of the first soldier's hand while the other handcuffed the second soldier.

Crouching behind his Humvee, Army Specialist Pete Holloway watched the action unfold a hundred feet in front of him. He couldn't leave now. *'Nemo resideo.' No one left behind!*

He eased around the front of his armored vehicle. As he crossed the headlight beams, the motion of his silhouette caught the attention of a third enemy fighter emerging from the compound.

"There's another one!" the fighter shouted the warning to his comrades. Grabbing his sidearm with both hands, he assumed a firing position. "SPD! Drop your weapon and get on the ground. *Now!*"

Specialist Holloway instinctively raised his weapon to engage the enemy . . .

POP! POP! POP! He heard a bullet whiz past his ear and another thud into the door post. The rear passenger window suddenly exploded with a loud crash. Pete blinked and came to his senses. He looked at his sedan, then back at the policeman.

"Throw down your weapon and get on the ground!" the officer screamed again, taking a step toward him.

For the first time, Pete noticed the Taurus in his hand. What was he doing? Did he just draw down on a cop? He slowly lowered his arm and let the gun hang limply in his hand.

I'm in serious trouble here! But I don't think they've seen my face yet. It's too dark. There's only one thing left to do. He made like he was going to fling the weapon aside but tossed it through the shattered rear window instead. Then he spun and dove into the driver's seat.

"He's running!" two of the officers yelled in unison. One of them holstered his weapon and sprinted toward his patrol car. Pete slammed the shifter into drive and gunned the engine. Gravel and dirt spewed from beneath the rear tires as he jerked the steering wheel hard left. The car leaped onto the pavement, found traction, and rocketed away. As he glanced over his shoulder, he saw the officer climbing into his car. But he caught sight of something out of the corner of his eye that made his blood run cold. It was the impound office building, no longer dark but ablaze with light. Flames were shooting through the windows.

Pete mashed the accelerator to the floor as he raced down the road away from the scene. Surely, he had enough of a head start. Utilizing all the evasive skills in his arsenal, he made several screeching, sliding turns onto random side streets. He cut through neighborhoods and sped down nearly deserted avenues, all the while keeping one eye on the rear-view mirror. To his relief he saw nothing but darkness behind him.

After five minutes of high-speed maneuvering, he slowed down to avoid drawing attention to himself. Doubling back from his initial heading, he zig-zagged his way toward the Holiday Inn at the other end of the city, being careful to avoid major thoroughfares, which were sure to be patrolled by other cruisers now on the lookout for a light-colored, four-door sedan with the left rear passenger window shot out.

When he reached the hotel, he drove around to the rear and parked in the far corner of the lot next to the dumpster, backing into the space to hide the shattered window from inquisitive eyes. He grabbed his handgun which had fallen onto the floorboards during the high-speed escape, and ran up to his room, taking the back stairs to avoid the lobby. Once inside, he bolted and latched the door, then pulled a bottled water from the mini-fridge and drained its contents in one drought.

Pete set his gun on the desk and fell into the chair. He leaned back and put both hands on his head. Blood pounded in his heart and temples. Questions raced across his mind like a stock exchange ticker run amok.

Did I just flee after being shot at and ordered to surrender? Was I really going to shoot a policeman? Did Richard and Vince set that fire to cover their tracks? Is Richard dead or alive? Am I guilty of aiding and abetting a crime? What have you done, Pete Holloway? Have you lost your ever-lovin' mind?

At some point, he knew he would have to step back and assess where he'd gotten off track and determine what needed to be done in order to correct the present situation. But there was no time for any of that now. The entire city would be crawling with cops on the lookout for the man who fled the shootout in the middle of the night while the rest of the population slept peacefully in their beds. He needed to get out of town, and fast.

Pete jumped to his feet and began tossing clothes into his suitcase. But in the middle of packing his toiletries, he was struck by a moment of clarity. The streets were almost deserted. If he left now, he would never make it out of the city. He'd be seen for sure. What he needed to do was wait until morning, when the chances of him being spotted during rush hour would be much less.

Having convinced himself of that strategy, he lay down on the bed and attempted to get some shuteye. He tried blocking out the memories of what he'd just been a party to, but it was as if he'd watched a violent 3-D horror picture on a large movie screen, and the graphic scenes were now permanently etched in his psyche. All he could see were the flames shooting skyward from the windows, all he could hear were the bullets striking way too close to his head, and all he could feel was the knot in his stomach as he watched Richard stagger and fall lifeless to the ground.

Pete stirred and rolled over in bed. He stretched his tense body beneath the covers. Gradually, like fog fleeing a harbor as the rising sun chases it away, sleep left him. What a realistic nightmare! That was so vivid, so lifelike. He pushed himself to a sitting position and looked around the hotel room. The truth provided a painful wake up call. That was no nightmare.

He checked the time. 6:25 a.m. He arose and stepped into the shower, hoping to wash the night's troubles down the drain along with the lather. Then he dressed and shaved and went down to the lobby for breakfast.

About a dozen people were already seated or going through the line when he entered the room. He felt self-conscious and conspicuous as he grabbed a plate and selected his breakfast items. He was being ridiculous. Nobody knew what he did last night. He took a seat facing the wall-mounted television. A family with two young children sat at the next table. The small boy about four-years-old watched him for a moment, then made a silly face and stuck out his tongue. Any other time Pete would have responded in kind, but this morning he just didn't have it in him. The local news broadcast came on the television.

"Go-o-o-d morning, Sacramento!" the overly cheerful and apparently over-caffeinated newscaster began. "I'm Sandra Tarkington, and this is your WSLN Channel 6 morning news at seven. It's a comfortable sixty-eight degrees climbing to an expected high of eighty-two across the capital city area, with sunny skies and low humidity. It's going to be another beautiful day!"

"Speak for yourself," Pete mumbled, taking a sip of his coffee.

"Here's this morning's top local story: Overnight, Sacramento police interrupted a break-in at the department's Stockton Road impound lot on the city's southeast side." Pete stiffened and stared at the screen, his fork halfway to his mouth. "Responding to a silent alarm, officers engaged three suspects in a gun battle that left one forty-two-year-old man dead and another in custody."

Pete got a prickly sensation on the back of his neck. The camera cut to a video of the impound lot sometime after he'd fled the scene. The night sky was illuminated by the red and blue flashing lights of emergency vehicles, as well as the yellowish-orange glow of flames that had engulfed the office building and several nearby cars.

"The suspects set fire to a wooden structure, and the blaze quickly spread to a dozen impounded vehicles. The building and vehicles appear to be a total loss." The picture of a car similar to Pete's flashed on the screen. "A third suspect fled the scene in a light-colored, four-door sedan with the left rear passenger window shot out. He is approximately six-foot tall and is still at large and believed to be armed and dangerous. Anyone with information on the suspect's identity or whereabouts is urged to contact the Sacramento Police Department immediately."

Pete didn't stay around for the rest of the news. He tossed his breakfast into the trash and retreated to his room. He closed the door and hastily finished packing. Then he threw himself on the bed to wait for the rush hour to commence. He was tense and anxious. Although not the exact make or model as his, the car in the news photo was very similar in style and color. But if there was a silver lining in this whole sordid affair, it was the fact that there were probably thousands of vehicles in the city that looked like his. That, coupled with the fact that the police had been able to describe him only as "approximately six-foot tall," gave him a small measure of relief. But as he lay on the bed waiting for eight-thirty to roll around, he could not relax. He half expected a knock on his door at any moment.

At eight twenty-five Pete scooped up his belongings, descended the back staircase, and walked out the rear exit to his car. He threw his things into the trunk and cleaned up the shattered glass on the rear seat and floor as best he could. He surveyed the remaining fragments stuck in the gasket around the window frame. He would never make it out of the city with it looking like that! He opened the trunk and selected a small pair of needle nose pliers from a toolbox he kept on board in case of emergency. Then one by one, like a dentist extracting a mouthful of loose teeth, he pulled the pieces of glass from around the window frame and threw them into the dumpster. He glanced around the parking lot before pulling the Taurus from his waistband. As he stared at the dull black weapon in his hand, a feeling of utter revulsion swept over him. He started to dispose of it in the dumpster, but his training alerted him to the inherent dangers in that action. Spying a small retention pond on the other side of the chain link fence, he instead removed the magazine, and chucked it and the pistol into the water.

After checking out at the front desk, Pete returned to his car and drove through the parking lot. As he pulled onto the busy street, now choked with cars, trucks, and Regional Transit buses, he powered down all four windows as an added safety measure against detection. Driving amid the heavy traffic through downtown Sacramento, Pete began perspiring. He cranked up the air conditioner, which did little to alleviate the situation. It wasn't the heavy traffic—he was used to far worse in San Francisco. It was the thought of having his car identified by the police, who seemed to be omnipresent. He frequently checked his rear-view mirror for the familiar black and whites. At one point an SPD cruiser with a single occupant pulled up behind and tailed him for two blocks. He held his breath, waiting for the red and blue lights to begin flashing. But the officer finally drove around him without so much as a glance in his direction.

Heading east on Lincoln Avenue, he kept in the center of a cluster of cars, using them as shields from suspicious eyes. A sudden dinging sound emitted from his dashboard, startling him. Glancing down, he saw a blinking red light, informing him that he was nearly out of fuel. In all the excitement of fleeing San Francisco, he'd forgotten to fill up.

"Great! All I need is to run out of gas and draw the attention of a Good Samaritan cop!" he bemoaned loudly. "Why are the police always around when you don't want them?"

He began looking for a gas station, but there weren't any nearby. He continued driving for a few miles, keeping his eyes peeled for one of those tall roadside signs that informs passersby of the automotive sustenance awaiting beneath.

"Why is there never a gas station around when you need one?" he complained again. Nothing seemed to be going right for him lately.

Pete Holloway, relief flooding through him, pulled his sedan up to the gas pump and checked the fuel gauge one more time. The needle rested squarely on "E." *I must be running on fumes!*

He shut off the engine and got out of the car. After inserting his credit card into the slot, he selected the grade and began filling the tank. As he waited, he scoped out his surroundings. The parking spaces in front of the convenience store were full. Through the window he could see the cash register and a number of people waiting to pay for their gas and snacks and super-sized cups of coffee. He turned toward the street, which was still choked with vehicles driven by people in a rush to get to work. So far so good. Another fifteen minutes and he would be outside the city limits and free of the manhunt. He returned the nozzle to its holster, grabbed his receipt, and headed inside to buy a soft drink. Driving always made him thirsty.

Pete selected a large, insulated foam cup, added ice, and filled it to the top with Coke from the self-serve machine. He grabbed a candy bar on the way to the cashier and got in line behind two plumbers in dirty gray overalls. As he waited for the men to finish their transactions, he glanced out the large plate glass window and nearly dropped his soda. A black and white police cruiser had pulled up behind his car, and the officer was running his license plate number through the on-board computer. Pete watched in shock as the uniformed policeman got out of the cruiser and approached the driver's side of his sedan. The officer ran his hand around the left rear window frame, as if feeling for bits of glass. Then he noticed the bullet hole in the door post. After examining it closely with his index finger, he tilted his head and spoke into his shoulder microphone. Then he leaned through the window frame and surveyed the interior of the car. Suddenly, he straightened and looked over the sedan's roof at the convenience store window.

In full panic, Pete turned his face away and stepped back out of the officer's line of sight. With heart pounding, he frantically looked around for the back exit. Setting his drink and candy bar on the shelf, he darted down the aisle and into the dingy hallway, past the single bathroom, and out the rear service door. He stumbled over an empty cardboard box but managed to stay on his feet. With adrenaline shooting into his veins like an injection of nitrous oxide into a racing engine, he fled down the short alley, cut between two houses, and headed up a side street, glancing over his shoulder as he ran. He continued running until he came to a busy intersection at the end of the block and turned the corner. About twenty yards ahead of him, a dozen or so people were waiting at a bus stop. Breathing heavily, he rushed up to the group and quickly got in line. An elderly woman turned around and stared at the out-of-breath man behind her.

"Alarm didn't go off this morning," he explained between gasps. "Thought I'd missed the bus!"

His conscience made itself known. The lie had rolled off his tongue all too easily. She nodded and turned around. He nervously glanced behind him, fully expecting the officer to come charging around the corner any second now with his gun drawn. Instead, to his immense relief, he saw a colorful Regional Transit bus heading toward him. It drew up to the curb and stopped in front of the group. The bi-fold door hissed open, and the people began embarking. With one last look over his shoulder, Pete climbed aboard, paid the fare, and made his way down the aisle toward the rear of the bus. He slumped wearily into an empty seat. As the driver released the air brakes and eased the bus away from the curb, Pete purged the air from his lungs, leaned back in the seat, and closed his eyes.

CHAPTER SEVEN
A NEAR-FATAL MISTAKE

PETE'S RAPID BREATHING GRADUALLY RETURNED to normal, but his mind continued to race. That was close, too close! Why in the world did he have to get that drink? Why didn't he just get in the car and drive away from the pump when he had the chance? Now they had his car, and they knew who he was. He was no longer anonymous. It wouldn't be long before his name and photo were plastered all over the news. Every time the bus stopped to let riders on or off, his heart skipped a beat. How soon before somebody recognized him? How soon before the police started pulling over city buses to check the passengers for the six-foot fugitive wanted in connection with the overnight shooting?

Lost in thought, Pete stared out the window. Thankfully he still had his wallet and cell phone, but everything else was lost to him now. His car, clothes, toiletries, groceries, even his Bible, were all in the possession of SPD. What should he do? This keeping one step ahead of the law was wearing him down. He needed to get someplace where he'd have time to think, to sort through things, to figure out his next move. But to do that he'd need to get far away from the city.

How? He could take the bus to the end of the line, wherever that was, but then what? He couldn't just walk out of the city. Maybe he could hitch a ride. No, too risky. Somebody might recognize him, and SPD would spot him for sure. He felt hunted like a wild animal and targeted as if a huge red and white bull's-eye were painted on his chest.

Pete watched a couple of fast-food restaurants and a drive-through bank pass by his window, then an auto dealership and a rental car company.

Wait a minute. A rental car! That might be the quickest and safest way to put some distance between him and Sacramento.

He reached up and yanked the cord above his window. A block later, the driver pulled over and Pete stepped off the bus. As it left, he realized he was in plain sight of every driver in the vicinity. Fighting the urge to sprint, he began walking briskly back to the rental company, as running would attract too much attention. Only when he reached the rental lot and entered the front door of the office did he begin to breathe again.

Thirty minutes later, Pete drove off the lot in a dark blue two-door coupe. He sported a pair of chrome-tinted sunglasses and a green baseball cap, purchased from a rack of items bearing the rental company's logo. They weren't much of a disguise, but they'd have to do. Which direction should he go? By now the authorities would know he was from San Francisco, and that he'd fled a warrant there. Since he'd shown up in Sacramento, they might figure he was heading east. So to throw them off, he turned south and began driving toward Stockton on a less crowded state highway. His use of misdirection had worked so far. Hadn't he eluded police at the impound lot and at the convenience store using that tactic?

However, one thing was for sure. He couldn't expect to remain invisible in another city. Those state-of-the-art police departments would be on the alert for him now. No, he needed to find a smaller town, one that might not have the law enforcement resources of the larger metropolitan areas. But not one so small that an outsider would draw the locals' attention, where he would stick out like a sophisticated, tuxedo-clad urbanite crashing a simple, barefoot country wedding.

The little community of Murphys came to mind. He and Angela had spent a weekend there celebrating their tenth wedding anniversary. With just over two thousand residents, it was definitely a small town, but one relying heavily on the tourism industry. People from all over the state, and even the country, flocked to the former gold mining town known as the "Queen of the Sierra" to stay in the historic hotels and B&Bs, and browse the art galleries, restaurants, and eclectic shops up and down Main Street. It should provide the perfect sanctuary from the all-seeing eyes of Big Brother, he convinced himself.

Two hours later, Pete drove into downtown Murphys. He traversed the three short blocks and turned into the parking lot of the Murphys Historic Hotel. As he walked up to the 165-year-old building, pleasant memories of his previous visit came flooding back. He and Angela had stayed in one of the historic landmark's upstairs bedrooms, where notable personalities such as Mark Twain, Ulysses S. Grant, Susan B. Anthony, and Black Bart the "Gentleman Bandit" once rested their heads. He recalled strolling hand-in-hand with Angela down Main Street, visiting the art galleries, bakeries, and antique shops, and sitting under the cloudless evening skies enjoying fine outdoor dining. But those pleasant memories became painful reminders that she was not with him this time.

He stopped at the front desk and rented one of the less expensive rooms in the building adjacent to the original hotel. Since check-in was not for another three hours, he decided to walk down Main Street and get something to eat. Mingling with the mid-day tourists, he sauntered about a block and a half to a small eatery housed in an old fire station, where he purchased a hamburger platter and took a seat near the back of what used to be a pumper truck bay.

After lunch, he wandered aimlessly up and down the street, but he had no interest in window shopping. So to kill the remaining time before his room became available, he walked down the hill behind the hotel to the small municipal park and found an empty bench under a large, gnarled shade tree next to the narrow creek that marked the southern border of the green space. Several children were splashing and playing in the shallow, lazy water, and the sounds of their laughter as they chased one another brought a smile to his troubled face. Oh, to be young and carefree again. He watched two industrious boys, about eight or nine years old, pry up rocks, carry them upstream, and deposit them in a row perpendicular to the bank in a gallant attempt to build a dam. They were totally engrossed in their work, and he was sure that if given enough time, their labor would be rewarded. A slight smile creased Pete's face. *Two future engineers!*

His thoughts gravitated toward his own children. When they were younger, he and Angela had taken them camping in the mountains, where he'd wanted them to have the experience of trout fishing. But they'd been more interested in throwing rocks into the water, and sailing boats fashioned from anything that would float downstream. Those days seemed so long ago and so far away. Seven days had passed since he'd said farewell to his children before fleeing

San Francisco. Only one week? With everything that had happened recently, it seemed more like a month. His thoughts turned to Angela, and he suddenly found himself missing her every bit as much as he had during his Iraqi deployment.

He'd give his right arm to have her here with him right now, to see her smiling eyes, to hear her laughing voice, to lay beside her in bed holding hands. The pain in his heart rivaled any he'd experienced on the battlefield, but no Purple Heart could atone for the anguish he felt in her absence. *Why hasn't she phoned me yet?* Were the police still questioning her? She promised to call the first chance she got. How were Drew and Brie holding up? How was the church doing in his absence?

Unable to bear the disconnect any longer, he whipped out his cell phone to call home. But the screen showed only one bar, and he couldn't get a signal. Maybe it was because he was in a bit of a hollow. He got off the bench and walked back up the hill. At the top, he tried again, but the screen suddenly went black. He tried turning on the phone several times, and even removed and reinstalled the battery. Nothing. The battery must have run down. He tried to recall when he'd last charged the phone. It had to be four or five days ago at least. He walked back to the hotel parking lot to fetch his phone charger from the center console. But when he reached the rental car he stopped and groaned out loud. The charger was in his own car, which ironically was now probably on the same impound lot he'd visited in the wee hours of the morning.

Pete entered the hotel lobby and approached the reservations clerk. "Excuse me, I seem to have lost my phone charger. Can you tell me if there's a store nearby where I can pick up another one?"

The clerk thought for a moment. "Um, I'm not aware of any here in town, but there's a cell phone store in Angels Camp. I'm sure they'd have what you need."

He thanked her and went back to his rental car. As he drove the eight miles down Highway 4 to the larger community, he made a mental shopping list. He would need a phone charger, a few changes of clothes, some basic toiletries, food supplies, and a small suitcase or duffel bag. He thought about how he'd almost run out of fuel that morning and how that had cost him his car. *And gas! Don't forget to fill up on gas, you moron!*

By the time he got back to the hotel, it was 3:45. He carried the shopping bags into his room and pulled the tags off the purchased items. His credit card receipts were beginning to crowd his wallet, so he stuffed them into one of the duffel bag's side pockets instead. Then he plugged the phone charger into the wall, drew the curtains, and fell asleep on the bed.

Pete awoke three hours later and immediately called Angela. She and the kids would all be home by now, and most likely sitting down to dinner. His wife was a firm believer in schedules and routines.

"Hello, Pete?"

His heart nearly burst at the sound of her voice. "Ange! It's sure good to talk to you. You have no idea how much I've missed you."

"Oh, babe, I've missed you, too." She sounded extremely relieved. In the background, he heard Brienna cry out 'Daddy!' "I've been so worried. How are you doing? Are you all right?"

"Well, I'm okay, I guess. Not bad, all things considered. It's been a rather interesting week, to put it mildly."

"Where are you?" Angela asked anxiously.

"Um . . . hon, remember our tenth anniversary? I'm not going to say any more than that, in case you're questioned again. Then you can honestly say I didn't tell you *where* I'm staying. But until this morning I was somewhere else."

Angela hesitated, then responded somberly. "So I heard."

"What do you mean? Who did you talk to? Did Sarah Sutherland call you?"

"No, not her. I heard it from that SFPD detective. You know, the one who interviewed you last month."

"Detective Branch? When did he call?" Pete wondered.

"He didn't call. He just left here a little over an hour ago. He was waiting across the street in a police car with another officer when I came home from picking up the kids from school."

Pete shook his head. "News travels fast, doesn't it?"

"He said you're wanted in connection with a shooting in Sacramento last night!" Worry crept into Angela's voice. "Babe, what's going on? What happened? Are you in trouble? I mean, more than when you left here last Thursday night?"

Pete picked his words carefully. "Ange, I think it's best that I don't share a lot with you. For now, anyway. I'll fill you in on all the details when the time's right. The less you know, the better. But don't worry, I didn't shoot anyone. I was just in the wrong place at the wrong time." He hesitated. "I've been under a lot of stress this week, Ange. In fact, I . . . I've even had a couple of flashbacks since leaving home."

Alarm resonated in her voice. "Flashbacks? You mean the kind you had after you came home from Iraq? But you haven't had those for over a decade. I'm scared for you, Pete! It sounds like you're in this mess deeper than you were before."

"I'm afraid that I am. A lot has happened, and not much of it's good. There are some loose ends that need to be tied up before I can come home. Right now, I'm trying to figure out the best way to go about doing that."

"But you've had a whole week to think things over. Can't you come home *now*?" she begged. "Whatever the consequences, we'll face them together. I need you, babe. The kids need you."

"I haven't had much time to think, Ange. There's been no time to do anything but react. You wouldn't believe how crazy things have been the past couple of days. But I promise I'll make a decision soon. I should have time in the next day or two to figure it out." He changed the subject to divert her from the uncomfortable line of questioning. "How are Drew and Brie?"

"They're scared, too. Especially Brie. I've tried to shield them from all that I can. They were at school last Friday morning when the police tried to serve your warrant, but they were here when Detective Branch grilled me an hour ago. I sent them to their rooms, but they heard everything from the top of the stairs."

"Can I talk to them?" Pete asked, longing to reassure his children of his love.

"Sure. They're both right here. Here's Drew."

He spent the next twenty minutes talking to his son and daughter. Drew, like his mother, wanted to know all the details. Pete promised to explain everything when the time was right, and requested he pray for his father. Drew said that he would. Considering the breach in their relationship, that was a step toward reconciliation. Brienna, on the other hand, was more frightened than inquisitive, but he was able to assuage her fears with the promise that he would soon be home, and they'd all be together again. But he wasn't so sure he believed that himself. When they were finished talking, Brienna handed the phone back to her mother.

"Pete, is there anything you need?" Angela asked. "Can I bring you something? I'd really love to see you."

"Thanks, Ange, I'd love to see you, too. I really wish you were here with me. But I don't think that's a good idea right now. Since I'm wanted in two cities, they'd likely tail you to where I am. In fact, I'm sure of it. But I've got everything I need for now. Don't worry about me. Just keep praying for the situation."

"I have been, believe me. A lot!"

Pete laughed. "I'm sure you have. So, everything's okay at home, then? No other drama that I need to know about?"

Angela managed to return his laugh. "Drew's been a little withdrawn since you left, but all-in-all we're doing as well as can be expected with the drama we already have. To quote from the sermon on the mount, 'Sufficient for the day is its own trouble.'"

"Well, I've got enough trouble for today, that's for sure, and a few more days to boot. By the way, how's everything at church?"

"Good. People are praying daily for their pastor."

"Tell them I appreciate that."

"I will."

"Did John preach the sermon last Sunday?"

"Yes, he did a great job on such short notice. He's leading well in your absence, but he's no Pastor Pete."

Pete chuckled. "You're always so encouraging, Ange. That's one of the things that attracted me to you in college." He sighed. "I really miss you, hon."

"I miss you too, babe. When can we talk again?"

"Soon, I hope. God-willing I'll *see* you soon, too. Tell Drew and Brie I love them."

"I will."

"I love you, Ange."

"I love you, too, babe. Take care of yourself."

"I will. Good night."

"Night."

Pete shut off his phone and placed it on the nightstand. Then he lay back on the bed with hands clasped behind his head, unsure if the call had eased his longings for home or only intensified them. As he stared up at the little flashing red light on the ceiling smoke detector, he thought of everything he'd lost.

Would he ever get the car back? There were still twenty-three payments to make on it! He could replace the clothes, although he'd sure miss that jacket. But his Bible was irreplaceable . . . all those marked passages and margin notes. Would he ever see it again? He could sure use it right now.

Interestingly, the only thing he didn't miss was his handgun.

Pete slept soundly until ten-o-clock the following morning. His mind was weary from the stress, and his body tired from fleeing the Sacramento police officer. He felt exhausted in every sense of the word, but he also felt hungry. Realizing he hadn't had anything to eat since yesterday's lunch, he fixed a bowl of cornflakes purchased from the grocery store in Angels Camp. Then, as he showered and dressed, he formulated a plan for the day.

When he and Angela were here for their anniversary, they'd spent several days hiking through Calaveras Big Trees State Park, about fifteen miles up the Sierra Nevada mountainside from Murphys. He recalled how relaxing and refreshing that time had been for them both. That would be the ideal place to finally get away from everything and have the solitude and time needed to sort through the mess in which he found himself.

He hurriedly threw some fruit, snacks, and bottled water into a grocery bag. Then he opened the desk drawer in search of a notepad and pen which hotels usually keep on hand for guests. Those items weren't there, but something else was. He picked up the hardbound Gideon Bible and held it lovingly in his hands. He'd read accounts of how people's lives had been transformed after discovering the copy of God's Word in their hotel rooms: angry people blaming God for their problems or circumstances, lonely people hurting from damaged or destroyed relationships, hopeless people contemplating abortion or suicide. *And fleeing people seeking guidance and direction for their lives.*

Pete put the Bible in the bag and went out to the parking lot.

He drove up the winding stretch of Highway 4 to the 6500-acre wilderness preserve, eager to get out into nature and get alone with God. He parked the dark blue rental car in the visitor lot, grabbed the bag and a jacket he'd purchased the previous day, and picked up a trail map from the welcome center. Then he began hiking down the River Canyon Trail, inhaling the pure mountain air and enjoying the freshness of the pleasant pine scent that permeated the forest. As he walked along the footpath, which was covered with a soft layer of pine needles, he looked up at the giant sequoias overhead, some as big as three hundred feet tall and thirty feet in diameter. What an awesome part of creation! This was heaven on earth.

After hiking for nearly an hour, he came around a bend and spied an outcropping of rocks on the mountainside about fifty yards off the trail. That looked like a good spot to get alone by himself and spend time with God.

Leaving the trail, he scrambled up the steep incline to the top of the formation. It was relatively flat and covered with dry pine needles. He sat down and surveyed the area. Up here, he was hidden from the eyes of hikers on the trail below. Satisfied with the location, he took a drink from one of the water bottles and ate an apple. Then he removed the Gideon Bible from the bag.

"Lord, thank You for creating this sanctuary where I can be alone with You and seek Your guidance," he prayed. Closing his eyes, he pictured the view of the mountains from his Sacramento hotel room and recalled the words God had given him then. "Here I am, Lord, on the side of Your mountain. Speak to me through Your Word. Give me the direction I need. Show me the way." Turning to the book of Psalms, he thumbed through the pages until he came to the eleventh psalm. He read the words out loud.

"In the LORD I take refuge;
how can you say to my soul,
'Flee like a bird to your mountain,
for behold, the wicked bend the bow;
they have fitted their arrow to the string
to shoot in the dark at the upright in heart;
if the foundations are destroyed,
what can the righteous do?'

The LORD is in His holy temple;
the LORD's throne is in heaven;
His eyes see, His eyelids test the children of man.
The LORD tests the righteous,
but His soul hates the wicked and the one who loves violence.
Let Him rain coals on the wicked;
fire and sulfur and a scorching wind shall be the portion of their cup.
For the LORD is righteous;
He loves righteous deeds;
the upright shall behold His face."

Pete contemplated the lyrics to this psalm of David, who was singing about the trouble in his life at the time. Although Samuel had anointed David king over Israel, Saul was the one still on the throne, and seeking to kill him. As a result, he'd fled the wrath of the king, feeling like a hunted animal, or a bird fleeing the fowler. Pete could certainly identify with that sentiment. He'd even felt the arrows shot at *him* in the dark, too. But the police weren't the "wicked" ones. They were just doing their job. And as for him, could he truthfully be considered the "upright in heart" in this matter? What were his motives for fleeing the consequences of his actions? Could he honestly claim the Lord as his refuge if he was fleeing to the mountain like David had? The passage stated that God tests the righteous. Was he being put to the test to reveal some hidden fault or wrong motive? Did his present state parallel David's dilemma? What options did David have? He could fight, flee, or face the consequences.

Should I fight, Lord? David did not want to fight Saul, although he had the opportunity. God delivered Saul into his hand and he could have killed his enemy. But he refused to lift a finger against God's anointed. *No, I can't fight back using illegal tactics, like Richard and Vince did. I was wrong to participate in that. Look where it got me! From now on I'll have to use righteous means and honorable methods.*

Should I flee, Lord? Was David saying it was wrong to flee from Saul? Was running actually failing to trust God by taking one's personal safety into one's own hands? Yet others in the Bible did just that in times of persecution. For its faith, the early church was scattered because of persecution. Paul himself escaped from those seeking his life when he was let down over the city wall in a basket in the middle of the night. Why, even Joseph and Mary were told by the angel to flee to Egypt to avoid Herod's attempt on Jesus' life. *Should I, like them, continue to hide until my "Herod" is dead and it's safe to return home?*

Or should I face the consequences, Lord? Should he return home and continue to stand publicly for his faith, knowing he could lose his freedom and possibly his ministry? Daniel did and was thrown into the lions' den. Shadrach, Meshach, and Abednego did and were thrown into the fiery furnace. The apostles did and were thrown into prison, and later they were sentenced to death. But that didn't stop them. *Pete, are you able to trust God with the consequences, no matter what the cost? How much faith do you really have?* Maybe this was his test.

Pete closed the Bible and set it on the ground beside him. He lay back on the soft carpet of pine needles and looked up at the patches of blue sky peeking through the high canopy of branches. "Lord, I confess to You, I put myself in a situation last night where I nearly got myself killed, all because I was afraid of being thought of as weak. That was my pride. You tried to warn me, but I was too stubborn to listen to Your Spirit. Please forgive me! I've always thought of myself as strong, but maybe I'm just weak. Maybe I'm too weak to stand up for what's right. In the military I was taught to be smart about things, to give my all, but if possible, live to fight another day. I confess I don't want to lose my freedoms, or to be separated from my family and ministry, but in the end, I know they all belong to You. Help me to get to the place where I can say with the Apostle Paul, 'For to me to live is Christ, and to die is gain.' Direct my steps, Lord. Make my paths straight. In Jesus' name, amen."

Pete suddenly sat up and looked around. He must have dozed off for a while. He rose to his feet and studied the sky above. From the sun's position, he'd slept for about an hour he guessed. He glanced at his watch, confirming the fact. It was nearly one-o-clock.

He brushed himself off and picked up the Bible and his bag of snacks, and then looked for an easier way down. As he made his way around the back side of the ledge, he noticed a small cave tucked under the slabs of rock that formed the top of the outcropping. Curiosity got the better of him, and he crossed the sloped earth toward it and ducked into the narrow opening. Activating the flashlight on his cell phone, he looked around the interior of the cave. It wasn't very large at all, about six feet wide, five feet high, and maybe ten feet deep. But it appeared dry and cozy. Over time, pine needles had blown into the mouth of the cave, providing a comfortable cushion under his feet. Pete stepped out into the sunlight and descended to the trail below. He glanced back up at the rock ledge. The cave was on the opposite side, invisible to anyone hiking the path. *What a perfect place for a bear's lair . . . or a hideout for a fugitive from the law.*

As he hiked back to the parking lot, he began thinking about the indefinite expense of staying in hotels. As a pastor of an average sized church, he certainly wasn't a wealthy man, and the charges for the past week were beginning to mount: hotel rates, restaurant tabs, clothing and supplies, and now rental car fees. How long could he keep racking up debt at this pace? When he'd signed the Voluntary Compliance Agreement, he'd been concerned about good stewardship when it came to paying fines for his preaching, but now the decision to flee was costing him much more, with no end in sight. *Maybe it's time to look for ways to cut expenses,* he contemplated. *Or is it time to face the music and go home?*

CHAPTER EIGHT
BACK TO NATURE

PETE ROUNDED THE LAST BEND of the River Canyon Trail on the way back to his rental car. As he passed the small, log cabin-style restroom building at the trail head, something stopped him dead in his tracks. Not seventy-five feet away, two police SUVs had boxed in the dark blue coupe! Three uniformed officers, their backs to him, stood beside the driver's door discussing the situation. A fourth was in one of the vehicles on the radio with dispatch.

With his heart pounding rapidly, Pete ducked into the restroom and sequestered himself in one of the stalls. Hopefully they hadn't seen him. By now his description must have been broadcast to all the local law enforcement agencies within a hundred-mile radius.

He should have known better than to go out in public without a disguise. But he never imagined they'd look for him here! Through the high, narrow window screens he could barely make out their conversation. A car door slammed as the fourth officer joined the others beside his rental car.

"Reinforcements are on the way," Pete heard him announce to the other officers.

"How long has it been here?" one of them asked.

"Hard to say. It was rented yesterday morning in Sacramento, around ten, so not more than twenty-four hours at the outside."

"Then the suspect might still be around here somewhere," a third commented.

"I doubt it," the first officer replied. "More than likely he ditched it. Probably had an accomplice meet him here where they thought we wouldn't find it for a while."

Pete heard the fourth officer laugh derisively. "Some people are so stupid! All they can think about is getting as far away as possible, as if putting distance between them and the crime makes any difference. You'd think they'd know about GPS by now." The others laughed.

"The vehicle's locked but the keys don't appear to be inside."

"He may have tossed them, or they might be under the seat or in the glove compartment," the first officer suggested. "But if he's still in the area, he could be planning to return to the car. Central wants us to stake out the entrance until dark on the slim chance he shows up. If he doesn't, they'll send the tow truck in the morning. They're also sending some plain clothes up here to scour the trails, just in case. Should be here shortly." He grunted. "If the suspect's in the park, he's not going to be driving out today. We've got the area blanketed. Let's pull back to the entrance and wait for the reinforcements."

"I gotta hit the john first," Pete heard one of the officers say.

He panicked. The man was sure to check the stalls. Quickly he slipped out the door and hid beside the building just as the officer rounded the opposite corner and disappeared into the restroom. Pete held his breath. *What if he circles the building? There's nowhere to hide. I'm a sitting duck!*

He heard the urinal flush, and the water run in the sink, then the squeak of hinges as the officer checked the stalls. Footsteps sounded as the policeman emerged from the restroom and returned to his patrol vehicle the same way he'd come. Flattened against the log wall, Pete remained motionless. He heard a car door slam and listened intently as the two SUVs drove out of the parking lot.

Pete's legs gave way and he sagged to the ground, sucking dry air into his lungs. Another close call! But now what? He'd have to wait until sometime during the night, after the police called off their stakeout, in order to make his getaway via the rental car. But even if that was successful, they might still have Highway 4 covered. And how far could he expect to get with them tracking the vehicle, anyway? He'd need a different means of transportation, but there weren't many options this high up in the mountains. Besides, there was the more pressing issue of what to do and where to hide until nightfall. Any minute the plain clothes officers would show up and begin looking for him.

How would he identify them if they were dressed like ordinary hikers? He wouldn't be able to avoid them. And he couldn't afford to be seen by anyone.

He remained slumped against the wall, too confused to make a decision and too weary to get on his feet. His befuddled mind remained in a fog as thick as pea soup, and he lost track of time. Suddenly a car door slammed nearby, then another. He heard voices. Struggling to his feet, Pete cautiously peered around the corner of the building. To his horror, the parking lot was crawling with vehicles and hikers, hikers who all looked to be in their thirties and forties, hikers who all looked suspiciously like undercover cops. Just then he remembered the cave he'd found at the far end of the trail.

If only he could get back to it, he could hide out there until nightfall, after they ended the search. But there was just one problem. The trail head was in plain view of the parking lot. He thought about making a run for it, but he'd be spotted almost immediately. Frantically, he looked around, desperate for an escape route.

At the far end of the long, narrow parking lot, he caught sight of a caterer's truck backed up to another trail head. He watched a young man in a white jacket loading sealed containers onto a wheeled cart. It looked as if he might be setting up for some kind of outdoor venue, more than likely a destination wedding. Maybe he could crash it and pretend to be a wedding guest. He could think of no other option at the moment.

Pete chanced a peek around the corner again. The "hikers" had all gathered in a tight circle and were receiving instructions from the officer in charge. This was his chance. Keeping the small building between him and the group of plain clothes policemen, he stealthily angled through the trees toward the caterer's truck. Staying out of sight, he paralleled the young man in the white jacket pulling the wheeled cart along the trail. A hundred yards into the forest, he saw a clearing ahead. Remaining undercover, he crept closer, and noticed a white canopy to his left, under which tables had been set up for a food line. To his right, about seventy or eighty folding chairs had been placed in rows facing a huge sequoia with a base diameter of almost twenty feet. His heart sank. It would be impossible to mingle with guests at a wedding this small.

He observed a long-haired musician, dressed in black, setting up his sound equipment to one side. A guitar case lay on the ground next to him. Just then, the sound of female voices caught his attention.

Two women, one dressed in a white caterer's jacket and black slacks, the other in a three-quarter length purple pastel dress, entered the clearing. They were arguing loudly.

"I can only work with what I've got," the woman in white was saying, rather defensively. "You don't need to get so upset. We can handle it, I promise you."

"Well, that's not good enough!" the other woman replied angrily. "You should have had the tables ready by now. And you said you'd have *three* people for this wedding, not two. Two servers can't adequately handle a crowd of eighty people."

"I've done it before without any problems," the first woman responded. "Anyway, what was I supposed to do? My third server called half an hour ago and told me she was sick. You don't want someone throwing up all over your guests, do you?"

"You should have had a contingency plan for additional staff," the other woman retorted, jabbing her index finger at the jacketed woman. "That's what the *real* professionals do. Besides, I paid for three servers, not two."

"If you'd like, we can talk about a discount when this is over," the exasperated caterer shot back. "But if we keep standing here arguing about it, I can't guarantee anything!"

Beside herself, the woman in the dress glared at the caterer and threw her arms in the air before storming off in a huff.

Pete formulated a strategy that would kill two birds with one stone. Brushing himself off, he tucked in his shirt, smoothed down his hair, and stepped out of the forest into the clearing. He approached the angry woman in the dress, who had taken to realigning the rows of chairs and mumbling to herself.

"Excuse me, are you the wedding planner?" he asked politely.

The woman straightened and turned toward him. "Uh . . . yes. What do you want?" she asked abruptly.

"Well, I happened to be hiking the trail and couldn't help but overhear your conversation with the caterer. You seem to be in a bit of a pickle."

The woman scowled at him before returning to the task of straightening the chairs. "That's putting it mildly," she remarked sarcastically.

"Well, I don't mean to intrude, but I've had some experience in food service myself. I'd be only too happy to help you out of a tight spot." He smiled winsomely. "I used to wait tables in college, and I worked for the largest catering company in the state two summers in a row." He conveniently failed to mention the fact that his position with the caterer consisted only of janitor and night watchman.

The wedding planner stopped what she was doing and eyed him suspiciously. "Why are you so eager to lend me a hand?" she asked pointedly.

"No particular reason," he replied, as nonchalantly as possible. "It's just that my wife and I celebrated our wedding anniversary here, and I know what special memories this place holds for us. If I can help someone else create those same wonderful memories, then why not?" He grinned and shot a quick glance over her shoulder, fully expecting several hikers to come barging into the clearing waving his photo in the air. "Anyway, I'm traveling alone this time, and I have nothing else to do but go back to the hotel room and watch old reruns on TV. Besides, I could always use a few extra bucks."

The woman in the pastel dress sized him up while considering his offer. "All right," she acquiesced brusquely, "but you'll have to take up the matter of your wages with Amber. I've already paid her for the server you'll be replacing. I think she went back to the truck. Just tell her I sent you and see if she has an extra jacket or apron or something." She eyeballed him again and shook her head disapprovingly. "I'd rather have two properly attired servers than three if one of them is going to be dressed like *you*," she complained, before forcing a faint, stressed-out smile. "No offense."

Ten minutes later Pete, wearing a white server's jacket a couple of sizes too small, and sporting a stubby white chef's hat, assisted the other catering employee with transporting the food containers to the canopied area. He busied himself arranging the covered metal trays in the proper order and lit the warming candles as wedding guests began to arrive and mill about in small, conversational groups. Suddenly, two male hikers emerged from the trail and stood at the edge of the clearing, scanning the gathering crowd. Pete quickly turned his back to them, pretending to rummage through one of the coolers behind the serving table. He could almost feel their stares on the back of his neck, which was growing hotter by the second. He prayed they wouldn't notice that he was wearing jeans instead of black pants. Then he heard a familiar voice behind him.

"You gentlemen will have to move out of the area immediately!" it barked authoritatively. "This space is reserved for a wedding. There are signs posted on the trail to that effect." He heard a mumbled apology from one of the hikers, and out of the corner of his eye watched them retreat into the forest.

It was nearly five-o-clock when the last of the wedding party departed. Pete helped the caterer clear the tables and return the leftovers to the truck. He debated if he should ask his temporary employer for a ride back to Murphys, figuring the police wouldn't search the catering vehicle. But how would he explain leaving his own car behind, and how would he secure other transportation once he got back to the hotel? It wasn't worth the risk. After the caterer left, he hung around and lent a hand to the wedding planner, stacking the chairs onto a pneumatic-tired furniture dolly. Anything to give the impression he was part of the event staff. But he felt exposed and conspicuous without the white hat and jacket.

On his return to the parking lot, Pete noticed that a few cars were still there, but he was relieved to see that all the vehicles carrying the plain clothes policemen were gone. They must have called off the foot search. But no doubt one of the SUVs was still at the park entrance, like the uniformed officer had said. And the rental car might still be under surveillance, at least until dark. So to avoid detection he cut through the trees, giving his car a wide berth, and picked up the River Canyon Trail two hundred feet downhill from the parking lot. He walked for about twenty minutes, passing many late-afternoon hikers along the way. Thankfully, none of them offered more than a passing glance.

As daylight began to fade, he spied a large, fallen tree trunk approximately fifty feet or so off the trail. He might be able to rest out of sight behind it until after dark. He cut through the brush and discovered that the four-foot diameter log was hollow. Crawling inside, he found himself on a soft bed of dry wood chips that gave off a pleasant cedar scent. Pete placed the bag containing his water, snacks, and Bible beside him, then took off his jacket and rolled it into the shape of a pillow. He lay down and stretched out, allowing himself to relax. Within minutes, he fell asleep.

When Pete awoke, it was pitch black. *Where am I?*

He sat up quickly, bumping his head on the roof of the hollow tree trunk. He fumbled for his cell phone and activated the flashlight. As he waved it in a sweeping arc, his senses gradually returned. He checked the time. It was 10:45. He'd been asleep for almost five hours. Grabbing his jacket and bag, he crawled out of the log and stretched his stiff muscles. The sky overhead was clear and the moon nearly full. Stars twinkled here and there between the canopies of the tall sequoias and pines. Glancing around, he could make out the dark, ghostly shapes of the giant tree trunks, standing erect like sentries guarding their prisoner. He'd been held hostage here among them during the day, but now was his chance for escape. The moonlight filtering through the forest ceiling provided just enough visibility to navigate the area without having to rely too heavily on the cell phone for guidance. Besides, he needed to conserve the battery.

Locating the trail, Pete hiked in the direction of the parking lot. The night was absolutely still, without breeze or sound, save the occasional eerie hooting of a distant owl. As he walked, he peered into the forest around him, watching for any movement and listening for any snap of a twig that might alert him to the presence of a bear. While he knew black bears usually kept their distance from humans, he did not want to surprise one on the path. A startled bear might react by attacking rather than fleeing. *I wish I had my gun on me!*

Thirty minutes later, he made out the dark silhouette of the restrooms at the trail head. Silently and cautiously, he approached the rental car. To his immense relief, it was the only vehicle in the otherwise empty parking lot. He fumbled for the key fob in his jeans pocket and pressed the UNLOCK button. Then he quickly got into the driver's seat and shut the door. So far so good. He started the engine and let it warm up for a few minutes. But before he backed out of the parking space, he shut off the headlamps and running lights, just in case. He could navigate the road toward the park entrance by moonlight. Once he reached the highway it should be safe to turn them back on.

Pete inched slowly along the winding, asphalt road. He was almost home free. As he approached the entrance, a light suddenly flashed in front of him through the trees. Startled, he hit the brakes and came to a stop. The light emanated from the interior of a darkened vehicle parked just off the highway, illuminating its two occupants. He could make out the shape of a badge on the driver's side door. It was one of the police SUVs that had surrounded his car earlier. They were still here, and there was no other way out of the park. He was trapped! Holding his breath, Pete put the car in reverse and slowly backed away from the entrance. Once around the curve and out of sight, he made a three-point turn and drove back to the parking lot. He'd stay in the park overnight until they towed the car. Once they were gone, he would figure out some way to get out of there and back to town.

As he pulled into the lot, the realization suddenly hit him: he wasn't absolutely sure where he'd parked before! Was it the space directly in front of him, or the next one over? He couldn't remember.

In the darkness, he couldn't get his bearings. Tossing up a quick prayer, he made the decision, and parked and locked the car. Then, after one final glance around, he trudged through the darkness and back to the log.

Once inside the confines of the fallen tree trunk, Pete attempted to sleep, but the benefits of unconsciousness eluded him. So he spent the remaining hours of darkness thinking about his family and praying. He prayed for Angela and Drew and Brienna, for his deacons and church members, and for Jorge and Jim. He prayed for Richard's family, and for Vince and Colin, whose misguided motives and methods had spurred him into his present quandary. And he prayed for his country, that God's people would be the salt and light needed in this period of encroaching spiritual darkness.

As the blackness of night gave way to the grayness of dawn, Pete opened the Gideon Bible and turned to Matthew chapter five. Reading the beatitudes, three verses in particular resonated within his spirit: *"Blessed are those who are persecuted for righteousness' sake, for theirs is the kingdom of heaven. Blessed are you when others revile you and persecute you and utter all kinds of evil against you falsely on My account. Rejoice and be glad, for your reward is great in heaven, for so they persecuted the prophets who were before you."*

His current brush with persecution was nothing new. Throughout the centuries, many had faced much worse. Turning to the end of the eleventh chapter of Hebrews, he read the details of the suffering that Christians experienced in biblical times: *"Some were tortured, refusing to accept release, so that they might rise again to a better life. Others suffered mocking and flogging, and even chains and imprisonment. They were stoned, they were sawn in two, they were killed with the sword. They went about in skins of sheep and goats, destitute, afflicted, mistreated—of whom the world was not worthy—wandering about in deserts and mountains, and in dens and caves of the earth."*

Even hiding inside a hollow log in the middle of a 6500-acre wilderness, Pete knew he was not alone. He was surrounded by a great cloud of witnesses. The words of Jesus came to him in that moment. *"I am with you always, to the end of the age."*

He ate his last apple and drank from a bottle of water, then rested until ten o'clock, when he decided to hike back to the parking lot to see if the police had towed his car. Maybe he could hitch a ride with a park visitor back to Murphys today, although he had no idea what he'd do for transportation once he got there. With uplifted spirits, Pete hiked at a brisk pace back to the trail head, passing a young couple and a family of five along the way. As he came around the last bend, he was relieved to see that the rental car was gone. But something else caught his eye. The vehicles with all the "hikers" were back! And this time there were more of them.

Panic-stricken, he turned and ran back down the now familiar trail. *I thought they'd given up searching for me here! Why are they back?*

Maybe they had talked to the wedding planner or the caterer, or some hiker remembered seeing him. Maybe he had left a clue of some sort behind. This was definitely not good! He came to the hollow log, but it didn't look safe to him this time. It could be seen from the trail, and they'd be sure to check it out. Then where could he hide?

The cave! If he could just get back to the cave, he would be safe there. He had enough water and snacks left to hold him for another day. Surely this was the last time they were going to search for him.

Running faster than he had since his high school track days, Pete sprinted down the winding trail, reaching the rock outcropping in record time. Being careful not to break any branches, and covering his footprints, he ascended the slope around the side of the formation and located the almost invisible entrance to the cave. He stuck his head in and shone the light around, just in case a bear or skunk had decided to make a reservation for the day. It was empty. Crawling inside, he leaned back against the rear wall until his breathing slowed. Then he drank half the remaining bottled water and began the long, anxious wait.

CHAPTER NINE
NOT OUT OF THE WOODS YET

PETE HAD NO IDEA HOW long he'd been inside the cave when he heard a faint sound. At first it didn't register, but then he heard it again, louder this time. A dog barked. Then two more dogs began barking simultaneously. He shuddered violently. Tracker dogs! The police were searching for him with tracker dogs. They were sure to follow his scent right up to where he was hiding. He was not safe here after all! His only hope was to escape into the forest and throw them off track as much as possible.

Shifting into survival mode, he scrambled to his feet, grabbed the bag, and peered cautiously outside. He heard the barking again from somewhere back up the trail. His pursuers were getting closer. Glancing at the bag in his hands, he suddenly chucked it back into the cave. When they found it, they would stop to check it for clues. That should buy him a few extra minutes head start. Besides, it would only slow him down.

To create a new scent trail out of the cave, Pete cut across the top of the slope before wending his way down to the hiking path a hundred yards away. He crossed the path and pushed deep into the scraggly underbrush. He could hear the dogs behind him, much closer than before. His jacket snagged on a branch, but he yanked it loose, not caring if a shred of evidence had been left behind. The dogs would eventually pick up his trail anyway, so haste was his only ally. Pete ran through the dense forest, dodging bramble bushes and circumventing large sequoias that existed as saplings when Jesus walked the earth. He tripped over a large root sticking out of the ground, ripping the right knee of his jeans and drawing blood. Not bothering to check the wound, he began running again, kicking several pinecones the size of cantaloupes out of his way. As he continued to flee, the terrain gradually grew steeper. Thirty minutes later, he spied a river through the trees.

If I can make that, I might be able to throw them off my trail!

He picked up his pace, skidding and sliding down the steep slope. Suddenly he slipped and tumbled off a small rock ledge into a bramble bush, snapping several branches. A large thorn ripped the sleeve of his jacket and he felt a sharp sting as it pierced his flesh. Struggling to untangle himself, he incurred several additional cuts and abrasions in the process. Finally, free from the clutches of the bramble bush, he continued his descent toward the river. He could hear the rushing water now, and the sound rejuvenated his spirit. It seemed to be calling out to him, like a siren's song to a weary sailor. He eagerly ran toward it.

Reaching the river, Pete stopped to catch his breath, and took the opportunity to survey the damage to his knee and forearm. The wounds didn't look too bad, nothing requiring immediate care. He turned his attention to the river.

If he could make it to the other side, he just might be able to throw off his pursuers, or at least delay them long enough to put some distance between them. He recalled the map of Big Trees State Park he'd picked up at the visitor center the previous morning. It showed the North Fork of the Stanislaus River widening as it flowed southwest down the Sierra Nevadas into the San Joaquin, so his best chance for a crossing would be upstream where it was narrower and not as deep. He started in that direction, but suddenly stopped. Wouldn't the police come to the same conclusion? And wouldn't the dogs pick up his scent on the other bank regardless of where he crossed? His mind shifted into tactical mode.

What if I made a random decision right now, like I did when I left San Francisco? What if I made it appear as though I crossed the river, but I really don't? From where he stood, the river looked to be about thirty yards wide and waist deep. It was the perfect place to initiate Operation Misdirection.

He quickly removed his wallet, cellphone, and wristwatch, and zipped them into his jacket pocket. Then he rolled the jacket into a ball, and holding it above his head, plunged into the strong current. The shock nearly took his breath away. He'd forgotten how cold rivers could be at this elevation so late into spring. He completed the thirty-yard crossing and emerged onto the opposite bank, his water-logged sneakers squish-squish-squishing as he crossed the open, rock-strewn terrain toward the shelter of the tree line. Once under cover, he ripped off a small piece of his already torn left shirt sleeve and stuck it onto a sharp, low-hanging branch, leaving a visible clue for his pursuers. Then angling upstream, he ran into the woods about fifty feet before doubling back. Retracing his exact steps, Pete reentered the cold waters of the Stanislaus and began floating downstream. Above the sound of the rushing water, he could hear a dog barking somewhere behind him. His trackers were almost to the river! Keeping the jacket above water, he let the current carry him around the bend and out of sight.

Pete floated downriver for about twenty minutes. In a few places he had to wade through the shallows. At one point he slipped and fell heavily, bruising his left knee on a rock. As the river widened it deepened, and the current gradually slowed to a lazy pace. His plan was to exit the water a few miles ahead before reaching the dam he'd seen on the map.

Suddenly, from somewhere behind him, the faint sound of a helicopter assaulted his ears. He instinctively turned and looked upstream. The police were apparently conducting an air search as well as a ground search. And here he was fully exposed in the middle of the river!

Swimming with all his might, he made for the bank and dragged himself out of the water. He sprinted across the rocks and threw himself into the undergrowth just as the bird rounded the bend above the distant tree line. As the chuka-chuka-chuka-chuka of the blades grew louder, Pete looked around, desperate for a hiding place. His military training told him there was probably a thermal-imaging camera on board, so he needed some deep cover fast. Scrambling up the slope, he spied a large, standing sequoia about forty feet away with a small gap at the base. He raced toward the tree and squeezed through the opening. The space inside was barely large enough for his six-foot frame. *Lord, You once made blind eyes see. Now would You please make seeing eyes blind?*

He forced himself to breath slowly and listened as the chopper approached his position and flew past it down river. He waited, motionless. Five minutes later it returned, flying past him again heading upriver. Over the next twenty-five minutes it came and went twice more. Then the noise of the blades faded over the trees, and silence returned to the area.

Pete remained inside the tree for a full thirty minutes, listening intently. He heard no chopper blades, no barking dogs, no human voices. Nothing. All was quiet, except for the whisper of the mountain breeze and the burbling of the river's flow. Cautiously he emerged from his above-ground bunker and looked around. Apparently, his evasive maneuvers had been successful. But just in case the boots were still on the ground in the vicinity, he decided to hang near the hideout. He could make for the river on short notice if necessary.

From his position, Pete watched the shadows of the trees creep across the forest floor and lengthen as the sun arched across the California sky. By now the police must have called off the ground search as well. But they knew he was still in the area, so more than likely they'd be back in the morning. To play it safe, he decided to move further into the wild at sunup. With evening approaching, he ventured down to the river's edge and unrolled his slightly-soggy jacket, spreading it out on a sun-drenched boulder to dry. Then he did the same with his wet clothes. As he stretched out his jeans, he noticed the bulge in the left front pocket. It was the key fob to his rental car. Holding it up, he watched the water trickle out. *I guess I won't be needing this anymore.* It was probably shot, anyway.

He threw it as far as he could into the middle of the Stanislaus River.

As soon as his clothes were dry, Pete dressed and began looking for a warm place to bed down for the night. But he could find no suitable shelter. The mountain air was still too chilly this time of year to remain fully exposed overnight, so he fashioned a makeshift rake out of a branch from a nearby bush and busied himself with raking pine needles, wood chips, and bark into a large pile at the base of the sequoia tree. Then he curled up with his head and torso inside the hollow space and covered himself as best he could with nature's blanket. As he tried to sleep, his stomach kept reminding him that his last meal had consisted of only a single apple for breakfast.

At daybreak Pete turned his back on the river and pushed deep into the dense forest. He was feeling weak from not having eaten for twenty-four hours, so as he hiked through the heavy foliage, he kept an eye out for anything edible. If he didn't get some nourishment soon, he would lose his stamina. Forging ahead through the underbrush, he stumbled across an abandoned bear path which the omnivores had once used to traverse their dens and the river below. He followed it up the slope, hoping to find a discarded lair he could claim as his own for the next day or two. Along the way he discovered a few dandelions growing beside the path. He begrudgingly plucked a handful and forced himself to consume them as he continued his ascent.

After an hour of hiking, he stopped to rest. Leaning against a tree, he closed his eyes and listened for any telltale sounds of the previous day's pursuers. He heard none, but instead detected the sound of trickling water coming from somewhere nearby. Following the sound, he left the path and climbed up and around a steep embankment. At the top he was greeted by a small spring bubbling from a crevice between two rocks. Energized by the welcome sight, he scoured the area for leaves, twigs and small rocks, anything that could be used to build a dam. In short order the trickling spring had backed up enough for him to scoop the water to his parched lips. Using a cupped hand, he drank long and deep until his thirst was quenched.

Pete decided to set up camp near the spring. He made forays into the forest in a three-hundred-foot radius, looking for a suitable place to spend the chilly nights. To his delight he found two large rocks jutting from an overhang that provided just enough space between them in which to lay down. The ground appeared to be matted down and had the faint, musty odor of bear, but he was certain the lair had long been abandoned. He created a roof between the rocks by covering the span with branches, leaves, and pine needles.

"That should keep me warm enough tonight." He stood back and surveyed his handiwork with a measure of satisfaction.

Having secured his hotel room, Pete returned to the dam and drank again from the clear, cold mountain spring. Then he went in search of food. Not far away he located a patch of clover, which he harvested and transported back to his digs. Further up the slope, he was overjoyed to stumble upon a small blackberry bush from which he was able to glean about a cup of the delicious bramble fruit. Feeling very blessed, he sequestered himself in his new home and savored the feast God had provided for him.

Two uneventful days passed. He neither heard nor saw anything except for a few squirrels and chipmunks, and a lone jackrabbit. If the authorities were still searching for him, it must be further upstream near where he'd crossed. To pass the time, he spent much of his waking hours foraging for food. He stashed away a good supply of pine nuts and found a small patch of miners lettuce which proved to be a treasure trove of needed vitamins and Omega 3s. He thought constantly of Angela and the kids, wondering how they were holding up in his absence. Several times he tried calling them, but his phone had no reception this deep in the wilderness. To conserve the battery, he took to carrying it separately from his phone. Although he was without a Bible, he spent time quoting passages of Scripture from memory, grateful for the memorization program his parents had enrolled him in as a child. And he spent time praying for everyone he could think of, and for wisdom and direction for himself.

After a week's encampment at Shasta Base, so nicknamed for the "precious water" of the sustaining spring, Pete began thinking about hiking out of the mountains. *I can't last forever out here in the middle of nowhere.* The lack of proper nutrition was wearing him down, and he was not only sleep deprived, but losing weight, too.

Although law enforcement was probably still on the lookout for him in every town and hamlet up and down Highway 4, this was his only chance to get back to civilization. He'd have to take the risk and grab whatever opportunity presented itself in the moment. For a while he even considered turning himself in, but his pride prevented him from relinquishing total control just yet.

If I do surrender voluntarily, it's going to be back home to SFPD, and on my own terms!

A few days later, with all his food stores depleted and the area surrounding Shasta Base picked clean of anything edible, Pete broke camp. Following the abandoned bear path, he made his way further up the mountainside in hopes of finding something to eat. About mid-day he entered a pine grove and began rooting for nourishment among the shrubs and plants, but all he could find was a patch of dandelions. That would have to do for now. As he harvested the yellow weeds, a woman's scream shattered the stillness. He jerked upright, peering intently through the trees in the direction of the sound. It seemed to have come from his right, maybe a half mile or so away, it was hard to tell. He stood motionless for a full two minutes, straining to catch any hint of sound. But his ears met with nothing but silence.

Returning to the task of selecting the only item on the all-you-can-eat buffet, Pete forced himself to consume a handful of the earthy, bitter plants. Then he set out to locate a water source. As he navigated through the pine grove, a low growl stopped him in his tracks. With the hairs on his neck standing at attention, he slowly turned toward the sound. About thirty feet away and ten feet off the ground, a mountain lion crouched tensely on a large pine bough, its round, feline eyes fixated on him. Pete's heart beat wildly, but he knew not to show fear. That was a sign of weakness.

He held the big cat's gaze as he searched the archives of his brain for information. Cougar attacks were rare in this part of the country, but he remembered reading of one in Washington state a few years ago that resulted in the first human death in the United States in more than ninety years. *Maintain eye contact, Pete! Try to appear as big as possible.*

He raised his arms over his head like a referee signaling a touchdown and began swinging them in an arc. He spoke firmly. "Go on. Get out of here. Git! Git!"

The cat snarled, exposing its fangs, but did not move. *I definitely wish I had my gun on me now.*

Pete took several steps backward, looking for anything with which to defend himself. Out of the corner of his eye he spied a dead tree limb about ten feet away. He slowly inched toward it without breaking eye contact. As he squatted to pick it up, the mountain lion pounced, closing the distance between them in two bounds. Pete grabbed the four-foot stick with both hands and swung with all his might, knocking the cat to one side. With a shriek of surprise and pain, the mountain lion tumbled to the ground and somersaulted once before landing on its feet. Limping noticeably, it ran off into the pines and disappeared over a rise.

Still gripping the stick like a baseball bat, Pete stared after his attacker, too shocked to move. Then he began to shake violently, and his legs buckled beneath him. Dropping the branch, he collapsed on the ground, his breath coming in short spurts. For the first time he felt a searing pain in his left arm and noticed that the sleeve of his jacket was torn. Peeling it off, he discovered his shirtsleeve was shredded and the fabric wet with fresh blood. Gingerly, he removed his shirt and inspected the wound. There were two six-inch-long gashes in his bicep. Despite the pain, he spread apart the flesh with the fingers of his right hand to see how deep the cuts went. Fortunately, they were both just flesh wounds. The big cat's claws had struck only a glancing blow, thanks to his quick reflexes. Still, they would need tending to.

Pete grabbed his shirt between his teeth and tore a strip of cloth from the left sleeve. Then he tightly wrapped his upper arm with the temporary bandage to stop the bleeding and slipped back into his jacket. He had to get out of here as fast as he could. He needed to find someplace where he could get some antibacterial ointment and real bandages. Besides, if that cougar caught wind of the blood, it might come back and try to finish the job!

Moving as quickly as he could, Pete cut through the forest on a northwesterly path, heading opposite the direction the cougar had taken. He scrambled up the slope, looking over his shoulder every time he stumbled and fell. His wounds throbbed painfully from the exertion, and his mouth grew dry and parched. After forty-five minutes of hiking, he stopped to catch his breath and check his arm. The makeshift bandage seemed to be serving its purpose, and he was relieved to discover that the bleeding had slowed considerably.

But he had to get help soon. He needed water and something to treat these cuts before they got infected. He resumed his trek, hoping to intersect Highway 4 at some juncture.

"It can't be much farther," he said out loud to encourage himself. Suddenly a screeching sound came from somewhere in front of him. He froze instantly, fearing the mountain lion had circled and was coming in for the kill. Then he heard it again. It was not the scream he'd heard earlier, but rather a higher pitched, sustained one this time. It was the sound of a chain saw. Someone must be cutting down trees or clearing brush nearby!

Heaving a sigh of relief, Pete followed the sound of the power tool and soon spied a clearing ahead. Through the trees he detected movement. As he cautiously approached, he spied a man in a red plaid shirt, his back to him, bending over a twelve-inch diameter log and cutting it into firewood-sized lengths. Then Pete noticed the house. The clearing was actually someone's back yard. He looked to his left and right and saw the backsides of several more houses hiding among the trees.

He was finally out of the wilderness! But where was he? What town was this? And where was Highway 4? He fought the urge to approach the man and ask for a drink of water, telling himself it wouldn't be hard to convince the homeowner that he was a hiker who'd gotten lost in the wilderness. But by now the locals would be aware of the recent manhunt in Big Trees State Park, so they might be suspicious of any stranger who approached them from the direction of the forest.

Pete backed away and circumvented the man in the yard, keeping out of sight in the tree line. He skirted several more back yards before he realized that the houses were at the end of a cul-de-sac. At some point he'd have to leave the forest in order to reach the highway where the stores were, so he cut between two houses and began walking down the street. The heavily-wooded lots would provide him cover should any police cars happen to be cruising the neighborhood. He walked four blocks, crossed a golf course carved out of the hillside, and followed another winding street for about half a mile without passing a single car or person. He came to an intersection, and from the volume of traffic Pete could tell he'd reached Highway 4. Across the road on the opposite corner, a fuel truck was parked next to the pumps in front of a combination gas station and mini-mart. They should have what he needed. With renewed energy he crossed the two-lane road, checking both directions for any sign of the black and white SUVs he'd seen in the state park.

Pete entered the store and began searching the aisles for the needed items. People gawked as he walked by, making him extremely uncomfortable. Why were they staring at him?

Have they seen my picture on TV? What if somebody calls the cops?

He fought to remain calm and went about his business, selecting a hiker's first aid kit, some energy bars and beef jerky sticks, and a six-pack of bottled water. As he passed the freezer section, he caught sight of himself in the mirrored glass. The face staring back at him sported a two-week's growth of stubble, his skin appeared cracked and dry like old leather, and his clothing was filthy, torn, and blood-stained. His disheveled hair was matted with bits of leaves, twigs, and pine needles projecting in all directions, giving him the appearance of a deranged porcupine.

No wonder they were staring at him. He looked terrible! And he probably didn't smell all that good, either. He forced himself to meet their stares with a polite smile as he carried his purchases to the cash register. After paying for the items, he entered the small, one-person bathroom at the back of the store. Locking the door, he shed his jacket and shirt and gingerly removed the cloth bandage from his wounded left arm. The cuts were red and irritated, but thankfully the bleeding had all but stopped. After washing them with soap and water, he patted the skin dry with a paper towel, applied some antibacterial ointment, and covered the area with a large waterproof bandage. Then he wiggled back into his shirt and jacket and unlocked the door.

Once outside, he walked around the corner of the building away from prying eyes and sat down with his back against the wall. When he'd finished drinking a bottled water and devouring a couple of energy bars and a beef stick, he plotted his next move. First, he'd need some clean clothes and a disguise. There must be a thrift store around here somewhere. Then he'd figure out how to get out of Dodge. He picked up his bag and headed back inside to ask the cashier for directions. But just as he reached the front door, he glanced across the highway and spotted a black and white SUV with "Calaveras County Sheriff" on the door. The two uniformed officers inside were watching pedestrians and traffic go by. Pete quickly turned his face away and ducked around the corner again, praying they hadn't seen him. He could wait here until they drove away, but how long would it be until they spotted him somewhere else? As he worked through his options, he watched the fuel truck driver filling the store's underground storage tank. His eyes were drawn to the bright red "FLAMMABLE LIQUID" label on the truck's polished side, then to the company's logo: "Standard Petroleum, Inc., Stockton, California." *Hmmm. An out-of-towner. He wouldn't know anything about me. If I could only . . .*

Keeping the tanker between him and the policemen across the street, Pete approached the driver, who was watching the meter on the side of his truck.

"Excuse me, but do you think you could give me a lift when you're done here?"

The driver glanced up and gave him the once over. "Sorry, no riders. Company policy," he replied curtly, before returning to his work.

"Listen, I'm really desperate for a ride," Pete pleaded. "I'll even pay you for your trouble."

The man studied him for a moment, then glanced around before responding. "How much you willin' to pay?"

"What do you say to . . . fifty dollars?"

"Make it a hundred," the man replied.

"I don't have that much on me." Pete hesitated. "How about sixty?"

"Eighty," the driver countered. "Take it or leave it."

"That's almost everything I've got!" Pete protested. But he was out of options. "Oh, all right, eighty." He took out his wallet and forked over four twenties.

The man quickly folded the bills and stuffed them into his shirt pocket. "You must be real desperate askin' for a lift without knowin' where I'm headed." He nodded toward the front of his rig. "All right, wait in the cab," he barked gruffly, turning back to the meter. "But don't touch nuthin!"

Pete climbed into the passenger seat and closed the door. In the large side mirror, he watched the driver disconnect the hose from the fill valve and pack it away before disappearing into the store with the invoice.

What if he's in there calling the police? It was too late to do anything about it now. Besides, he was out of options. He had no choice but to trust the man.

A few minutes later the driver emerged from the mini-mart and climbed into the cab. He stashed the clipboard, fastened his seat belt, and started the engine. As it warmed up, he studied Pete's clothes. "So, what happened to you? You look like you been sleepin' in the woods, or mud wrestlin' or somethin'!"

Pete was tight lipped. "Well, actually, I'd rather not talk about it."

The driver stared at him for a second before raising both hands in surrender. "Sure, I gotcha, man. Ask me no questions, I tell ya no lies, right?" He gave a short, gravelly laugh. "For eighty bucks, I guess I don't need no answers."

"So, where *are* we headed?" Pete asked, revisiting the topic of their destination.

The man retrieved a well-chewed cigar stub from the ashtray and stuffed it between his lips. "Fresno," he muttered, leaning over and releasing the air brakes. Then he put the rig into gear and eased out onto Highway 4, driving right by the two deputies in the SUV. They continued down the road for about a mile before he turned and squinted suspiciously at Pete. "Say, uh . . . you ain't no escaped convict or serial killer, are you?"

Pete frowned at him. "Do I look like a criminal to you?"

The driver shrugged. "Hey, pal, just askin'. They come in all shapes and sizes, ya know."

Pete settled back in his seat and closed his eyes. Fifteen minutes later, he was out of the county and on his way to Fresno.

CHAPTER TEN
THE GOOD SAMARITAN

THE SUDDEN, SHARP PAIN CAUSED Pete to jerk awake and cry out. He grabbed his injured bicep with his right hand as the truck driver shook him again.

"Hey buddy, wake up! I need ya to get out here."

The throbbing wounds hastened the return of Pete's senses. Straightening in the seat, he looked around. They were stopped on the side of the road. "Where are we?"

"Stockton," the driver replied. "I need ya to get out here." He stared suspiciously at Pete's torn jacket. "You hurt your arm, mister?" Before Pete could respond he added, "Now wait a minute. How do I know you ain't got a slug in your arm or somethin'? Is that why you were in such a rush to get away? What did ya do, rob the bank back there in Arnold?"

Pete stared back at him. "Rob the bank?" He opened his bag of snacks and showed the contents to the driver. "If I did, all I got away with was some water and snack bars and beef jerky." He shot the man a knowing grin. "But I'll split the loot with you if you keep your promise."

The driver laughed coarsely. "Okay, you got yourself a deal, pal. So then, what *did* happen to your arm?"

"I was hiking this morning and got attacked by a cougar. It managed to give me a couple of nasty scratches before I scared it off."

The driver's eyes widened. "A cougar? For real? I never seen one before, but I heard there was some back up in the mountains. How big was he?"

"I don't know, five foot long, maybe. A hundred and fifty pounds."

"That big, huh? Did you report it?"

Pete hesitated. "Well, I uh . . . I'd rather not talk about it."

The driver raised both palms off the steering wheel. "I get it. Too many questions, right? Whatever. Anyway, I need ya to get out here." He pointed to some large above-ground storage tanks in the distance. "I can't drive into the yard with a passenger on board. I'd get sacked, sure as shootin.'"

It was Pete's turn to be suspicious. "You didn't say anything about dropping me off in Stockton. You said you'd take me all the way to Fresno."

"I will, I will," the man retorted, "but first I gotta pick up a fresh load. This rig holds only eleven thousand gallons, and that station back there just about took everything I had."

"How long will it take to refill your truck?" Pete asked, wondering what to do during the layover.

"'Bout thirty minutes. With all the paperwork and stuff, 'bout an hour, hour ten tops." He pointed toward a restaurant across the road from where they were stopped. "Wait for me over there. I'll pick you up when I'm loaded. Won't take but two hours to get to Fresno once we're on 99."

"Okay, I'll be waiting. Thanks." Pete got out of the cab and crossed the roadway as the tanker pulled back onto the pavement. He watched the rig make a right-hand turn into the fuel facility a half mile ahead before entering the restaurant.

Fully conscious of the stares of the other patrons waiting to be seated, Pete studied the menu posted on the lobby wall. To a man who hadn't had a decent meal in almost two weeks, everything sounded delicious. But he had only fifteen dollars and some change, and he'd need most of that for some thrift store clothes. He thought about charging the meal, but ever since he'd learned the police had tracked the rental car to Big Trees, he'd determined not to use his credit card if at all possible, in case they were monitoring his purchases. On the other hand, he'd be in Fresno before they could track him here, and he simply had to have something to eat. He approached the hostess stand.

"May I help you?" the girl asked, trying hard not to stare at his torn, filthy clothing.

"A table for one, please," he replied.

The hostess hesitated. "Um, just a minute, sir. I'll be right back." She turned and hastily retreated around the corner. A moment later she returned with the manager.

"How may I help you, sir?" the man inquired, flashing a patronizing smile.

"I'd like a table for one if you don't mind." Pete sensed what was coming.

The man looked him up and down. "Sir, I'd very much like to accommodate your request, but I'm afraid I can't seat you at the moment."

"Why not?" Pete's question was a mere formality at this point. He already knew the answer.

The manager lowered his voice to avoid being overheard by the other customers. "Sir, this restaurant has a favorable reputation in this area. Your presence might be . . . um . . . a bit upsetting to our regular patrons." He shook his head sympathetically. "I'm very sorry. I wish I could help you."

"Well, can I at least place a take-out order, then?" Pete argued. "And you don't have to worry, I can pay for it."

The manager shook his head again. "I'm afraid we don't offer take-out service here. This is a dine-in establishment only. But there's a fast-food place just up the road a quarter mile. I'm sure they would be happy to take your order there."

Pete decided it would not be wise to make a scene. Any further attempt to secure a meal might prompt a call to the local authorities. He shrugged in surrender. "Well, okay then, if that's the way it has to be. Thanks anyway." He forced a polite smile, and then turned toward the door.

"Have a nice day, sir," the manager called after him in an overly-polite voice, most likely for the benefit of the other patrons.

Pete walked the three blocks to the fast-food restaurant and ordered a large combo meal, paying for it with cash. Then he sat down in the far corner of the seating area and ate his food without so much as a glance from the other eat-in customers. In the first establishment he'd felt terribly incongruous, but in this one he felt totally invisible.

After finishing his meal, he refilled his soda and walked back to the first restaurant. With twenty minutes to kill, he sat down under a tree at the edge of the parking lot to wait for the truck driver. The twenty minutes passed, then thirty, then forty. He stood up and walked to the edge of the roadway, looking for a bright red-over-white cab pulling a shiny 11,000-gallon tank trailer. Nothing. He returned to the tree and continued his wait. After sitting in the shade for over an hour, Pete finally succumbed to his growing suspicions. The driver was not coming back.

What am I going to do, Lord?

Pete prayed, as he sat under the tree outside the restaurant. If he stayed here much longer, someone might report him to the management, and he'd be picked up for loitering. And he couldn't stay in Stockton. It was only an hour from where the police last searched for him, so he was not safe here.

He needed to get to Fresno. But how? *Lord, give me some sign so I know what to do. Show me the way.* Leaning back against the tree, he pulled his knees toward his chest, and placed his head in his hands. Overwhelmed by weariness and deluged with discouragement, Pete wished a police car would pull up next to him and put an end to this misery. He was tired of running and tired of being chased. He missed Angela and the kids, his church family, sleeping in his own bed, and the simple pleasure of taking a hot shower.

A jail cell would be better than this. At least then I'd get three meals a day, and the family could come visit me.

He remained in that position for some time, lost in a world of self-loathing. No longer did he feel like the brave man who faced difficulties and challenges head on, the one who had a keen sense of right and wrong and who displayed solid integrity and moral fortitude. He'd become fearful, weak, and cowardly, with no sense of purpose or direction. He silently prayed that it would all go away.

The sound of voices crashed his self-imposed pity party. Pete raised his head and observed two men who appeared to be in their early to mid-forties leaving the restaurant. Walking in his direction, they stopped beside one of the parked cars without noticing him. He caught the tail end of their conversation.

"It was really good catching up with you, Tom," one man said, shaking hands with the other. "Let's not wait so long to do this again."

The other man nodded in agreement. "You're right, it's been way too long. I'll give you a call in a month or so. Maybe we can bring the wives along next time. I know Bev would enjoy listening to your war stories."

The first man laughed. "Oh, I don't know about that. Lilly's heard them all a hundred times before. Anyway, she says I talk too much."

The man named Tom returned his laugh. "Then once more won't make any difference, will it?" He unlocked his car and opened the door. "I'll be in touch. Take care of yourself, Eddie."

"You, too, Tom. Hooah!" Eddie said, making a fist.

"Hooah!" Tom replied immediately.

"Hooah!" Pete responded instinctively.

The two men turned and stared at Pete. Glancing at each other, they approached him.

"Hey buddy, you ex-military?" the man named Eddie asked.

Pete quickly stood up. "Yes sir! 101st Airborne, 586th Forward Support Battalion," he announced.

"327th Infantry Regiment, 3rd Battalion," the man responded warmly, shaking Pete's hand. "I'm Eddie Marshall. This here is Tom Barrett."

"2nd Battalion, 70th Armor Regiment, C Company," Tom introduced himself.

"I'm Pete Holloway," he said, shaking the man's hand.

"586th, huh? Then you must have seen action in Iraq."

Pete nodded. "Plenty! I was over there almost a year. Spent most of my time in Baghdad and Mosul."

"No fooling? I'll bet you've got some interesting stories to tell," Eddie offered. "I wish I could stay around and hear some of them, but I've got an appointment I need to be at in half an hour." He looked at Pete's deplorable condition. "Say, Pete, you look like you could use a hot meal." He removed his wallet and took out a twenty-dollar bill. "Why don't you take this and get something off the menu?" He gave the restaurant a nod. "I can vouch for the food."

Pete looked at the bill in Eddie's hand, and managed a weak smile. "I appreciate your kindness, but the truth is, I just ate." He held up the soft drink cup as proof.

"Well, take it anyway," Eddie insisted, forcing the twenty into Pete's hand. "I'm sure you can use it down the road." He patted Pete on the shoulder. "Thank you for serving your country. It was good meeting you. God bless you, brother." He turned to Tom. "I've got to run. Don't forget to call me."

"I won't," Tom replied. Eddie hurried away toward his own vehicle which was parked a few spaces away. Tom turned back to Pete. "Are you from around here, Mr. Holloway?"

"No, I'm from San Francisco." Pete wanted to say more but checked himself. "I uh . . . I'm just passing through. Heading south."

"Do you have transportation?" Tom asked. Then he hastily added, "I don't mean to pry or anything, but it appears as though you might be down on your luck at the moment."

Pete resisted the temptation to lie. "Mr. Barrett, I know I probably look homeless to you, but I can assure you I'm not. However, things haven't exactly been going my way lately." He looked down at his torn, filthy clothing and forced a wry grin. "I guess that's pretty obvious, isn't it?"

Tom held up one hand. "You don't have to explain yourself. But I'd like to help if I can. I've got to run down to Fresno tomorrow on business. If you need a ride, I'd be happy to give you a lift."

Thank You, Lord, that sure was a fast answer to prayer! "Actually, Fresno is where I'm headed. But I wasn't sure how I was going to get there. Thanks for the offer, that's very generous of you."

"No problem, glad to help. I'm leaving around eight in the morning. Where would be a good place to pick you up?"

Pete hesitated. "Well, um . . . how about right here?"

Tom cocked his head. "Pete, do you need a place to stay tonight?"

"Oh, don't worry about me," Pete responded quickly, "I'll be fine. I'm used to it by now."

Tom became resolute. "Nonsense! You're coming with me." He motioned toward his car. "Get in. There's a motel a couple of miles from here. I'll put you up there for the night." Without waiting for a response, he turned and walked back to his car. Too tired to argue, Pete obliged. They pulled out of the parking lot and headed up the road, past the entrance to the fuel facility.

"I'll pay you back for your kindness," Pete promised.

Tom glanced over at his passenger. "Tommy rot!" he blurted out, "you'll do no such thing. I'm just glad for the chance to help out a fellow Screaming Eagle." They approached a neon motel sign with the words "CATTLEMAN'S TRAIL MOTEL" on it, and the word "VACANCY" flashing underneath. "This isn't the Ritz-Carlton, mind you." Tom laughed. " . . . But you can get a good night's sleep and a free continental breakfast here." He drove past the motel without slowing down.

Pete watched the sign recede in the passenger side mirror. "Um, wasn't that the motel back there?" *Where is this guy taking me?* He fought the familiar feeling of growing panic.

"Yeah, that's it," Tom replied casually, "but I thought you could use a change of clothes first." He turned into a thrift store lot and parked next to the building.

It dawned on Pete what his benefactor was planning to do. "Mr. Barrett, you don't have to do this. Really, you've done enough already."

Tom gave him a sly look. "Well, to be honest with you, this isn't just for *your* benefit," he explained reluctantly. "After all, we're going to be traveling together for over two hours tomorrow . . . in an enclosed vehicle . . . "

Pete nodded. "I catch your drift," he said with a knowing grin. "But I'm guessing you don't want to catch mine!"

At eight o'clock the following morning, Pete was waiting in front of the motel for his ride to Fresno. He'd used the twenty dollars Eddie had given him to buy a disposable razor and miscellaneous toiletries at a drug store a block away. That, along with a good night's sleep, a hot shower and breakfast, and the change of clothes, made him feel like a new man. The two strangers' acts of kindness were an answer to prayer, and their generosity buoyed his spirit and encouraged his heart. He'd also been able to finally get a hold of Angela again, this time placing the long-distance call from the telephone in his room to conserve the battery in his cellphone, which was once again without its charger.

SFPD had informed her that the various law enforcement agencies were now interested in him primarily for his role in the

Sacramento shooting, something he'd already deduced. So many resources would not have been wasted on a manhunt for a mere hate speech violator. He'd learned that several people in his church had also been questioned regarding his whereabouts, a fact which made him grateful for having decided to keep them in the dark as well. He and Angela had discussed his return to San Francisco, but he'd thought it best to contact his lawyer first. He was certain Mr. Murdock would advise him to surrender, but he wanted to review his options as well as provide the lawyer with a full statement regarding his involvement in the Sacramento incident.

A few minutes after eight, Tom Barrett drove up to the front of the motel and Pete got into his car.

"Good morning," Tom greeted him cheerfully. "You look refreshed. How were the accommodations?"

"Best night's sleep I've had in two weeks!" Pete told him honestly. "I can't begin to thank you for doing this for me, Mr. Barrett. You're a godsend, a true Good Samaritan."

Tom shrugged self-consciously. "Like I said before, I'm happy to help out a fellow soldier. Besides, I was already going to Fresno. Having a passenger will help pass the time." Several minutes later they merged onto Highway 99 South and put Stockton in the rear-view mirror.

After ten days alone in the wilderness, and being betrayed by the tanker driver, Pete felt the need for conversation. "You said you were going to Fresno on business," he began. "What line of work are you in?"

"I'm in sales. Medical equipment," Tom replied, keeping his eyes on the road. "I used to own a small insurance agency, but I sold that five years ago." He chuckled. "I'm not one for sitting behind a desk all day long. With this job I get to travel a bit and still be home most evenings."

"How big of an area are you responsible for?" Pete asked.

"My territory covers Sacramento to Fresno, including San Francisco, San Jose, and all points in between." He glanced over at his passenger. "Didn't you say you were from San Francisco? St. Francis Memorial is one of my biggest accounts there."

"My daughter was born at St. Francis," Pete replied, feeling the connection. "I've lived in San Fran most of my life, except for my time in the Army. I was stationed at Fort Campbell for four years after high school, and again when I re-enlisted after 9/11."

"You're not career military?" Tom seemed surprised. "I just assumed you were on the twenty-year plan."

Pete laughed. "No, I went to San Jose State after my first hitch. Got a degree in management. After my second hitch I went to seminary before moving back home."

"Seminary?" Tom appeared surprised. "So then, you used to be a minister?"

Tom's use of the past tense jolted him as much as if he'd stuck a fork into a light socket. Staring blankly out the passenger window, Pete fought unsuccessfully to block the questions that forced their way in his head.

Am I still a minister? Do I still have a church, or a congregation, or a job to come back to? Or is that all over now? Have I ruined everything I've worked for all these years? Have I failed God?

Pete's lack of response prompted Tom to retreat. "Hey, I didn't mean to pry into your personal life," he apologized, "I was just making conversation. If you'd rather change the subject, that's okay by me."

Pete turned away from the window and sighed. "No, it's all right. The truth is, I *am* a minister. At least, up until three weeks ago I was. But now I'm not so sure."

"I hope you don't mind me saying so, but a lot must have happened in a short time for you to end up like this," Tom surmised. "Would it help to talk about it? I'm a pretty sympathetic listener."

Pete desperately wanted to unburden his soul to this man, to tell him everything. But something deep inside held him back. Although Tom had shown amazing kindness, he was still a stranger, and lately, opening up to strangers hadn't exactly been good for him.

"I appreciate that very much." He smiled politely. "I'd like to tell you about it, but I don't want to involve you in my problems. I've got to work them out on my own. Anyway, your generosity has already helped me more than you will ever know. Let's just leave it at that, if you don't mind."

Tom appeared to let a comment die on his lips. "Okay, no problem. I just thought I'd offer in case you were interested." They drove in silence for a few miles. Then he glanced at his passenger. "So you were in a forward support battalion in Baghdad. That must have been quite the experience. What was that like?" He grinned and added, "If you don't mind me asking."

For the rest of the trip, the two men shared their combat experiences in Iraq. It wasn't long before the skyline of Fresno began to rise from the horizon. "Where would you like me to let you out?" Tom asked, as they approached the downtown district.

"Anywhere is fine, it doesn't matter to me," Pete replied. "Whatever is convenient for you."

Tom stared at him for a moment. "Pete, if you need a place to stay, may I suggest the Good News Mission on Ventura Street? It's got a pretty good reputation among the homeless veteran population, although I know you're technically not homeless. In any case, they'll provide you with a bed and a hot meal. But you'll have to agree to listen to preaching every night."

Pete grinned. "I think I can handle that. Thanks, that would be just fine."

Ten minutes later, Tom pulled to the curb in front of an old brick storefront bearing a sign with the words "Good News Mission" and "Jesus Saves" on it. As Pete opened the door, Tom handed him a business card. "Here's my cell number. If you're ever in Stockton again and you need anything, anything at all, don't hesitate to call me."

Pete accepted the card. "Thank you, Mr. Barrett. I won't ever forget your kindness to me. God bless you!"

"Take care of yourself, Pete." He raised a fist. "Hooah!"

"Hooah!" Pete responded, with a grateful smile. He watched the car drive away from the curb. Then he turned and entered the Good News Mission.

CHAPTER ELEVEN
RESCUE ME

PETE STOOD JUST INSIDE THE front door of the mission and surveyed the long, narrow, L-shaped room. To his right, between plastered square columns, several rows of old church pews faced a hand-built pulpit with a wooden cross mounted to the front. A large painting of a lighthouse hung on the wall behind the pulpit, with the words of Matthew 11:28 underneath: *"Come to Me, all who labor and are heavy laden, and I will give you rest."*

An ancient upright piano, its dark mahogany finish cracked and chipped, was parked in the corner with several stacks of well-worn church hymnals piled on top. Above it, a flat screen television was mounted to the wall. Several men sat slouched among the pews, one dozing, another reading a newspaper, the others watching TV.

On the opposite side of the room was a large wooden desk with several chairs lined up along the wall. A man who looked to be in his late fifties sat behind the desk, writing something in a manila folder. Pete crossed the creaky wooden floor to the man at the desk.

The man looked up at him through thick glasses and flashed a warm smile. "Welcome to the Good News Mission. I'm Jack. How can I help you?" His tone was sincere and inviting.

Pete cleared his throat. "I was wondering if you might have room for me to spend the night here."

Jack studied him for a moment. "Are you from the Fresno area or just passing through?"

"Passing through," Pete replied. "I just got into town and I don't have a place to stay at the moment. A guy I know, Tom Barrett, suggested this place."

Jack raised his eyebrows. "Tom Barrett's a friend of yours?"

"Well, not exactly," Pete confessed, "I met him only yesterday afternoon. But he put me up in a motel last night and gave me a ride from Stockton this morning."

Jack shook his head and laughed. "That sounds like Tom, all right. He's got a real knack for finding people in need of a hand up. Did he mention that he's on our board of directors?"

"No, he didn't," Pete acknowledged, "but I can tell he's got a real heart for this kind of ministry."

"That he does," Jack said with a vigorous nod. He tilted his head. "I didn't get your name."

"Pete. It's Pete Holloway."

"Well, Mr. Holloway, if Tom referred you here, then I'm sure we can find a place to put you up for a while." He motioned to one of the chairs beside the desk. "Please have a seat." As Pete sat down, Jack opened a desk drawer and pulled out a single sheet of paper. "We have some guidelines we ask everyone staying with us to abide by." He closed the drawer and handed the paper to Pete. "As a Christ-centered, gospel-focused ministry, our purpose is not only to meet a person's physical needs but his spiritual needs as well. We seek to offer a hand *up*, not a hand*out*. In addition to providing meals and shelter, we offer recovery programs, counseling, and spiritual guidance." He pointed to the paper in Pete's hand. "In order to stay with us, everyone is expected to attend a half-hour service here in the front room every evening. We also assign tasks such as housekeeping or kitchen help as a way to offset the cost of your room and board. And if you plan on staying with us more than three nights, we require that you meet with a counselor to determine how we can best help you going forward. Does that sound like something you can agree to?"

Pete nodded. "Sure, I've got no problem with any of that. I'm just grateful to have a place to stay."

"Good. Then why don't you take a moment to read through those guidelines and I'll get you set up for tonight."

Pete read the rules. In addition to the mandatory evening service, no drugs, alcohol, or weapons of any kind were permitted on the premises, and smoking was allowed only in the alley out back. He chuckled inwardly when he thought of the required church services. This was so much better than being forced to attend the state's reeducation program!

After Pete signed the guideline agreement, Jack led him through the door at the back of the room and showed him the dining area before taking him up a back stairway to the sleeping quarters. The upstairs consisted of two large areas with about twenty single beds per room, and a large bathroom with four shower stalls.

"This will be your space." Jack pointed to an empty bed against the back wall near a boarded-up window. "You can store your belongings underneath if you like, but I'd caution you to keep anything of value with you. We're not responsible for any stolen property during your stay with us. You'll get a towel and washcloth, a bar of soap, and some toiletry items your first night here, but after that it'll be up to you to replace them as needed. Any questions?"

"No, that's fine," Pete replied.

"The service is at six-thirty and supper's at seven. Remember, if you want to eat tonight, you need to attend the service first."

"I'll be there," Pete promised. The two men left the room together. "Oh, one more thing. Do you have an extra Bible I could use while I'm here?"

Jack turned and stared at him, a look of surprise on his face. "A Bible? Sure, I can get you a Bible. You can keep it if you like." As they descended the narrow staircase, Jack looked over his shoulder and gave Pete a friendly smile. "You know, you're the first person who ever asked me for a Bible his first night here."

Pete spent the remainder of the afternoon sitting on his bed reading from his new Bible, and meditating on parts of Psalm 119: "*I have stored up Your word in my heart, that I might not sin against You . . . I will delight in Your statutes; I will not forget Your word . . . Deal bountifully with Your servant, that I may live and keep Your word . . . My soul clings to the dust; give me life according to Your word . . . My soul melts away for sorrow; strengthen me according to Your word . . . Let Your steadfast love come to me, O Lord, Your salvation according to Your promise; then shall I have an answer for him who taunts me, for I trust in Your word.*"

When he headed downstairs for the evening service, his soul was as full as a person leaving a sumptuous buffet. With about thirty-five men present for the half-hour meeting, a large, jovial man calling himself Big Ben led in the singing of a couple of hymns. His wife, whom he introduced as Sandy, accompanied him on the piano which, although woefully out of tune, produced a certain comforting sound in her skilled hands. Then Big Ben opened his appropriately large Bible and preached from Exodus 10:16-17 on Pharaoh's insincere confession, saying that if one merely acknowledges his sin against God to avoid the consequences, he is not truly repentant. He concluded by quoting Second Corinthians 7:10, *"For godly grief produces a repentance that leads to salvation without regret."*

Following a meal of meat loaf, mashed potatoes, and peas, which wasn't nearly as bad as he'd anticipated, Pete went outside for some fresh air. He meandered around the nearby downtown area for a while, but after spotting three police cars cruising the streets, he got cold feet and returned to the mission, fearful of being identified as the fugitive from Sacramento.

He passed the next two nights at the Good News Mission. The bed to which he'd been assigned was surprisingly comfortable but being in a room full of strangers who mumbled to themselves, or coughed and hacked all night, or who didn't smell all that great made sleep rather difficult. During his waking hours he read his Bible and drafted a statement to his lawyer, using the spiral notepad given to him by Jack, the mission front man. He made himself available for whatever work needed to be done, volunteering with the meal prep and cleanup, and passing out hymnals at the evening services.

On day three, Jack arranged a meeting between Pete and Big Ben to determine how the mission could best serve Pete's needs going forward. The two men sat down across an old oak table from one another in a small first floor office off the main room.

"So, tell me a little about yourself," Big Ben said casually, leaning back in his chair so far that Pete feared it might tip over. "I heard Tom Barrett gave you a ride here from Stockton. Is that where you're from?"

"No, I'm from San Francisco," Pete answered, deciding to be totally up front with the large man. He was tired of hiding the truth. Besides, Big Ben appeared to be someone he could really trust this time. "I was born there, and I've lived there most of my life. Actually, for the past thirteen years I've pastored a medium-sized church in Diamond Heights."

Big Ben grabbed the table edge with both hands, narrowly averting a disaster. His look of surprise gave way to a warm smile. "I *thought* there was something different about you," he confided. "I was told that you asked for a Bible your first night here, and you've been volunteering so cheerfully in the kitchen and with the church services. Are you a born-again Christian, Mr. Holloway?"

Pete nodded. "Yes, I accepted Christ when I was ten years old."

"That's wonderful!" Big Ben beamed. "I was saved in college. That was the most important decision I've ever made. Changed my whole life." He shifted in his seat. "Do you have family back in San Francisco?"

"My wife Angela, and my two kids, Andrew and Brienna. Plus, my congregation. I count them as family."

"How long since you last saw them?"

Pete wasn't sure. "What day is today?"

"Thursday the fourteenth," Big Ben said.

"Well, um . . . let's see, it's been three weeks then." Pete wrinkled his brow. "Can that be right? It seems more like three months!"

Big Ben placed his elbows on the table and leaned forward. "So then, I guess the obvious question would be, 'How did you go from being a husband, father, and pastor in San Francisco to being a resident here at the Good News Mission in only three weeks?' Something drastic must have happened in between." When Pete was slow to respond, he added, "It might ease your mind to know that I'm a certified nouthetic counselor. I've been helping people with serious life issues for over twenty years."

"That's good to know," Pete said, "but that's not really the problem. As a pastor, I've been the one giving the advice for over a decade. It's difficult for me to admit that I might now be the one in need of counseling for a change. I suppose that's my pride getting in the way."

"That's understandable," Big Ben replied gently. "Pride can be a big stumbling block. But you're not alone. Pastors bear a heavy responsibility caring for their flocks. Everyone expects them to always be ready to listen to other people's problems and offer biblical advice. But pastors are human, too. Who do they go to with *their* burdens?"

"We're supposed to take our burdens to the Lord. That's the pat answer, isn't it?"

"*'Casting all your anxieties on Him, for He cares for you,'* right?" Big Ben grinned. "But that's not just for pastors, that's for all believers. And so is this: *'Bear one another's burdens, and so fulfill the law of Christ.'* Pete, just because you're a pastor doesn't mean you have to carry your own burdens by yourself. It's a two-way street, my friend." He tapped the tabletop with one of his large palms. "That's why I'm here, to help you with your burdens."

Pete's shoulders sagged and his eyes brimmed with tears. Here was a fellow believer, a brother in Christ, another Jim Sutherland, who was willing to listen to him and help carry his heavy load. He decided to be totally transparent.

"Are you familiar with the Hate Speech Reparation and Elimination Act?" he asked his newest confidant.

Big Ben quirked his eyebrows. "Um . . . yes I am, actually. Why do you mention that?"

Pete launched into his narrative, starting with his interview by Detective Branch. As he began to explain the sequence of events that unfolded thereafter, Big Ben stopped him with an upheld hand.

"I don't mean to cut you off, Pete," he said, "but before you continue, would it be all right if I asked my wife, Sandy, to join us? I'd like for her to hear how the state has intimidated and threatened you and your pastor friends."

"Well, I'm a bit uncomfortable sharing this, even with you," Pete confessed.

"I'm sure it's not easy, but I think you'd benefit from her being here. You see, before we came to the Good News Mission six months ago, we both were in a ministry together in Los Angeles."

"What kind of ministry?"

"We ran a not-for-profit biblical counseling center with a staff of eight in an impoverished neighborhood in central LA, funded entirely by private donations. We offered counseling for drug and sex addictions as well as women's health, but our ultimate goal was to point people to Christ as the only permanent solution for their sin problem." A look of sadness crossed Big Ben's otherwise jovial face. "However, because we refused on religious grounds to accept, endorse, or promote abortion and homosexuality in our programs, the state accused us of hating women and the LGBTQ community."

Pete scowled. "That sounds familiar."

"And that's not all. They eventually forced us to close our doors."

Pete shook his head in disbelief. "Seriously? Then the detective wasn't bluffing when he said I could lose my church if I didn't comply with the state. It's already begun."

"Yes, it has," Big Ben agreed. "So, do I have your permission to invite Sandy to sit in on our discussion? She's got some skin in the game just like you and I have. Besides, she's very insightful on this topic."

"I guess that would be all right," Pete capitulated. "It sounds like you've experienced the same opposition I have."

Big Ben smiled appreciatively and sent his wife a text. The two men chatted until a knock sounded on the door. Sandy stuck her head into the office and Big Ben motioned her inside. After introducing her to Pete, Big Ben asked him to share his story with them, beginning again with the SFPD interview. As the husband and wife listened intently, Pete told them everything he'd been through in the past six weeks. What a relief it was to share his burden with others of like precious faith who not only could sympathize with his trial, but who also were willing to help him bear it.

"Pastor Holloway, I'm so sorry that you and your friends are being persecuted for the faith," Sandy said, when he'd finished his narrative. "Ben and I understand what you're going through." She looked at her husband. "The truth is, we're under the same gun as you are."

"What do you mean?" Pete wanted to know. "What did they do to you?" He feared their answer.

Big Ben was the one who replied. "At first, the state levied fines for each day we remained open without complying with the law. We couldn't afford to pay them. Then they said they would waive the fines if we agreed to do community service at an abortion clinic and help organize a gay pride march as part of our 'reparations' under the law. Of course, we couldn't in good conscience do that either, so they revoked our license and shut us down." He paused, as if conflicted. "Pete, I'm reluctant to share this with you, but since you're facing the same consequences we are, I feel I can trust you. When we challenged those actions via legal means, the state retaliated by flexing its muscle and issuing warrants for our arrest."

Pete's mouth dropped open. "You both were arrested? What happened? Did you spend time in jail?"

"Well, not exactly." Big Ben hesitated, glancing at his wife. "We, ah . . . we fled LA to avoid arrest. That's how we ended up here."

"You both have open warrants, same as me?" Pete was amazed. "Then you're on the run, too. Only . . ." He paused and frowned. "Then why aren't you in hiding? You openly preach and counsel here at the mission. Aren't you afraid of being discovered?"

A smile creased Big Ben's face. "I confess, we sometimes feel like the Apostle Paul must have felt when the Jews sought his arrest in Damascus. But he fled that city and ended up in Jerusalem. We fled LA and ended up here. I don't know how long we'll be able to serve the Lord before they catch up to us."

"One thing we've learned since being at the mission," Sandy added, "is that the state doesn't much care what goes on here, so long as we continue to feed and shelter the homeless. They pretty much leave this place alone because we're doing them a favor by taking a liability off their hands. But it's not been easy. Any day could be our last if we're found out here. That begins to wear on you after a while, especially after six months of looking over your shoulder."

"No wonder you were hesitant to share your story with me." Pete stared thoughtfully at the table in front of him. "You know, all these years I thought I was pretty well-informed on this issue. But now I'm beginning to see that I've been asleep at the wheel." He looked at the sympathetic couple sitting opposite him and frowned. "How did we get to this point in our country, anyway? Where have we failed?"

"I think the church has been too busy trying to appeal to the world instead of proclaiming the gospel," Big Ben replied sadly. "Many so-called 'Christians' have drunk the Kool-Aid of social and political reforms, often to the exclusion of the need for repentance and faith in Christ. The church in general has failed to be the salt and light in this dark world. We seem to have forgotten that apart from the life-transforming work of the Lord Jesus, there is no lasting hope or peace for this world."

"Mr. Holloway, your question reminds me of a quote from a movie about an old itinerant preacher named Robert Sheffey," Sandy said, pulling out her phone and scrolling down the screen. "Here it is. *'Every time we give up a part of our faith to try to fit into the ways of the world, we lose it forever. We lose a precious part of God's promise, sacrificed to the world—and the world will never give it back. And someday when the world tells us we can no longer have our religion, except where they say, and God is driven from our schools and our government and our homes, then God's people can look back and know that our religion was not taken from us. It was given up, handed over, bit by bit until there was nothing left.'*"

She looked up at him. "How true that statement has proven to be!"

"Yes, and it seems as though the church's response to the lack of persecution in America has been to stop contending for the faith,"

Pete commented. "We have let down our guard and grown content and complacent in our prosperity. We have allowed the world to define our reason for existence. For millennia, people have been attacked for their faith. From the killing of the Old Testament prophets to the slaughter of the early Christians, to the persecution of the present-day world-wide church, those who identify with Christ have always been targeted. Jesus warned His disciples, *'Indeed, the hour is coming when whoever kills you will think he is offering service to God. And they will do these things because they have not known the Father, nor Me.'*"

"It comes as no shock then, that Christians in post-modern America should eventually face the same opposition," Big Ben concluded. "There are lots of recent examples of religious persecution in America. A fire chief in Atlanta was terminated for conducting a Bible study away from the job on his own time, and businesses like ours have been sued into bankruptcy or forced to shut down for taking a biblical stand on marriage or abortion."

"What about that teacher in New Jersey who was suspended for giving a student a Bible," Sandy interjected, "or the coach in Washington who was placed on leave for praying after a high school football game? And then there was the educator in North Carolina who was fired for simply refusing to use the pronoun 'she' when referring to a boy-identifying-as-a-girl."

"Have you heard about the seventy-nine-year-old man who was recently assaulted on a New York subway?" Big Ben posed the question to Pete.

Pete shook his head. "No, I haven't. What was he doing that was so offensive?"

"Nothing more than quietly reading aloud from his Bible. He was attacked by a trans-gendered man with a stiletto-heeled shoe and needed thirty stitches to sew up his face!"

Pete pursed his lips. "Based on the history of Christian persecution around the world, I guess it was only a matter of time before this two-hundred-and-forty-year bubble of religious liberty in America burst," he bemoaned. "But I never thought I'd live to see it in this country. However, two thousand years ago Paul warned his young protégé, *'Indeed, all who desire to live a godly life in Christ Jesus will be persecuted.'* That's a rather sobering thought."

"It is, but I think there is also a modicum of comfort in those words," Sandy offered with a slight smile. "And that can be found in the fact that we are in good company. Lots of it! Even Jesus reassured His disciples, *'I have said these things to you, that in Me you may have peace. In the world you will have tribulation. But take heart; I have overcome the world.'*"

Following his conversation with Big Ben and Sandy, Pete decided to contact his lawyer. He went out into the alley behind the mission and found a secluded spot next to a large metal dumpster. His hands shook as he placed the call on his cell phone. When Mr. Murdock's secretary put him on hold, Pete prayed the man would be available to speak with him. The next voice he heard was the lawyer's.

"Mr. Holloway? This is Walter Murdock. I've been expecting to hear from you. I understand you've got a bit of a problem."

"I sure do," Pete replied, grateful for someone in the legal system who was on his side, "and I need your advice on what to do about it."

"Your wife called me last week and told me everything she knows about your circumstances. Are you aware that there are now two outstanding warrants for your arrest?"

"Yes, I figured as much. I should have taken your advice to stay put when I told you about the first one. Now I'm in over my head. However, there are definite extenuating circumstances that will likely play into my favor. I'd like to give you a statement about what happened so you can start preparing my defense."

"I aim to do that, Mr. Holloway," the lawyer promised, "and I'll take your statement in a minute. But first, I need to go on record as urging you to surrender yourself to the proper authorities. You understand the importance of that, don't you?"

"Yes, I do. But what's the best way to go about doing that?"

"Before I can give you any specific advice, I need to ask you a few questions. First, are you asking me to be your official legal counsel and represent you in this matter?"

"Yes, I am. I'm hiring you as my defense lawyer."

"Okay, fine. Second, without divulging your exact location, would you agree that you have knowingly fled the jurisdiction, or jurisdictions plural, where the crimes you are alleged to have committed occurred?"

"Yes, I agree."

"And have you undertaken, or are you now undertaking, any steps to intentionally conceal yourself in order to avoid arrest or prosecution?"

Pete hesitated before answering. "Um . . . yes."

"Then it should come as no surprise that you are legally classified as a fugitive from the law, and as such, there is no statute of limitations that applies to you. In other words, Mr. Holloway, there is no benefit whatsoever in remaining at large. Additionally, this places me in a very precarious position as well. As your defense counsel, I must take into account the boundaries of permissible advocacy. Anything as seemingly minor as knowing your location and not reporting it could put me in danger of being charged with harboring or concealing a fugitive, which would constitute a criminal violation on my part. I'm afraid you've left me with very few options."

"I understand that, Mr. Murdock, and I'm terribly sorry to have put you in this position," Pete apologized, "but will my statement about what happened in Sacramento help me at all, now?"

"That depends on the circumstances, and your involvement and intentions," the lawyer cautioned. "But in order to represent you I must have complete honesty from you. Are we clear on that?"

"Absolutely. You have my full cooperation," Pete assured him.

"Good. Then with your permission I'm going to record your statement. I'll ask you some guiding questions, and I want you to answer them as truthfully and completely as possible. Do you understand?"

"Yes."

For the next fifteen minutes Mr. Murdock questioned Pete about his flight from San Francisco and Sacramento, and his involvement in the police action shooting. Pete explained that he'd only agreed to drive Richard and Vince to the impound lot, and that he had no prior knowledge of how they planned to recover their cars, or that they intended to set the fire to cover their tracks. He explained how the situation triggered his flashback, and that it was never his intention to fire upon an officer of the law. Mr. Murdock was particularly interested in that point of his narrative.

"Mr. Holloway, are there any eyewitnesses who can corroborate your statement that you were suffering from a PTSD episode when you exited your car that night and drew your firearm?"

"Not that I know of," Pete replied. "I don't believe I displayed any symptoms until I heard the first gunshots, and by then I was alone. And I think I was too far away from the officers for them to notice anything. Besides, I was in the shadows and they didn't get a good look at me."

"That's unfortunate," Mr. Murdock said. "Then there's no way to substantiate your claim to having a flashback. It's your word against theirs. But even if they *had* noticed anything amiss, I doubt if it would be of much help, because you still engaged them after they identified themselves and ordered you to drop your weapon. If you had obeyed those commands, your claim might have carried more weight. As it is, I don't believe your PTSD will be very helpful as a defense for your actions that night."

"I've been wondering the same thing. By the way, do you know what they've charged me with?"

"Not yet. I needed to confirm you as a client first. But if everything you've told me is true, I would venture to say that you've been charged with involvement in a police action shooting, resisting arrest and aggravated fleeing of a police officer, and—I have to say this—possibly attempted manslaughter." Mr. Murdock's voice grew even more somber. "Mr. Holloway, the fact that you pointed a gun at an officer *after* he identified himself and ordered you to surrender definitely won't help your cause. But if there is any hope, it would be that you didn't actually fire it. We might be able to use that fact to create doubt about your intent to shoot, but that in itself is not enough to prove the point."

"Are there any other reasons for hope that you can see?" Pete asked, fighting to restrain his discouragement.

"Well, your lack of a criminal history and your status as a minister will help to establish your good character. And I plan to get statements from Vince and . . . what's that other gentleman's name . . . Colin? They might be able to verify that you were a reluctant participant who only intended to drop off your two passengers across from the impound lot. Plus, the fact that you met them only a few days before the shooting might work in your favor, at least as far as premeditation is concerned. But all that is on rather shaky ground, if you want my honest opinion. And then there's the matter of the first warrant, although those charges won't be as serious. I think we should focus your defense on the more serious charges in the Sacramento warrant."

"I agree," Pete said. "So, what do you want me to do?"

"I advise you to surrender to the local authorities wherever you are now," his lawyer urged him.

"But shouldn't I return home and surrender to SFPD?"

"I wouldn't do that if I were you. If you were to get picked up while on the move, you would be unable to prove that you were planning to turn yourself in, and further charges would likely be added. The local authorities will return you to San Francisco. After that, we can discuss our strategy before they extradite you to Sacramento County. If we can get them to drop the charges on the first warrant in favor of the more serious charges on the second, that will help your case considerably."

Pete let out a sigh of relief. He was tired of running, tired of looking over his shoulder, and tired of being separated from his family. He just wanted to go home. He congratulated himself. It was finally over. But in that moment, a sliver of fear pierced his heart. *Is it really over? Or is it just beginning?*

CHAPTER TWELVE
FAKE NEWS

TWICE PETE STARTED TO CALL the Fresno Police Department to turn himself in. Twice he interrupted the call before the connection could be completed. Each time, something kept him from following through. Maybe it was fear that stopped him cold. Maybe it was pride. Maybe it was the idea of placing his new friends at risk by having the police come to the mission. *Sometime tomorrow I'll talk to Big Ben again before I do what I know I have to do,* he convinced himself. However, the jovial giant beat him to the punch.

Early the next morning, Big Ben approached him. "Pete, could Sandy and I meet with you again today?"

"Sure. I was wanting to talk to you anyway. When would be a good time?"

"Sandy will be here around ten," Big Ben replied. "Can we talk then?"

Pete noticed the strain in his friend's face. "Okay. Same room?"

"That would be fine. See you then." Big Ben smiled weakly and walked away, leaving Pete to wonder what had happened overnight to drain the bighearted man's enthusiasm.

Pete entered the office at five after ten to find Big Ben and Sandy waiting for him. He shut the door and took the seat he'd occupied the day before.

"Thank you for meeting with us, Mr. Holloway." Sandy displayed the same weariness he'd seen in her husband.

"My pleasure. What did you folks want to see me about?" Pete sensed the inner turmoil in the couple.

"Pete, Sandy and I did a lot of talking and praying after our meeting yesterday," Big Ben began. "In fact, we both spent a relatively sleepless night thinking about it. You said one of the reasons you fled San Francisco was to distance yourself from your ministry in hopes of protecting it. Well, our ministry had already been shut down when we decided to flee LA, but you got us thinking about how our presence here could jeopardize *this* work if we stay."

"Yes," Sandy interjected, "we've closed one ministry, and we don't want to be the reason for closing another one."

Pete leaned forward in his chair, a pained expression on his face. "I didn't mean to discourage you two in any way. That certainly wasn't my intention."

"You didn't discourage us," Big Ben assured him, "but you did give us a fresh perspective on the matter. You see, the Good News Mission isn't our ministry. It was started by several churches nearly twenty years ago. We've been here only a short while. Through mutual friends we heard that they were looking for a couple to run the kitchen, conduct the services, and help with the counseling. The timing coincided with our decision to leave LA, and since we were qualified, we took the opportunity as coming from the Lord."

"But since then, both Ben and I have grown increasingly troubled about our fugitive status," Sandy explained. "While we love serving here, we've had second thoughts about our decision to go on the run. We've become weary of living outside the law, even if it is a bad one."

"Several times before you showed up, we contemplated turning ourselves in," Big Ben added, "and we think God sent you here to encourage us to do just that."

Pete was gobsmacked. "How have I done that?"

"Didn't you say yesterday that you were seriously thinking of surrendering?"

"Yes, I've been aware for a while now that I need to do that. In fact, I spoke with my lawyer yesterday after our conversation, and he said that's the only option. But I haven't been able to bring myself to actually follow through with it. I planned to talk to you about it again today, only you beat me to it."

Big Ben laughed. "Then that's another indicator that we're doing the right thing. But there's something else that's led us to believe this is the right time to surrender."

"What's that?" Pete wondered.

"Are you aware of the state's amnesty offer?" Big Ben asked.

Pete's ears perked up. "Amnesty? Amnesty for whom?"

"Violators of the hate speech law," the large man replied. "For a short period of time, the state has agreed to waive all charges against those who have been accused of hate speech."

"Even those with open warrants?" Pete was definitely interested now.

Big Ben nodded. "Yes, all charges will be dropped once they complete the state's reeducation program."

"What about the fines and unreasonable community service requirements?" Pete pressed.

"All that will be dismissed for anyone voluntarily surrendering," Big Ben said.

"Where did you hear about this?" Pete wanted to know.

"It was in the LA Times about three weeks ago," Sandy answered. "One of our close friends whom we still keep in touch with sent us a copy of the article."

Pete recalled his lawyer's words from yesterday's phone call. "*If we can get them to drop the charges on the first warrant in favor of the more serious charges on the second, that will help your case considerably.*" This must be it, the confirmation he needed to make the call. "So, if we all agree to this, do you think we should surrender separately," he suggested with a slight quaver in his voice, "or all together?"

Big Ben smiled broadly. "We were hoping you'd agree to surrender with us."

"But won't we be putting the mission at risk?" Pete asked.

"We thought about that, so we've decided to drive back to LA instead and turn ourselves in at our local precinct. Of course, if you'd rather return to San Francisco to do that, we'd understand."

Pete grimaced. "My lawyer cautioned me against going anywhere. He said to surrender right where I'm at. But I agree we can't have the police come here to the mission." He thoughtfully tugged on his ear. "What about the deli around the corner? It's a public place. Couldn't we have the Fresno police meet the three of us there?"

Big Ben looked at his wife. Sandy shrugged, then nodded in agreement. "Okay, let's do that, then. We'll need about an hour to clear out our things here at the mission. Why don't we meet at the restaurant at, say . . . twelve-o-clock?"

"That's fine," Pete agreed. "That will give me time to shower and shave."

The trio of fugitives walked into the L-Street Delicatessen at noon and ordered lunch. Then they took their food outside and sat down at one of the round, umbrella-covered tables on the sidewalk patio. Big Ben prayed over the meal, then he and Sandy began to eat their sandwiches.

Pete stared at the club sandwich in front of him. "Why do I feel like a death row inmate about to eat his last meal?" he opined, his appetite suddenly gone.

Big Ben chuckled nervously. "I'm a little anxious myself," he confessed, "but I think I'll be able to deal with this better on a full stomach. Besides, it could be tomorrow before the county gives us our first meal."

Pete watched the couple finish their sandwiches. When they were done, Big Ben got up and stepped around the corner of the building to place the call to the Fresno police department. A few minutes later he returned to the table.

"Well, the deed's done," he announced. "I told the dispatcher the three of us would be waiting here. She said a couple of patrol cars will be here in about ten to fifteen minutes." He sighed and reached for Sandy's hand. "I'm sorry it's come down to this, sweetheart."

"We both knew this moment had to come," she reminded him, squeezing his hand and forcing a sad little smile. "But it's the right thing to do. Whatever happens now is in the Lord's hands. Don't you agree, Mr. Holloway?"

Pete felt a twinge of nausea. "Yes, it's the right thing to do." The trio sat quietly for a few minutes, considering what was about to happen, and contemplating the changes to their lives that were sure to follow. He suddenly got to his feet. "I need to use the restroom once more before they arrive," he said, reaching for the meal leftovers. "I'll return the tray on my way in."

"Thanks," Sandy said with a smile.

Pete tossed the trash in the under-counter receptacle and stacked the tray on top, then headed down the hall to the restroom. Once inside, he stood at the sink and splashed cold water on his face before entering the stall. Someone had left a dog-eared section of the Fresno Bee draped over the grab bar. Out of curiosity, he tilted his head sideways to read the headlines. The words "Fake News" caught his attention. Pulling the newspaper off the bar, he folded the section in fourths and stared at the article's title: "State Amnesty Email Proves to be Fake News." As he began to read, a chill came over him.

> "An email sent to all media outlets across the state on April 21st has now been proven to be fake news. The original correspondence, first thought to be an official announcement from the state, declared that anyone charged with hate speech crimes who voluntarily surrenders to state or local authorities would have all pending charges dropped, and any consequences such as fines, reparations, or incarceration would be waived. It said that those complying would only be required to complete the state's hate speech reeducation program.

> "However, when pressed in an interview Wednesday, Alicia Cunningham, director of the State Media Relations Bureau, admitted that the email was false and apologized for the error, alleging that the notice was the work of extremist right-wing hackers who were able to gain access to the state's information network. She categorically denied the offer of amnesty, saying instead that 'the state of California

takes each violation of the Hate Speech Reparation and Elimination Act seriously, and is committed to punishing those who flaunt it to the fullest extent of the law.' She went on to say that the department was launching an internal investigation into the breach of security.

"Spokespersons for several conservative right-wing organizations opposed to the hate speech law were quick to denounce the official explanation, suggesting instead that the email was nothing more than a ploy by the state to trick those with open warrants into surrendering. Representatives of the California Free Speech Alliance and the Christian Legal Society are calling for an independent investigation into the allegations that the email was the work of hackers. A statement released by Governor Stevenson yesterday quoted him as saying, 'I not only stand by the Bureau's explanation, but I have the utmost confidence that an internal investigation will confirm the truth.'"

Pete broke out in a cold sweat. *So there's no amnesty! They're coming after us with full vengeance. I've got to warn Big Ben and Sandy!* With the newspaper tucked under his arm as proof, he hastily washed and dried his hands. Exiting the restroom, he hurried toward the door leading to the sidewalk patio. As he reached for the handle, he looked through the glass and stopped short. A black and white cruiser was parked at the curb, and two uniformed Fresno police officers were conversing with the couple seated at the round table. *What should I do?*

An all-too-familiar feeling of alarm swept over him. It was too late to help them now. But he could still make a run for it himself!

With the blood pounding in his temples, Specialist Pete Holloway spun around on his heels and hastily retreated. *Gotta get away. Can't let myself be captured by the enemy!* He ducked down the hallway and pushed through the double swinging doors into the DFAC kitchen. One of the cooks glanced up from his food prep station, a look of surprise on his face.

"Hey, customers aren't allowed back here!" he shouted. Without a word, Pete ran past him and out the back door.

He looked around in a confused panic. *Where's my APC? Gotta get out of here and rejoin my squad!*

He sprinted down the alley and turned the corner. A bright yellow taxi caught his attention, and he stepped into the street to flag it down. As it pulled up next to him, Pete jumped into the back seat before the driver was able to come to a complete stop. "Go! Go! Go!" he shouted to the man behind the wheel, as he slammed the door.

The driver turned and stared at him, sizing up his fare.

"Step on it!" Pete urged, pounding the seat beside him.

The man shot him a contemptuous look and shook his head. "Whatever you say, boss." He turned back around, glanced over his left shoulder, and merged into traffic. He drove a few blocks, glancing frequently into the rear-view mirror. Finally, he broke the silence. "Where to?"

"Bravo Base," Pete replied, breathing hard.

"Where?" the cabbie asked quizzically.

"Bravo Base. On the double!"

"Bravo Base? Never heard of it. You got an address?"

Pete twisted in the seat and looked out the side and back windows before replying. "Uh . . . I think it's south of here. Just head south."

"Look, Bub," the driver said over his shoulder, a tone of impatience in his voice, "I don't know what's going on, but if you don't give me a legit address, I'm going to let you out right here! I don't know where this 'Bravo Base' is, or *what* it is. Where's it located?"

"I don't *know* the exact location," the frustrated Specialist Holloway replied, "but you should. It's south of here somewhere. Just take me to my home base!"

The cab driver frowned at him in the mirror. "You talking about a military base? The only one anywhere close in that direction is NAS Lemoore. Never heard it called Bravo Base before. But that's outside my range, almost forty miles from here. I'm just a city cab."

"Then take me as far as you can," Pete insisted, settling back in his seat.

The driver shrugged his shoulders and shot him a look of resignation. "Whatever you say, boss."

Twenty minutes later the driver turned into a restaurant parking lot and stopped the taxi. He threw an arm over the seat and turned to his fare. "This is as far as I can take you, boss." He glanced at his meter. "That'll be fifty-nine dollars and seventy-five cents."

Pete fished through his wallet for a credit card and handed it to him. "Where are we?" he asked, looking around.

"Selma," the driver replied, as he ran the card through his scanner. "This is as far south as the company will let me go." He returned the card along with a receipt. "I wish you luck, boss," he said, as his passenger got out. "I hope you find whatever it is you're looking for." With that the man drove away, leaving Pete standing in the middle of the parking lot.

Pete sat down on a concrete bench next to the flagpole in front of the fast-food restaurant. He breathed deeply and allowed himself to relax. With the pressure of the narrow escape behind him, his appetite gradually returned. His wallet informed him that he had the grand total of six dollars left. He went inside and purchased a small combo meal, then returned to the bench to eat his lunch.

With his mind once again functioning normally, he took stock of his situation. *Well, it looks like this isn't over after all!* He was still on the run and there was no chance for leniency now. Not even Mr. Murdock could save him this time. But it might count for something if the taxi driver would be willing to testify to his state of mind.

He pulled the fare receipt out of his pocket and slipped it into his wallet for safekeeping. It might come in handy if the man needed to be tracked down for his testimony.

Pete finished his meal and contemplated his next move. As he watched the American flag rippling lazily in the breeze, his thoughts returned to the free speech rally he'd attended in Sacramento three weeks ago. He recounted what the state senator and the lawyer had promised the crowd, that they and their colleagues were challenging the constitutionality of the law and would keep fighting to have it repealed.

If he could just hold out long enough for that to happen, then the hate speech warrant would be invalid. And the charges against him in the police shooting might be reduced as well, since he was there as a direct result of the first warrant.

Pete reentered the restaurant and approached the teenage girl at the cash register. "Is there a bus terminal here in Selma?" he asked.

"Uh, I wouldn't know," she replied, shrugging her shoulders. Turning away from him, she yelled to one of the other employees behind the divider wall. "Hey, Sam, is there a bus terminal around here somewhere?"

"Bus terminal?" Pete heard the invisible man reply. A moment later the manager came around the wall and approached the counter. "What kind of bus are you looking for? City transit or over-the-road?"

"Is there anything going to LA?" Pete wondered.

The manager thought for a minute. "There's no actual bus terminal in Selma, but I've seen a Greyhound stop at the Rx on Whitson Street several times. I think it's out of Fresno, so it must be heading south. You might be able to pick it up there."

"You talkin' about the Family Drug Mart downtown?" the teen interjected. "There's a Greyhound sticker in the front window. I've seen it."

"Then you should be able to buy a ticket there," the manager suggested.

After getting directions to the store, Pete thanked them both and left the restaurant. Fifteen minutes later he entered the drug store and purchased an economy one-way ticket to LA. With an hour to kill before the next scheduled departure, he decided to do some shopping at the Walmart he'd passed earlier.

Once inside the store, he grabbed a cart and went in search of some toiletries, a couple changes of clothes, a few snack items, and a new phone charger—his third in three weeks.

As he shopped, the urge to phone Angela began to grow. At first, he resisted the temptation, but eventually it overtook him, and he made the call anyway. To his dismay, his wife did not answer, and the call went to voicemail.

"Ange, it's me," he began after the beep. "When you get this message give me a call, okay? Man, I really miss you, sweetheart. How are Drew and Brie? I miss them, too. A whole lot's gone down since our last conversation. I'll tell you about it later. I spoke with Mr. Murdock and agreed to surrender, along with some other believers I met recently who are in similar circumstances, but those plans just went south a little while ago. Can't say too much now, but hopefully we can talk soon. I don't know how this is all going to turn out, or when it will end, but just keep praying. I know you will. Love you, Ange. Call me back. Bye."

He slipped the phone into his pocket and resumed his shopping. When he'd found everything he needed, he pushed the cart to the front of the store and got into the self-checkout line. Three or four people were ahead of him. His phone suddenly rang. Pete quickly pulled it out and looked at the screen. It was Angela.

"Hello, Ange?"

"Babe, you've got to stop using your phone!" his wife blurted out immediately.

"What? Why?" Pete felt a sudden premonition.

"I think the police are tracking you through your cell phone!"

Her statement sliced through him like a knife. "How do you know that?"

"They had me come in for questioning again. The detective was wrapping up his interrogation when another officer asked him to step into the hall for a moment. I overheard him say something about a phone trace, but I couldn't make out anything else they said. That's when you called. I couldn't answer it or warn you then. I only had time to silence my phone before he returned."

"Where are you now?" Pete asked his wife.

"In my car outside the station. I would have texted, but you said not to do that."

"You did right." He lowered his voice to avoid being heard by the person in line ahead of him. "A text could have proven you complicit."

"How are you going to contact me if you can't use your phone?" Angela sounded concerned.

"Don't worry," Pete reassured her, "I'll find a way. I'd better go." He dropped his voice to a whisper. "I've heard the longer the call, the more accurately they can pinpoint your location. I don't know if that's true or not, but I don't want to risk it. I love you, Ange."

"I love you, too, babe. Please, please, *please* be careful!" she begged earnestly.

"I will." With that he ended the brief call.

Pete was in the process of checking out and had just scanned his fourth item, when the sound of screeching tires arrested his attention. He glanced out the large plate glass window in time to see a police car with flashing lights come to a stop out front. The doors opened and two uniformed officers got out.

Pete quickly turned to the self-checkout attendant. "I forgot one thing," he lied. "Would you watch my cart? I'll be back in a jiffy."

Without waiting for a reply, he turned and walked hastily toward the nearest aisle. Once out of sight, he broke into a sprint and dashed up the aisle to the back of the store. That didn't take long! They must have tracked his voice message. He followed the back wall to the far corner of the store. There was no way out.

What do I do now? I'm trapped!

Panicking, Pete looked around. In a matter of seconds, the officers would come charging around the far corner of the aisle and put an end to his fugitive status . . . and his freedom. No doubt they were using a portable tracking device to zero in on his cell phone. He'd read that tracking technology was now so sophisticated that a phone's location could be pinpointed within twenty or thirty feet.

Wait a minute. His phone. They were tracking his phone, not *him!*

In desperation, he yanked the phone from his pocket and hid it behind a bottle of car polish on the shelf. Then he turned and forced himself to casually walk away from the corner along the back wall. As he passed one aisle, he glanced toward the front of the store and caught a glimpse of the two policemen running in the opposite direction. One was holding an electronic device in his hand; the other was unsnapping the strap on his holster.

Wanting to break into a run, but not wanting to draw attention, he forced himself to walk briskly until he came to the swinging double doors leading to the stockroom. After a furtive glance around, he ducked into the back, located the rear exit, and hastily made his getaway.

CHAPTER THIRTEEN
THE STREETS OF LA

AS THE GREYHOUND LEFT THE Family Drug Mart parking lot, Pete sank wearily into the high-backed seat and massaged his tense neck muscles. Ten minutes later the bus was cruising down Highway 99 toward Los Angeles, scheduled to arrive at the Central City East terminal at 9:55 p.m. He looked at the young woman cradling her child in the aisle seat next to him, glad that the infant was asleep and not screaming its head off. The mother met his gaze with a polite smile, which he returned. Then he adjusted the air nozzle and reclined in his seat. He might as well try to get some sleep. He closed his eyes, but he had never been able to get too comfortable on public transportation, and sleep eluded him.

He felt badly that Angela had experienced the unpleasantness of being interrogated a second time on his account, but he was thankful not to have divulged any details that might have put her in a more precarious position. He wondered how Jorge Gonzalez was doing. Was he still incarcerated, or had he posted bail? Had Jim Sutherland been released to begin his reeducation yet? And what were Big Ben and Sandy doing right now? Probably sitting in intake, waiting to be processed by the Fresno Police Department. Were they ever in for a big surprise! He wished he had been able to warn them in time, although the truth about the fake amnesty notice might not have been enough to change their minds. But now he'd never know for sure. Feelings of survivor's guilt washed over him, but he quickly dismissed them by reminding himself that *he* was still in the thick of things, too. His own troubles were far from over.

Upset that he'd been forced to sacrifice his cell phone, Pete consoled himself with the knowledge that it was either that or surrender his freedom. However, if the authorities were tracking his phone, they were likely tracking his credit card purchases as well. He'd had the foresight to withdraw cash from an ATM before going to the drug store, so even though that transaction might lead them to the ATM, it would not directly link him to the Greyhound ticket. But he was not out of the woods yet. It would be almost five hours before the bus reached LA, and in that time the police might discover where he was headed through eyewitness accounts or camera surveillance.

A chilling thought struck him. Would they be waiting for him at the terminal, or worse yet, before he arrived? After all, there were several more stops along the way!

The closer the bus got to Los Angeles the greater Pete's anxiety grew. At every stop he anticipated seeing flashing red and blue lights out the window. He held his breath whenever the doors opened and a new passenger embarked, and he heaved a sigh of relief when the doors closed, and the bus began moving again. As daylight faded into twilight, he grew so tense that his body ached all over. Every muscle was taut, every nerve on edge. Even the cuts on his left bicep began throbbing again. His seat felt hard and uncomfortable, and he grew restless and miserable. But there was nothing he could do except sit still and wait it out.

Several hours later the dark horizon began to glow with an unnatural luminescence, and when the bus cleared a rise, the twinkling lights of the LA skyline broke into view. As the Greyhound approached the city limits, the clusters of lights expanded across the horizon until, like a vast starry galaxy opening its arms to the USS Enterprise, they completely engulfed the tiny transport. Pete stared out his window, watching whole neighborhoods flash by one house at a time. After a while commercial buildings replaced the single-family residences, and before long the bus exited Highway 5 onto the surface streets. He glanced at his watch. In about ten minutes they would be at the terminal. He felt like a man playing Russian roulette. At each stop he'd squeezed the trigger on an empty chamber, but now there was only one chamber left, and it was sure to hold the lone, fatal bullet.

There's only one way this game is going to end, unless . . .

Pete craned his neck to look out the front window and saw a traffic light turn red a block ahead. As the bus came to a stop, he suddenly got up and pushed past the sleeping mother and child, causing her to stir and the baby to let out a whimper.

He stumbled toward the front of the bus and addressed the driver. "I need to get off here. I feel sick!"

The driver looked startled, then scowled at him. "Can't you wait 'til we get to the terminal? It's only three blocks away."

Pete shook his head and grabbed his stomach. "I don't think so. I'm going to heave any second!"

The driver hastily opened the door. "You got any luggage on board?" he asked nervously.

Clamping a hand over his mouth, Pete shook his head and stepped down off the bus. The driver quickly closed the door, and as soon as the light turned green, he drove away from the intersection, leaving Pete standing alone on the sidewalk at ten-o-clock at night in the middle of downtown East Central LA.

Pete looked around, unsure of what to do next. He was convinced the police were waiting for him at the terminal, and once the bus arrived it would only be a matter of minutes before they learned from the driver that he'd gotten off three blocks back. He needed to get away from the intersection fast!

He turned the corner and ran away from the terminal on a tangent. A few blocks ahead he spied several overpasses. As he approached, he noticed the tangle of homeless shelters underneath. There were makeshift cardboard lean-to's and blue tarps everywhere, under the bridges and lining the sidewalks. Occupied sleeping bags lay along the edge of the sidewalk among the many homeless wrapped in nothing but tattered coats or jackets. He began looking for someplace, anyplace, to hide from the police cruisers that were sure to be driving past any minute now. Spying a weathered piece of cardboard propped against a chain link fence, he lifted it up, hoping to find the space empty. But there was a sleeping bag underneath, and someone was in it, whether a man or woman he couldn't tell. He kept looking for some cover, but every shelter was occupied, some by more than one person.

On the other side of the fence was a dark, narrow, trash-filled lot. Weeds three feet tall covered the ground. In desperation he scaled the eight-foot chain link and dropped down into the vacant lot. Dodging broken orange crates, cracked plastic buckets, and piles of damp, moldy insulation, he waded some forty or fifty feet into the weeds. At one point he stumbled over a body lying on the ground. Out of the darkness beneath his feet a gruff male voice cursed at him, and he hastily moved away.

Suddenly, a brilliant light flashed across one of the concrete bridge supports adjacent to the lot. Pete threw himself to the ground and held his breath as the beam from the passing police car's spotlight slowly swept the lot and then continued down the street.

He lay still in the weeds for fifteen or twenty minutes, but the light did not return. A nearby scurrying sound caused him to raise up on one elbow, and he kicked away the rat that was investigating his shoes. Cautiously, he stuck his head above the tops of the weeds and looked around. Near the back of the lot, against a rickety wooden fence, he noticed a pair of rusty appliances nearly hidden by the growth. Scrambling to his feet, he carefully navigated the jungle toward the old washer and dryer, which were dented and missing their doors, as well as any salvageable copper wiring or aluminum components. He pulled them apart and curled up between them on the bare earth.

Letting out a weary sigh, Pete closed his eyes and allowed the tension to evaporate. He was home for the night.

Pete awoke to the blinding glare of the southern California sun. The washer and dryer had provided shade until the blazing orb was almost directly overhead. The ground underneath him had been cool and damp all night, and the sun felt really good on his face and arms. He let its warming rays soak into his body until he began to perspire.

Then he got to his feet and stretched, an action which revealed multiple aches and pains caused by lying in one position on the hard ground for the past twelve hours.

Surveying the area, he took stock of his location. The back of the lot was about ten feet higher than street level, giving him a good view of the immediate surroundings. The lot was flanked by the two-story brick wall of an abandoned business on the left and the embankment of the highway overpass on the right, the chain link fence being the only barrier between him and the cluster of temporary residences under the bridge. He climbed onto the rusty dryer and peered over the dilapidated, weather-beaten fence. On the other side, the ground plunged steeply down into an alley littered with trash and makeshift homeless shelters, making the back of the lot impregnable to invasion. While he could be seen from the street standing up, the weeds gave him adequate cover should the police happen to cruise by again.

Convinced that this was where he should stay for the time being, Pete made his way back to the fence at the front of the lot, wary of the body he'd tripped over earlier. He came upon a dirty, tattered blanket, but the man was not there. Once at the fence he spent the better part of an hour prying loose the twisted wire fasteners that kept the chain link attached to the corner post. If this was going to be his home for a while, he didn't want to have to scale the eight-foot fence every time he came and went. Besides, the flap would come in handy should he need to make a quick escape from the lot. Then he loosely secured the chain link to the post and went in search of something to eat.

Dodging the temporary shelters and sleeping bags lining the sidewalks, he wandered the area for a while, wondering what he should do for money. He was out of cash, having used it to purchase the bus ticket, and after being tracked through his cell phone, did not want to risk using his credit card again. He chastised himself for not having the foresight to withdraw extra funds from the ATM.

Pete approached a man who was panhandling on the street corner. "Excuse me, could you tell me if there's a rescue mission or shelter around here that provides free meals?"

The man looked at him through bloodshot eyes and silently held out a coffee tin containing a few coins. Pete fished in his pockets and came up with eleven cents. Dropping the change into the can, he repeated his question.

The man pointed to the east with a dirt-caked finger. "Six blocks. San Mateo St." With that he turned his back and walked away.

"God bless you," Pete called after him, but the man dismissed the comment with a wave of his hand and continued on his way. Pete began walking in the direction the man pointed until he came to the aforementioned street. He glanced up and down but didn't see anything resembling a mission, so he started north. A few blocks up he noticed a line of people on the sidewalk outside a storefront. As he approached, he saw a sign attached to the building which read, "East Central Rescue Mission."

Getting in line, he waited nearly twenty minutes before reaching the front door. Inside, the place was packed with homeless people eating off paper plates, some occupying the picnic tables, others sitting on the floor against the walls. The room smelled strongly of cornbread and body odor. When he finally reached the serving line, he addressed the man in a white t-shirt with rolled-up sleeves, his long locks captured in a hair net.

"Is there room for me to spend the night here?" he inquired.

"We're only a day shelter," the server replied, his tattooed forearms glistening from the steam rising from the metal pan in front of him.

"Well then, do you know of any place around here where I can get a bed?" Pete pressed.

The man looked at him and cracked a wry smile. "Arthur's Furniture Mart on Santa Fe," he offered with a chuckle. Then he shook his head. "You ain't gonna find free lodging anywhere in central LA. Every place I know is full up. Has been for a long time."

"That's okay," Pete replied, "thanks anyway. And thanks for the meal. It smells really good."

"You're welcome," the man replied, with a look of mild surprise, as if the expression of gratitude was an unexpected rarity.

Pete carried the plate of food and the paper cup of black coffee outside. He found an empty spot on the sidewalk in front of an adjacent building and sat down with his back against the wall. He set the cup beside him, and after thanking the Lord for the food, began to eat. Several minutes later, a man in his mid-thirties with short-cropped red hair sat down about ten feet away from him and began eating as well.

Pete glanced at him as he ate. Except for the condition of his clothes, the man could have passed for a young professional. He was relatively clean-shaven and wore what appeared to be designer slacks, now wrinkled and showing signs of wear. His shoes, no doubt once shiny and clean, were scuffed and covered with dry mud. When the man leaned over to pick up the roll that had fallen off his plate, Pete noticed the monogrammed initials "D.J." on the breast pocket of his shirt. He might well have been a stockbroker or a salesman at one time. As he took a bite of the roll, Pete noticed something else: the needle marks on the man's forearm.

Pete ate in silence for a while, processing what he'd witnessed since getting off the bus. Here were hundreds of people—no, literally thousands of people—living day to day on the streets. He was not totally unfamiliar with the homeless crises facing most cities in the United States. His church had supported a homeless shelter in San Francisco for a number of years, and he'd led several evangelistic excursions into the Tenderloin district to minister to the needy there. He was vaguely aware of the common myths about street people, but he knew enough to know that they were not all drug addicts or mentally ill, nor were they all homeless because of bad personal choices. Some were victims of abuse or neglect, or other unfortunate circumstances beyond their control. But he had never spent any significant time living among them, and he began to wonder what he was in for here in the heart of LA.

The man next to him finished his roll and started sipping his cup of hot coffee. Pete decided to engage him in conversation. "Is this place open all the time?"

The man shot him a wary glance, then resumed eating before replying. "Nope. Eleven to seven."

"Seven days a week?" Pete continued. The man gave a slight nod of his head. "They serve dinner, too?"

"Yup, six-o-clock."

The two men fell silent for a moment. "What can a person do around here to earn a few extra bucks?" Pete inquired, with a friendly tone.

The man stared flint-eyed at him. "Panhandle or pick pockets," he muttered gruffly, his mouth full of food.

Pete got the distinct impression the brief conversation was over. "Thanks."

He rose to his feet. The man ignored him and continued eating as Pete picked up his trash and walked away.

For an entire week Pete spent his days at the rescue mission or wandering around East Central LA, and his nights sleeping between the rusty appliances at the back of the vacant lot. During one dumpster dive behind a furniture store, he emerged with a torn mattress from a child's crib which he used to pad the ground where he slept, and a cardboard box which he flattened and used as a roof over his shelter, anchored down by two bricks found among the lot's weeds. It was a huge culture shock to experience life on the streets firsthand, and he didn't think he could ever get used to the deplorable living conditions where trash and debris littered the sidewalks, and where used needles and human excrement seemed to be everywhere he stepped. And he was convinced that he would never be able to get the images out of his mind of men and women, young and old alike, selling their bodies on the streets for a few dollars, or of human beings openly urinating and defecating in the gutters. For the first time in his forty-six years, he began to understand what daily life looks like for most of the half-million-plus homeless in the United States.

Several days later, Pete was thrilled to discover a mobile shower trailer that the city provided for the homeless every Friday. The water pressure was low and the temperature barely lukewarm, but he was nevertheless grateful for the opportunity to bathe. He became familiar with several people whose tents were pitched on the sidewalk in front of his back lot shelter and engaged in conversations with others at the rescue mission during mealtimes, thankful for whatever friendliness was extended to him amid the vast sea of calloused indifference and cold-shouldered rejection.

One evening, he sat down for supper across from a man in his late seventies or early eighties. The man, dressed in a worn pair of filthy overalls, was thin and gaunt with dark, hollow eyes, long, matted hair, and a grayish-white beard. His leathery skin was dark and weather beaten. Pete silently watched the man devour his meal for a while, and then decided to strike up a conversation.

"You want an extra piece of bread?" Pete asked, holding out the thin white slice that had been on his plate. The man glanced at the handout and then at Pete.

"Sure," he muttered, taking the bread and returning to his meal.

"I'm not very hungry today for some reason," Pete explained, "although I don't know why. This is the only place I've found so far where I can get a free meal."

"Ain't no other place," the older man replied, looking up from his food. "Only soup kitchen in East Central LA."

"That's good to know," Pete said, with a nod. "I've been here a only bout a week myself. How about you?"

"Couple o' years," the man responded, biting into his newly acquired piece of bread.

"You from around here?" Pete asked, in a friendly attempt to further engage the old man.

"Nope. All over, mostly. But I was raised on a cattle ranch in West Texas."

"Really? I'm from San Francisco," Pete offered. "Lived there all my life, except for the time I spent in the Army."

"I was in 'Nam," the man replied, looking at Pete with sudden interest. "Third Marine Division. We were among the first Americans sent to protect Da Nang Air Base in '65."

"That must have been quite an experience. How old were you then? In your twenties?"

"Just turned twenty-five the week before we shipped out," the old man said. "I'd just finished grad school when I was drafted."

Pete's ears perked up. "Grad school? Where did you attend college?"

"University of Arizona. Earned a Bachelor of Science in Geology and a Masters in Geosciences."

Pete caught himself staring. "No kidding?"

"Yup. While I was there, I was part of a team that created maps of the moon's surface. NASA used those maps to find suitable places for the Apollo astronauts to land on." When Pete's jaw dropped, the man flashed a grin and chuckled. "Betcha never figured *this* old bum to be party to anything like that, did ya?"

Embarrassed, Pete shook his head. "To be honest with you, no I didn't." He took a deep breath as he surveyed the room. "You know, I have to confess that it's very easy to judge people by their outward appearance. I mean, as I look at those in this room, I see people who are homeless, desperate, and in need of help, for whatever reason. I see people who may have drug or alcohol addictions, or mental illnesses, people who are victims of crimes or circumstances, or just plain down on their luck. But what I see on the outside might not accurately reflect who they are on the inside."

212 FUGITIVE OF FAITH

The old man grunted. "I wish more people felt that way," he acknowledged, with a tinge of sadness in his voice. He studied Pete for a moment. "So, my friend, which of those categories do *you* fit into?" His question caught Pete off guard. "Me? Wow, how do I begin to answer that?" He thought long and hard. "Well, I can tell you that I'm not here because of a drug or alcohol addiction. And I'm not here because of a mental illness." He paused and then chuckled self-consciously. "Although, there might be a few people who would question that last one. And technically I'm not homeless, or the victim of a crime. I guess you could say I'm here as a result of some rather unusual circumstances, some of which I hate to admit are my own fault."

"There are exceptions of course, but most of us on the streets are here because of the choices we've made," the ex-Marine admitted. "I know I'm here because of some bad decisions I made in the past, decisions that cost me my marriage, my family, and my career." He squinted across the table at Pete. "But you strike me as someone who doesn't belong here. What kind o' work did you do?"

The man's question using the past tense jolted Pete, just as Tom Barrett's had on the ride to Fresno. He fumbled for a response. "I, um . . . I'm a . . . I was a pastor."

The former geologist arched his brow. "You were a minister? I'da never guessed, not in a million years." He broke into a sheepish grin, revealing a couple of missing teeth. "Guess I'm guilty of judgin' *you* from the outside, too." Staring intently at Pete, he asked bluntly, "So, what happened that caused you to end up here?"

Conflicted, Pete hesitated. The events of the past few weeks had not only made him wary of personal inquiries but had revealed his growing paranoia about strangers. He didn't know anything about this man. There was great risk in saying too much. However, his longing for some kind of connection and relationship got the better of him. "Well, you might say, uh . . . my preaching put me at odds with the state."

"You mean you ran afoul of the hate speech law," the old man replied candidly.

Pete startled visibly, then leaned forward. "How did you know about that?" he asked, with a slight tremor in his voice.

"Even the homeless read the Times," the man replied matter-of-factly. "Haven't you heard? The state is offerin' between five hundred and a thousand dollars to anyone turnin' in a violator. They even went around passin' out fliers a few months ago. All the street people know about it. That's how some of 'em make a living. Two women actually got into a fight tryin' to claim the same reward. One of 'em ended up in the hospital. And there's a guy over on East 5th Street who's pulled in over fifteen hundred bucks just for huntin' down and reporting violators. That kind of money goes a mighty long way on the streets, my friend!"

Pete sat back in shocked silence. He was stunned not only to learn that the state would go so far as to put a bounty on the heads of people like him, but that he had so foolishly offered his personal information to a total stranger.

The old man must have sensed his inner angst. "Hey, you don't have to worry about me, pal. I'm no rat!" He leaned toward Pete. "Although, a thousand bucks is a big chunk o' change in anybody's book. That would set me up for a long, long time. But I've got my principles, ya know? Besides, I'm a firm believer in the first amendment. And I don't agree with a lot of what the government is doin' these days. I served my country to protect our freedoms, not so they could be taken away."

The man sounded sincere, but that did not alleviate Pete's fears. A thousand dollars was a huge temptation for anyone, even someone with principles. He recalled a saying by an old southern preacher: *The test of your character is what it takes to stop you.* He had no idea what kind of character this man possessed, let alone what it might take to stop him from yielding to the temptation of cashing in on such a windfall.

"I hear you, sir. That's why I served my country, too," Pete responded, hoping their mutual military experience might somehow bond them together in a way that would dissuade the ex-Marine from pursuing a chance for a big payoff at his expense. He extended a hand toward the man sitting opposite him. "My name is Pete, by the way. What's yours?"

The old man shook his hand. "Just call me Bing."

"Bing? As in . . . Bing Crosby?

The man chuckled. "Nope. Bing as in 'cherry'. My given name is Bryan Cherry, but I've been called Bing ever since I was a kid."

"Okay, Bing. It's nice to meet you," Pete said, getting to his feet. "I'm sure I'll be seeing you around. Especially since this is, like you said, the only place to get a free meal around here."

"If it's chow time, you'll find me here. But let me give you a bit of friendly advice."

Pete put his hands on the table and leaned toward Bing. "What's that?"

The old man lowered his voice. "If I were you, I'd keep my troubles with the state to myself. Most people wouldn't hesitate to turn you in if they thought they stood to benefit from it. Watch your step, young man. And your back!"

"Thanks, Bing, I'll be sure to do that." Pete forced a smile. Then he threw away his trash and walked out of the mission into the fading light of the evening.

CHAPTER FOURTEEN
INNER-CITY EVANGELISTS

PETE SLEPT FITFULLY THAT NIGHT between the two rusted appliances at the rear of the weed-covered lot. He dreamed he was back in Iraq, alone and hunkered down in a dark, abandoned building, hiding from a group of heavily-armed Iraqi soldiers who were scouring the area for him in the inky blackness of night. Without warning, a blinding light flashed across his position. His heart pounded and he jerked upright and froze, his heightened senses straining to identify the source. Holding his breath, he watched as the LAPD cruiser continued down the street below him, the bright beam of its spotlight sweeping past his location. Pete slumped back onto his dirty, torn mattress and waited for his pulse to return to normal. Were they conducting their routine nightly sweeps, or were they looking specifically for him? Did the old man follow him there and then report him to the police? Would they come back in the morning to arrest him?

Realizing that sleep was impossible now, he leaned back against the washing machine and beat himself up for being foolish enough to have shared such sensitive information about himself with a total stranger. Then he pondered his next move. He best avoid any future contact with Bing, but that would mean staying away from the mission. Then where would he eat? To be on the safe side, perhaps he should relocate to a different part of Los Angeles. Surely there were additional food sources in other areas of the city. He remained lost in thought until the dead of night began to show faint signs of life.

Pete stood up and stretched his legs. Then he gathered up his meager belongings, pushed through the weeds, and squeezed through the flap in the corner of the chain link fence. After tossing a quick glance back at the shelter he'd built for himself, he headed off down the sidewalk in search of another residence. His own words, spoken defiantly when fleeing San Francisco, echoed in his head. *I'm not going to be here when they come to arrest me!* Sadly, not much had changed in the past five weeks.

Tired, hungry, and frustrated, Pete wandered the streets of East Central Los Angeles until the sun reached its zenith in the cloudless California sky. Scorching light burned into his head and face, while the blistering heat of the pavement bore through his scuffed and worn shoes, finding an unimpeded route to the soles of his feet via the holes in his socks. Too weary to formulate a plan, he searched for a shady spot where he could at least get some relief from the midday inferno. At last, he stumbled across a small park about half a city block square. Within the green space stood a dozen large oak and hickory trees, extending their broad, leafy branches like innkeepers beckoning weary travelers to seek shelter beneath their welcoming arms.

Many homeless had already claimed most of the shade, but he managed to find an unoccupied patch and threw himself down onto the sparse grass. He inhaled deeply and the accrued heat of the day began evaporating from his body. Lying on his back with his hands behind his head, he closed his eyes and envisioned Angela and the kids. How he longed to see them. He missed them as much as he had during his year-long deployment, and it seemed as though he'd already been separated from them for that length of time. His thoughts drifted to his church and the thirteen years he'd spent building up that ministry. Would he be able to return as the pastor of Diamond Heights Baptist Church, or was that opportunity lost to him now? Had he destroyed everything he'd labored for? Would he ever stand before *any* congregation again?

Pete lay paralyzed with doubts and fears. His mind flashed back to the faith crisis he'd experienced upon his return from Iraq. During that time, he'd questioned his faith, and for a brief period, the very existence of God. Yet now, although sure of his salvation, he doubted his usefulness for God. The emptiness gnawing at his soul was every bit as real as the hunger that had gnawed at his stomach three weeks ago in the wilderness. The story of Jonah came to mind. The Old Testament prophet had tried running from God, Who had miraculously captured his attention and steered him toward obedience. Although Jonah had warned the Ninevites of God's impending judgment, which led them to repent of their wickedness, he'd gone out of the city to sit in the shade of a plant to see what would become of them. God caused the plant to wither, and he nearly fainted under the hot sun, becoming so despondent that he told God, "*It is better for me to die than to live.*" And that's where the narrative of Jonah ended, with him feeling sorry for himself.

Pete folded his hands across his chest and prayed. *Lord, right now I can identify with how Jonah felt. I'm hot, hungry, and discouraged. I don't know what to do. I thought I needed time to think, but time hasn't shown me the answer. Now here I am, with no food for today, and no plans for tomorrow. Have I really blown it this time? Can You ever use me again? Please give me a sign that You aren't finished with me yet. Please!*

Gradually he became aware of voices nearby. Opening his eyes, he sat up and looked around. A number of youth were making their way through the park in pairs, talking to the homeless and handing out paper bags. He watched them for a while as they drew closer. There were ten or twelve of them, along with four adult supervisors. Eventually, a couple of young men about Drew's age approached him and introduced themselves.

"Hi, I'm Wes," one of the boys said in a friendly tone, "and this is Terence." He motioned toward his friend, who nodded and smiled. "We're part of the New Hope Community Church youth group, and we're out here today sharing good will and good news with those who might be in need."

"Yeah, we're giving out these bags of food and stuff to anybody who wants it," Terence explained, offering Pete one of the bags he was carrying.

Pete reached out and accepted the bag. "Thanks." He opened it and looked inside.

"There's a Bible in there, too," the boy named Wes added. "The food will help meet your physical needs for a few days, but the Bible tells you how Jesus Christ can meet your spiritual needs for eternity!"

Tears welled up in Pete's eyes. Ashamed, he quickly wiped them away with a dirty shirt sleeve.

Terence knelt on one knee in front of him. "Did you know that God loves you and sent His Son, Jesus, to die on the cross for your sins?" He pointed to the paperback copy in the bag. "It says in there that we all have sinned and fall short of God's glory. That's the bad news."

"It also tells us that the wages of sin is death," Wes tag-teamed, "but the free gift of God is eternal life in Christ Jesus our Lord. That's the good news!"

"Sir, do you know what you need to do to have that free gift of eternal life?" Terence asked, looking intently at him.

Pete smiled warmly and nodded. "Yes, I do. If I confess with my mouth that Jesus is Lord and believe in my heart that God raised Him from the dead, I will be saved."

The boys looked at each other, dumbfounded. Finally, Wes spoke up. "That's the very next verse we were going to share with you! Did someone in our group already talk to you?"

Pete couldn't help chuckling. "No, you're the first. Let's just say, uh . . . I've read and studied the Bible much of my life."

"Then you already know that everyone who calls on the name of the Lord will be saved!" Wes added excitedly.

"Yes, I do. In fact, I received Him as my personal Savior when I was ten years old. I placed my trust in the blood of Jesus to cleanse me from all my sin, and now I'm a child of God."

The boys' faces lit up like marquees during a power surge. "That's awesome!" they exclaimed in unison.

"Then the three of us are brothers in Christ," Wes acknowledged, also dropping to one knee.

"When were you two saved?" Pete asked.

"When I was seven," Wes replied. "I come from a Christian home where I've heard about Jesus for as long as I can remember."

"I gave my heart to God two months ago." Terence beamed. "I never went to church or knew anything about Jesus growing up." He glanced at his friend. "That is, until Wes shared the good news with me at school last year."

Pete was profoundly touched and humbled. "Well, God bless you for having the kindness and courage to share the gospel with me. You guys are doing an amazing work for the Lord. And you've not only convicted me by your boldness, but you've also encouraged me by your faithfulness. I can't thank you both enough."

"Would you mind if we introduced you to Mr. Russell?" Wes asked. "He's our youth pastor, and I'm sure he'd like to meet you."

"Sure, I'd be happy to meet him." The boys scrambled to their feet and scurried off to find their leader. Pete stood up and brushed himself off. He peeked into the bag and found a bottle of water. Unscrewing the lid, he took a long drink as he waited for them to return. A minute later the boys came back with a man who looked to be in his early thirties.

"Hi, I'm the boys' youth pastor, Ted Russell." He shook hands with Pete.

"Nice to meet you," Pete replied, conscious of his own unkempt appearance. "I'm Pete."

"Well, Pete, Wes and Terence tell me you're a fellow believer in Christ. Is that right?"

"Yes, I was born again when I was younger."

"That's wonderful! So then, you have the assurance that if you were to die tonight, you'd be with the Lord in heaven tomorrow?"

Pete grinned confidently. "Actually, I'd be in heaven *tonight*! To be absent from the body is to be present with the Lord."

Ted smiled broadly. "Amen! I'm glad to hear that." He placed a hand on Pete's shoulder. "Brother, is there anything we can pray with you about? Anything at all?"

Pete thought for a moment. "Yes, there is. I'd appreciate your prayers for wisdom. I'd rather not get into the details right now, but I could sure use His guidance to lead me back to where I need to be, in more ways than one."

"Absolutely," the youth leader responded fervently, "you can count on us to do that, Pete." He pointed to the bag in Pete's hand. "But just remember, that Bible in there is a lamp to your feet and a light to your path. It says in the gospel of John, *'when the Spirit of truth comes, He will guide you into all the truth.'* You received God's Spirit when you accepted Christ, so now you have the double-barreled promise of God's Word and God's Spirit to show you the way."

"Thank you, Ted, thank you," Pete replied softly. He turned to Wes and Terence. "And thanks again for taking the time to talk with me."

The four stood in a circle under the oak tree as Ted prayed for Pete and his request. Then, after pointing out their church flier in the bottom of the bag and inviting him to the services, the three left Pete in search of someone else in need of good will and God's good news.

Pete was thrilled to hold a Bible in his hands again, the third since losing his own in Sacramento. He spent the next several hours munching on the snacks given him by the two boys and reading from the Psalms for encouragement. Around four in the afternoon he started thinking about where to spend the night. He wandered the streets looking for a suitable place, but the longer he searched the more he missed his old shelter between the appliances. Finally, he abandoned the effort altogether and resigned to return to the vacant lot, willing to risk running into Bing or being caught by LAPD in exchange for the familiar space he'd called home the previous nine nights.

It was past seven when Pete squeezed through the corner of the chain link fence and climbed through the weeds to his beloved hovel. He was relieved to find it unoccupied. Grateful for the solitude and security it afforded, he curled up on the mattress between the washer and dryer and drifted off to sleep. For the next few days, he stayed in or around his home, reading, sleeping, or eating out of the paper bag. When its contents ran out, he decided to go back to the East Central Rescue Mission for his meals.

Pete got into the supper queue, collected his food, and then sat down at an empty picnic table. He'd just finished praying over his meal and had taken a few bites when he heard a familiar voice.

"Hey, Pete! Mind if I join you?" Without waiting for an answer, Bing sat down facing him.

"Oh, hello, Bing," Pete replied, feeling a twinge of apprehension. "Uh . . . be my guest."

The two ate silently for a while. Then Bing spoke up with a mouthful of food. "Haven't seen you around the last couple o' days. I was beginnin' to wonder if you'd decided to move on."

"I thought about it," Pete confessed, "but I had nowhere to go. It's kind of hard to relocate without money."

"Tell me about it!" Bing snorted, refilling his mouth. The two focused on their food for a few moments before the old man broke the silence. "You play checkers?"

"Checkers? Yeah, sure, I play checkers. But it's been a while."

Bing suddenly seemed excited. Rummaging deep into the plastic garbage bag he always carried with him, he pulled out a square piece of cardboard and set it on the table between them. It had been crafted into a makeshift checkerboard using a black marker to color the squares. Then he dumped the contents of a can onto the game board.

Pete picked up one of the game pieces and smiled to himself. They were lids from plastic water bottles, half of them colored red, the other half black. "You make these yourself?"

"Sure did," Bing replied proudly. "But it's hard to find anyone who wants to play." He eagerly began setting up his pieces.

"Didn't you say you were from all over?" Pete inquired, as he arranged his own pieces on the board. "How did *you* manage to move around without any money?"

"Didn't say I was broke when I moved around." Bing took a sip from his paper coffee cup. "I had jobs back then."

"Oh, my bad," Pete apologized quickly. "I assumed you were talking about when you were homeless."

"I've been homeless for only the past nine years or so. When I got back from 'Nam, I taught at the University of Arizona for twenty-two years. Then I worked as a geologist for a Nevada mining company for almost a decade. That was back when I was married, of course. Raised three girls and a boy. They're all grown now, with families of their own. I even hear I have some great-grand kids, but I've never met them. Haven't had any contact with my family for over twenty years."

"I'm sorry to hear that," Pete commiserated. "If you don't mind me asking, how'd you lose touch with them?"

Bing gazed into space before answering. "I suppose I could tell you all sorts of reasons, but I might as well be straight up with you." He sighed. "I was an alcoholic, pure and simple, although I wouldn't admit it until it was too late. Lost my job, my marriage, and my family. After that I drifted from job to job but couldn't stay sober long enough to hang on to one for very long. I finally gave up altogether and wound up here on the streets." He looked Pete squarely in the eye. "But don't go feelin' sorry for me or anything! I've got nobody to blame but myself." He turned his attention to the game. "You start."

Pete made his move. "Sounds to me like you've already taken responsibility for your mistakes," he said, hoping to encourage the old man. "A lot of people won't even do that."

Bing laughed. "You're beginnin' to sound like my old AA instructor. It took a while, but I finally owned up to it. I even kicked the habit all by myself two years ago."

"You've been sober for two years? Congratulations!" Pete reached out and shook Bing's hand. "What motivated you to stop drinking?"

Bing answered while studying the board. "I've seen too many people die of alcoholism out here on the streets, and it scared me." He made his move and then looked up. "I'm an old man, Pete, and I'm not gonna be around much longer. But I don't want to go like my friends did. I want to face death head on, sober, with both eyes wide open!" He leaned over the game board. "Your move."

Pete started to comment, but then thought better of it. In his mind's eye he pictured the two young men sharing the good news with him and heard the youth leader asking him about his soul. He moved one of his checkers. "Bing, I can tell you're being straight up with me, and I appreciate that. Can I be straight up with you, too?"

"Please do," the old man replied, grabbing a quick bite of food before returning his attention to the game.

"You say you want to face death head on. Then let me ask you a direct question. If you were to die tonight, do you know for certain where you would go?"

Bing didn't waste any time answering. "Probably straight to hell! That's what I deserve for the mess I've made of my life."

Pete nodded somberly. "I'm afraid I have to agree with you, Bing. But I need to tell you something else. The truth is *all* of us deserve to go to hell. Every last one of us."

Bing looked up from the board and squinted skeptically. "I don't know about that," he replied with a shake of his head. "I can understand someone like me goin' to hell, but what about all those people who live good lives, who live moral lives, decent lives, know what I mean? Are you sayin' that the folks who follow the golden rule, go to church, get baptized, do good deeds, and love everybody will end up in hell, too? That's pretty hard to believe, my friend."

"I wouldn't expect you to believe it just because I told you. But would you be willing to see what God says about it?" Pete reached into the paper bag he carried with him and pulled out the Bible the two boys had given him.

Bing eyed the inexpensive paperback and chuckled. "Oh, that's right, I forgot you were a preacher. Well, Preacher, I'm in a pretty good mood tonight. Go ahead with your spiel, I'll listen. But don't expect to convert me." He wagged a finger at Pete. "And don't expect me to give you any quarter when it comes to checkers, either!"

Pete laughed heartily. "Fair enough." He found Isaiah 53 and turned the Bible around. "Would you mind reading verse six for me?"

Bing leaned over the Bible and searched for the verse with a bony, dirt-caked finger. "*All we like sheep have gone astray; we have turned, every one to his own way; and the* Lord *has laid on Him the iniquity of us all.*'"

"Notice the words *'all'* and *'every one'?*" Pete flipped over to the New Testament. "Now read Romans three and verse twenty-three."

"*For all have sinned and fall short of the glory of God.*'"

"There's that word *'all'* again. God makes it clear that every one of us is a sinner." He turned back several pages. "Now read verses ten and eleven."

"*As it is written: None is righteous, no, not one; no one understands; no one seeks for God.*'"

"Did you catch the change?" Pete asked intently. "It goes from '*all are sinners*' to '*none is righteous, no, not one.*' That's God's answer to those who seem to be what we call good. That covers even the best of us. Our own goodness doesn't make us righteous enough to satisfy God's standard of perfect holiness. Do you see the huge dilemma we all face here?"

Bing's eyes narrowed. "What are you tryin' to say? That we're *all* goin' to hell?"

"Yes! Unless Someone greater than us intercedes on our behalf, we have no hope. You said you thought you were going to hell. If you believe in hell, then you must also believe in heaven."

Bing waved a dismissive hand. "When I said I was goin' to hell, I didn't necessarily mean literally. To be honest with you, I don't know *what's* on the other side of death. Maybe we're all annihilated, or cease to exist, or just . . . turn to dust. I don't know." He laughed awkwardly. "Guess I'll find out soon enough."

"The Bible says our *bodies* return to dust," Pete explained. "That's because God originally made us from the dust of the earth. But you're much more than just a body, Bing. He also gave you a *soul*. In Genesis we're told that *'God formed man from the dust of the ground and breathed life into him, and man became a living soul.'* That's what they call intelligent design. You are fearfully and wonderfully made by God Himself. That means He not only cares about you personally, but you're here for a reason and a purpose—a purpose greater than yourself."

Bing put an elbow on the table and propped up his chin with his hand. "If God created me, then why would He make it impossible for me to be good enough to go to heaven? That is, if there really is such a place."

"I could show you many passages where heaven is mentioned. But the fact is, there are many more references to hell in the Bible than heaven. Why do you think that is?"

The old man shrugged. "I don't know. Maybe He's tryin' to warn us about it."

"But why would He do that if everyone automatically goes there anyway? Or if there *is* no hell? That would be terribly cruel. The only reason God would warn us about hell is if He didn't want us to go there and if there was a way to avoid it!"

"You mean by believin' in God?"

Pete turned the Bible back around and flipped to John fourteen. "Let me read a few verses that answer that question. *'Let not your hearts be troubled. Believe in God; believe also in Me. In my Father's house are many rooms. If it were not so, would I have told you that I go to prepare a place for you? And if I go and prepare a place for you, I will come again and will take you to myself, that where I am you may be also. And you know the way to where I am going.' Thomas said to him, 'Lord, we do not know where you are going. How can we know the way?' Jesus said to him, 'I am the way, and the truth, and the life. No one comes to the Father except through me.'"*

Bing stared at him. "So you're tellin' me that Jesus is the only way to heaven? That's pretty narrow-minded, don't you think? Leaves all the other religions out in the cold."

"The Bible says the way to eternal life *is* narrow, and few find it. Did you notice the use of the phrase *'no one'* again? Not only is no one righteous, no one can come to God except through His Son, Jesus Christ. That's because Jesus came to earth to take our punishment on the cross. He atoned for our sins with His blood, something we could never do. The just One paid the debts of the unjust. You probably know John three sixteen: *'For God so loved the world, that He gave His only Son, that whoever believes in Him should not perish but have eternal life.'"*

"Yeah, I've heard that before," Bing acknowledged. "But one minute you're tellin' me that all have sinned, and none are good enough to escape hell, and the next you're tellin' me that God died for all of us. Then why aren't we all goin' to heaven instead of hell?"

"Because we must believe in Him, as the verse says. Elsewhere we're told, *'But to all who did receive Him, who believed in His name, He gave the right to become children of God.'* Did you get that? All who believe in Him and receive Him as Lord and Savior are given the right to be His children. But sadly, many reject that invitation and choose not to believe in Him."

Bing studied Pete across the table, then leaned back on the bench and crossed his arms. "Let me play devil's advocate for a minute. Nobody really knows what's on the other side of death, do they? I

230 FUGITIVE OF FAITH

mean, I know some people claim to have had near death experiences, and some even claim to have come back from the other side, but I personally don't believe those subjective accounts. There's really no way to verify them. How can you be so sure there even *is* a literal heaven or hell, or eternal life and all that? I would like to think there is, but no one can know for sure until they die."

"I disagree," Pete responded passionately. "Based on what God's Word says, you *can* know for sure before you die. The apostle John said, *'I write these things to you who believe in the name of the Son of God, that you may know that you have eternal life.'* Bing, he wrote those words to people who were still alive! The trouble is, if you wait until you die to find out, it'll be too late to do anything about it. Let me have you read one more verse, and then I promise we'll call it quits and get back to our game." He located Hebrews nine and pushed the Bible across the table again. "Read verses twenty-seven and eight."

Bing squinted at the page. *"'And just as it is appointed for man to die once, and after that comes judgment, so Christ, having been offered once to bear the sins of many, will appear a second time, not to deal with sin but to save those who are eagerly waiting for Him.'"*

"We all have an appointment with death, Bing, that's an indisputable fact. But after that comes judgment. That's when all of us will be judged, either for our sin or for our acceptance of Jesus as Lord and Savior. Your decision in this life determines your destiny in the next." Pete tapped the tabletop with his finger for emphasis. "So, you see, you *can* know for sure before you die whether you'll spend eternity in heaven with God or in hell without Him. Think of it another way. If there's no heaven or hell on the flip side of life, then you've gained nothing and lost nothing. But if there *is* a heaven and hell, if there *is* a God, if there *is* a coming judgment, and you do nothing about it, then you've gained nothing and lost *everything*! The big questions are, 'Do you believe it?' and if so, 'What are you going to do about it?'"

Bing stared pensively at the Bible in Pete's hands. "I guess I'll have to think about that for a while. But you bring up some very good points," he admitted honestly. Then the old man turned his attention back to the board and took his turn. "Your move."

CHAPTER FIFTEEN
PAWN SHOPS AND PERPS

OVER THE NEXT TWO WEEKS Pete's days came and went with pleasant regularity. Each day he ate two meals at the mission, took walks in different directions for exercise, scrounged for discarded materials with which to enhance his domicile, and read his Bible. He concluded that Bing was a man of his word and not a threat, since the old man had been given ample opportunity to turn him over to the authorities, but apparently had chosen not to. Pete eagerly anticipated their stimulating mealtime conversations in which he continued to talk to Bing about his soul. Although the ex-geologist seemed to enjoy the dialog and even asked a number of thoughtful questions, he remained noncommittal, showing more enthusiasm for the game of checkers than their frank spiritual discussions. However, on one occasion he went as far as to admit that he was leaning toward believing what the Bible said about his need for salvation but added that he was not ready to take such a "giant leap of faith" as he put it. Pete could tell that God was working in the man's heart but didn't press the matter. Knowing that salvation belongs to the Lord, he opted instead to pray daily for Bing.

Late one Friday afternoon, after enjoying his weekly luke-warm shower courtesy of the city's mobile trailer, Pete hurried toward the mission for supper. As he approached the old brick-faced building, he noticed a small group of people huddled on the sidewalk out front. They appeared to be reading something attached to the door.

"What's going on?" Pete asked, unable to get close enough to see what they were looking at.

"They gonna close their doors," a disheveled woman in tattered clothing said, turning toward him. He'd seen her several times before, pushing a rusty grocery cart around the area. "Gonna shut down on Wednesday!" Shaking her head and mumbling to herself, the women disappeared into the mission. Pete stepped forward and read the notice.

> "Due to the continuing shortage of donations and financial support, the East Central Rescue Mission will be forced to suspend all services to the community effective Wednesday July 4th. We are deeply saddened to be closing our ministry, but we hope to reopen at some point in the future should the proper funding be secured. God bless all those who have passed through our doors, and may He go with you."

Pete's heart sank. Just when he was getting into a routine. Now what was he going to do? How was he going to get money to buy food? He recalled what the man with the monogrammed shirt had told him his first day here. "Panhandle or pick pockets," he'd said.

Pete's pride had taken such a beating lately that the idea of panhandling, though once abhorrent to him, now seemed almost appealing. But he drew the line at theft. He would never compromise his convictions for something so clearly forbidden by God. If only they would hurry up and repeal that stupid hate speech law, or at least declare it unconstitutional, then he would be free to go home.

Grumbling, Pete pushed open the door and went through the food queue. He found Bing, already half done with his meal, and sat down next to him. "What do you make of that notice on the door?"

"Of all the rotten luck!" Bing muttered forcefully. "An awful lot of people depend on this place."

"What are you going to do?" Pete wondered, concerned for his new friend.

"Don't rightly know," Bing replied introspectively, as he sipped his coffee. "Guess I'll have to be movin' on like everybody else. But where? And how?" He patted his thigh. "These old legs don't take me as far as they used to. Besides, I've gotten used to hangin' around here the past couple o' years."

Pete mulled over their dilemma for a moment. "Have you ever thought about trying to reconnect with your family?" he asked. "Now that you've been sober for a while, maybe one of your children would be willing to take you in."

Bing shook his head emphatically. "Wouldn't do any good. They want nothin' to do with their old man, and I don't blame them one bit. They hate me for the way I treated their mother, and the way I ignored them for so many years."

"But that was a long time ago," Pete argued. "A lot can change over time. *You've* changed! You're not the same person you were back then, you said so yourself. Maybe they've changed, too. It's worth a try, isn't it? There comes a time when you just need to take that 'giant leap of faith' you mentioned earlier."

Bing grinned good-naturedly. "Now you're usin' my own words against me, Preacher."

"Then let me use *my* own words against you," Pete replied, returning the old man's grin. "If you make the effort and they reject you, you've neither gained nor lost anything. Everything would remain the same as it is now, just as it's been for the past twenty years. But if they *are* willing to reconcile with you and you don't make the effort to contact them, you've gained nothing and lost everything!"

Bing didn't reply. He was staring at the ceiling with a faraway look in his eyes, which glistened with moisture.

Pete put a hand on his friend's shoulder. "Listen, Bing, I don't mean to pressure you, not about your family, and certainly not about your soul. It's your decision. I just care about you making the right choice, that's all. On both accounts."

The old man wiped his eyes on the dirty sleeve of his shirt before replying. "Do you play chess as well as checkers?"

"Well, yes I do. Why do you ask?" Pete wondered, confused by the seemingly irrelevant question.

"'Cause you got me checkmated, Preacher. I'm trapped! If I agree with you that it's worth reachin' out to my kids, then I have to agree with you that it's worth reachin' out to God."

Pete answered the old man with a compassionate smile. "Bing, if you reach out to your kids, you don't know how they're going to respond. But that's not true with God. Jesus said, *'Whoever comes to me I will never cast out.'* And in the book of Romans we're told, *'Everyone who calls on the name of the Lord will be saved.'* That's not a 'What If and Maybe,' my friend, that's a 'Yes and Amen'!"

Bing hung his head. Pete held his breath and waited, praying silently. Finally, a heavy sigh escaped the ex-Marine's lips. "I'm so tired of runnin'," he admitted at last. "I'm tired of runnin' from my family." He raised his head and looked Pete squarely in the eye. "And to be perfectly honest with you, I'm tired of runnin' from God, too." A tear broke free and streaked his dirt-caked cheek. "I just . . . I just wanna go home, Preacher," he pleaded, his voice cracking with emotion, "I just wanna go home!" He sniffled and wiped his nose on his sleeve. "But I don't know how. Will you show me the way?"

When Pete awoke late Saturday morning, it was already quite warm, even in the shade of the cardboard roof that spanned the washer and dryer. He crawled out into the open, stood to his feet, and stretched his arms and legs. He used to be stiff and sore after spending the night in his makeshift home, but his body had adapted fairly quickly to sleeping on the thin mattress laid directly on the ground. He looked down toward the sidewalk in front of his weed-covered lot and watched the homeless population stirring and moving about. What were they going to do once the mission closed its doors? In the few weeks spent living among them, he'd learned that not everyone on the streets availed themselves of the free meals. Some received disability checks or public assistance of some sort. Some had part-time or low-paying jobs. One man he'd met received a rather fat pension, but for whatever reasons had chosen the carefree lifestyle of the streets. Many lived simply by their wits, scratching and clawing for their very existence, not to mention the few who, he recalled with loathing, made their living at the expense of unfortunates like himself.

Then there was Bing. He was thrilled that Bryan "Bing" Cherry, ex-Marine and family man, ex-professor and geologist, had finally surrendered his life to Jesus Christ last night. And he was grateful that by using *him* to share the gospel, God had shown that He was not yet finished with Pete Holloway, either. But he wondered what the old man was going to do next. Bing had mentioned trying to locate his oldest daughter, whose last known address was in Tucson, but even if he found her, how would he get there? She lived nearly five hundred miles away, and it didn't appear as though he had any money or income with which to buy a bus ticket. Why not? Surely a college professor who'd taught for twenty-two years would have a pension. And wouldn't a ten-year employment as a geologist generate at least a small amount of retirement benefits? Perhaps he'd taken a lump-sum payout and squandered it on alcohol or high living, maybe even gambled it away. He'd been pretty tight-lipped about the details of his past life.

Pete held a deep compassion for his friend. The old man's heart-wrenching plea that he was tired and just wanted to go home had touched him deeply, and he wished he was in a position to help him get there. For two frustrating days, he tried in vain to think of a way to get some cash. He even considered using his credit card to buy Bing a bus ticket to Tucson, but he'd determined not to use it, certain that by now the authorities were tracking his purchases.

On Tuesday morning, the day before the mission closed its doors, Pete was still contemplating how to help Bing when an epiphany struck him. He grabbed his balled-up jacket which doubled as a pillow and shook it. Unzipping a pocket, he pulled out his Seiko wristwatch, the only possession of any value he had left. Since coming to LA, he hadn't worn it in public for fear it would attract unwanted attention.

But he might be able to sell it to a jeweler, or at least hock it at a pawn shop. That would generate enough cash to buy Bing a bus ticket home, plus some. He studied the timepiece in his hand. It had been a gift from Angela on their twentieth wedding anniversary last summer. It was very precious to him, but he knew that if she were aware of his reason for parting with it, she would want him to pay it forward. That was the kind of woman she was.

Excited about the prospect of helping his new brother in Christ, Pete slipped the watch into his right front jeans pocket and pulled his faded, wide-brimmed cotton hat, a gift from Bing, low over his ears. Then he headed off in search of a buyer. He spent the better part of the morning visiting jewelry stores within a ten-block radius, but no one was interested in buying the used wristwatch. Pete could tell from the glances most sales associates gave him that they didn't believe someone so "homeless-looking" could be the rightful owner of such a fine piece of jewelry. In desperation, he located a pawn shop a few blocks away and entered the dingy establishment through the heavily-barred front door. The apron-clad proprietor was busy with a customer at the moment, so he waited at a respectable distance, observing the other people browsing the assortment of items on the shelves and walls and in the glass display cases. One was a man in his late thirties or early forties, about Pete's height and weight, wearing a dirty baseball cap and muscle shirt. Tattoos covered his arms and neck. He looked like one of the street people from the area, and Pete speculated that he was either there to get an item out of hock or to sell something he'd stolen.

When the customer at the counter turned to leave, Pete hesitated, glancing around at the others in the store. But when no one stepped forward, he dug the watch out of his pocket and approached the counter.

"Yeah, what can I do for you?" The proprietor looked him over cautiously.

"What can I get for my watch?" Pete asked, setting his Seiko on the counter between them.

The man wiped his hands on his grimy gray apron and picked up the watch. He studied it, turning it over in his hands and holding it up to the light. "Presage Automatic. Rose gold and silver. Nice timepiece," he acknowledged. "Looks fairly new. How much you pay for it?"

"It was a gift from my wife last summer," Pete replied honestly. "She paid two hundred and ninety-five dollars for it. But that was on sale."

The man cocked his head and squinted at him, as if assessing his story. "Sounds about right for this model." He took another look at the watch. "I can give you, ah . . . sixty-five bucks for it."

"Sixty-five!" Pete blurted out, reacting to the low-ball offer. "It's less than a year old. That watch is worth at least three or four times that!"

"Look, pal," the man replied impatiently, "this is a pawn shop, not a jewelry store." He handed the watch back to Pete. "If you want that much for it, take it to a retailer."

Pete grimaced, wrestling with his decision. He'd figured bus fare from LA to Tucson would be about sixty or seventy dollars, and he'd hoped to have some money left over to cover his own needs for a while. But he was out of options. And time. "Um . . . will you give a hundred for it?" he countered.

The man shook his head. "Seventy-five max. Take it or leave it. And that's the best price you'll get anywhere in Central LA."

With a reluctant sigh, Pete nodded. "All right."

"Good. Then all I need from you is some kind of ID and the money's yours," the man said, grabbing a pad of sales receipts from under the counter.

Pete hesitated. "I need ID? What kind of ID?"

"Driver's license, utility bill, something showing proof of address."

"I didn't know you had to show ID to pawn your own watch," Pete complained.

"State law, pal," the man replied flatly.

It was risky. The proprietor noticed his hesitation and motioned him closer. He glanced at the others in the room. "I gotcha, pal." He lowered his voice to a whisper. "Tell you what I'll do. You're hard up for the cash and I need the business. I'll give you fifty bucks, no paperwork, no questions asked. But you didn't hear that from me, got it?"

Pete grimaced. Fifty dollars would not even cover Bing's bus fare. Reluctantly, he pulled out his wallet and handed the man his driver's license. Five minutes later, convinced he may have just signed away his freedom, Pete walked out of the pawn shop with seventy-five dollars in his back pocket. Lost in thought, he vaguely noticed the customer in the ball cap follow him out of the building.

Pete headed down the sidewalk in the direction of the mission, where the "last supper" would begin in a couple of hours. He was eager to tell Bing that he would be going home after all. As he neared an alley in the middle of the block, someone roughly bumped into him from behind. He turned around and instantly recognized the tattooed customer from the pawn shop.

"Sorry, dude," the man muttered. Before Pete could reply, some-one else grabbed him from behind and dragged him into the alley. With his arms pinned at his sides by the crushing embrace, Pete lifted both feet and kicked at the tattooed man, knocking him to the ground. The massive arms around his chest tightened their grip, and he struggled to breath.

Unable to twist loose, he snapped his head backward, connecting with his unknown assailant's nose. The man cried out in pain and relaxed his grip. Pete wriggled free, spun on the balls of his feet, and punched the man in the face as hard as he could. The mugger staggered back, blood dripping from his nose and mouth. Before Pete could land another blow, something hard crashed against the back of his skull. Colorful flashes of light danced before his eyes and his turbid senses roiled with confusion. His arms dropped limply to his side, his body swayed, and he slumped to his knees on the crumbling pavement. A pair of rough hands shoved him to the ground, and a heavy knee planted itself in the middle of his back, pinning him down and knocking the wind out of him.

As he fought to catch his breath, he felt a hand pull his wallet from his hip pocket and the knee lift from his back. Too dazed to fight back, he sucked in a deep, painful gulp of air, hoping the attack was over. Without warning, a heavy shoe kicked him violently in the side, forcing a loud groan from his lips and doubling him up in agony on the uneven asphalt. He heard the bloodied man curse him repeatedly, and more strategically-placed blows followed in swift succession. Racked with pain, Pete felt himself slipping closer and closer toward unconsciousness with each kick.

When his senses returned, so did the pain. He lay curled up in a fetal position, eyes closed, praying that his attackers had fled. Opening one eye, he scanned the pavement from ground level and saw nothing. Cautiously he turned his head to the other side. He was alone. With great effort and pain, he rolled himself into a sitting position and gingerly explored the back of his throbbing head. Beneath the matted hair was a knot the size of a golf ball. When he pulled his fingers away, they bore traces of fresh blood. He gingerly probed his side and winced deeply, the pain informing him of the possibility of a cracked rib or two. Struggling to his feet, Pete limped to the entrance of the alley. The muscles in his legs screamed their protest with each step. He couldn't recall where all the blows had landed, but every part of his body hurt.

I'll probably be one massive bruise come morning.

It took Pete nearly an hour to cover the ten blocks back to the mission. During one rest break on a bus stop bench, he assessed the loss of his wallet. Gone were his driver's license, credit card, and cash, along with a few other club membership and retail discount cards, as well as the taxi receipt he'd hoped could be used to locate the driver who had witnessed his PTSD episode. His driver's license and other ID cards could easily be replaced, but he was upset at the theft of the credit card. There was no doubt in his mind that it was already being used by the two thugs who'd robbed him. But what could he do about it? He couldn't report the theft and mugging to the police.

He'd have to find a phone and tell the credit card company to place a hold on the account. And he'd have to somehow get word to Angela so she wouldn't worry that something had happened to him when the card suddenly quit working.

What really nauseated him was the theft of the seventy-five dollars—Bing's ticket home. He was so looking forward to giving the new believer some hope, but now that opportunity was lost, along with the extra money for himself. And so was his watch.

What a waste! An all-too-familiar cloud of discouragement began to settle over him. Pete chose to resist it. After all, he was no quitter! He bowed his head in silent prayer.

Lord, here we go again. Another trial, another difficulty, another setback. I didn't plan on this happening. But I believe that You're in—no, I know that You're in control. You are sovereign, and I claim Your promise that 'for those who love God all things work together for good.' You have a purpose in this, not only this but everything I've gone through recently. It's been a journey I never could have imagined I'd be taking. I'm still not sure what all You're doing, but please don't let me miss the lessons You're trying to teach me. My life is in Your hands. Work it all out for Your glory, Father. In Jesus' strong name, amen.

"What on God's green earth happened to you?" Bing exclaimed loudly, as Pete gingerly eased onto the bench next to him.

"What do you mean?" Pete replied, holding his side with one hand.

Bing was staring at him. "You're an absolute mess! Your shirt's ripped, your eye's swollen, your face is all scraped up, and there's blood on your collar and knuckles." He frowned. "Did you get mugged?"

Pete turned over his hands and noticed the split skin and dried blood on his right knuckles. He touched his forehead and cheek and winced. His attackers must have continued their assault after he lost consciousness. "Yeah, two men. One followed me out of a pawn shop and the other was waiting for me in an alley. Together they worked me over pretty good."

"Anything broken? Maybe you ought to get checked out at the clinic," Bing suggested.

"No, I'll be all right," Pete replied quickly. "I may have some seriously bruised ribs, but I don't think any are actually broken. And I *don't* want to go to the clinic!"

"Did they get anything?"

"Just my wallet. But it had my credit card and some cash in it."

"Sorry to hear that." Concern showed on Bing's face. "What are you gonna do?"

"I'll be fine," Pete assured him. "God will take care of me."

The old man gave him a puzzled look. "Now there's a statement I honestly don't understand. Why would God allow something bad like this to happen to you, Preacher? You're one of the good guys."

"None of us is good, remember?" Pete replied. "Only God is good, and He regularly showers His children with good gifts. But sometimes He allows bad things to happen to us, not to punish or discourage, but to teach us lessons we might not learn through His blessings alone. Besides, He's sovereign. In the long run, He works it all out for our good and His glory."

"I admire your faith, my friend." Respect tinted Bing's reply. "I'm new at this Christianity business. Guess I have a lot of catchin' up to do."

Pete smiled warmly and placed a gentle hand on Bing's shoulder. "You'll do fine. Just keep reading the Bible I gave you. God's Spirit will guide you in all the Truth. As you learn and grow, He'll give you exactly what you need."

The two ate in silence for a while, enjoying their last meal together.

"What were you doin' at the pawn shop?" Bing asked suddenly, as if the thought had just occurred to him. "Were you tryin' to get some cash to go home?"

Pete hesitated. What should he say? The truth might still be of some encouragement, even though Bing wouldn't benefit from it as originally planned. He decided to be up front. "I pawned my watch," he confessed. "With this place closing down tomorrow I figured it was time to liquidate my assets. The plan was to buy you a bus ticket to Tucson so you could try reconciling with your family." He crinkled his nose. "But apparently that's not how God intends to work that out."

Bing seemed gobsmacked. "You mean you pawned your watch just so *I* could go home?"

"Well, there would have been some money left over for me, too," Pete explained. "Not enough to get to San Francisco, but enough to last a while around here."

Bing's eyes brimmed with tears. "I . . . I really appreciate that. Nobody's ever done anything like that for me before." He dabbed at his eyes with his napkin and let out a sigh. "You're the real deal, Preacher."

"Thanks, Bing. I'm sorry things didn't work out. But without any money, how will you be able to get out of here to go visit your family? I'm worried about you."

Bing looked up at the ceiling, as if mulling something over in his mind. Then he turned to Pete. "My friend, I've been livin' on the streets for over a decade. I should be worried about *you*!" He shook his head resolutely. "But you don't need to be concerned about me. I'll make it to Tucson, trust me." With a twinkle in his eye, he shot Pete a sly grin. "Where's your faith, Preacher?"

Pete broke into laughter. "All right, Bing, you've got me there. God's going to take care of *both* of us. I don't know when I'll get back to San Fran, or what will happen when I do, but I'd sure like to stay in touch with you. Before we go our separate ways, could I give you my cell number?" He suddenly remembered his lost phone. "Or how about my address?" he added, somewhat lugubriously.

"Thank you, I appreciate that. God bless you!" Pete said with a smile, as the woman in the business suit dropped a dollar bill into his coffee can. She acknowledged his response to her generosity with a silent nod of her head before continuing down the sidewalk. Pete stared into the can and stirred its contents with his index finger. After four hours sitting on the hot pavement under the relentless burning sun, he'd managed to collect all of five dollars and sixty-eight cents. Being careful not to touch his still swollen and now black-and-blue eye socket, he wiped the sweat off his brow with the back of his hand. Then he struggled to his feet, an exercise that proved to be a painful reminder of his still-mending injuries.

Feeling a little light-headed from the heat, he sought out the shade of a four-story building around the corner from his very public panhandling position and sank down on the sidewalk with his back to the wall. The act of swallowing his pride in order to beg for assistance was nearly as painful as the knot on the back of his head. He had convinced himself that he would never get used to doing that. But what else could he do? He'd spent two days looking for some kind of work, any kind of work, that paid cash under the table without having to divulge his identity. Finding none, his hunger had driven him to take this drastic measure as a last resort. He seriously considered going home, but the eleven plus dollars he'd collected over the past two days had barely provided one decent meal a day. At this rate, it would take several months of near starvation to save up enough for a bus ticket home. There had to be a better way.

Tired, sore, and hungry, Pete got to his feet and went in search of a food mart or convenience store. A few granola bars and bottles of water would tide him over until tomorrow, when he'd begin the humiliating business of panhandling all over again. He'd walked about three blocks when he happened to glance across the street. A man passing in the other direction caught his attention. Peeking out from underneath his bright yellow and white Hawaiian shirt were massive tattoos. An electric current shot through Pete's body, and his heart began to thump ferociously in his chest. It was one of the men who'd pounded him into the pavement!

CHAPTER SIXTEEN
STREET JUSTICE AND ANGELS

PETE'S FIRST INCLINATION WAS TO yell to draw the man's attention, but then he remembered how bruised and sore he still was. He'd have no chance of catching the thug if a foot chase ensued. Wisely, he silently crossed the street in the middle of the block and began tailing him at a distance. After three blocks, the man turned and disappeared down a side street. Pete sped up as best he could and cautiously leaned around the corner. He watched the man cut diagonally across a parking lot and disappear into a small grocery store.

No doubt the dirtbag was using *his* credit card to buy food! Anger welled up within him. He couldn't let the man get away with that. Besides, this might be the only chance to get his card back.

Keeping parked cars between himself and the store entrance, Pete maneuvered closer. He had no idea what he was going to do once the man left the store. Maybe he could pretend to have a gun under his jacket and bluff his attacker into surrendering the card. Spying a waste receptacle near the corner of the store, he went over to see if there might be something inside that would make a believable "gun." As he rummaged through the trash, the desire to get even with his attacker began to grow. He tried justifying the emotion by telling

248

himself it was merely a matter of justice, not revenge. But deep down in his heart he knew better.

To his delight, he found a bag of used galvanized pipe fittings that some handyman must have tossed. He picked out a six-inch length of threaded pipe and stuck it underneath his shirt so that it looked like a gun barrel. It would have to do. With the element of surprise, the bluff just might work. Pleased with his MacGyver-like ingenuity, Pete hid around the corner of the building to await the confrontation. Ten, then fifteen minutes passed. Several customers exited the store, but not his assailant. What was he doing in there? Buying out the whole store? And he probably had his card to thank for those new clothes of his, too!

A few minutes later the man emerged from the store carrying several loaded grocery sacks and started walking toward him. As soon as he passed him, he would grab the man from behind, shove the pipe into his back, and demand he fork over his card! But to his chagrin the mugger sat down on a bench just outside the door, placed the sacks beside him, and pulled out a box of snack cakes and a carton of chocolate milk. How could he rob the man in plain view that close to the front door? He'd have to wait for a better opportunity. Pete's irritation grew as he watched the thug enjoying the food.

An LAPD cruiser entered the parking lot at a high rate of speed and screeched to a stop right in front of the bench. Pete flattened himself against the side of the building, senses on heightened alert. He heard one of the patrolmen address the man on the bench.

"Hey buddy, can we talk to you for a minute?"

"What about?" he heard the mugger say.

"Do you mind standing up?"

Pete peered cautiously around the corner. The man stood facing the two officers with a snack cake in one hand and the chocolate milk in the other.

"How'd you pay for those groceries?" the second patrolman wanted to know.

"Hey, just 'cause I look homeless don't mean you gotta target me!" the mugger complained.

"Just answer the question."

"Okay, cash. I gave the clerk cash."

"Mind showing us your receipt?"

The man hesitated. "I uh . . . tossed it in the trash on my way out."

"Sir, I'd like you to empty your pockets, please."

"What for? I didn't do nothin'. You got no right!" he protested loudly.

"Just do as he says," the first officer replied firmly. From his position around the corner, Pete watched the drama unfold.

Mumbling under his breath, the man set down his food on the bench and turned his two front pockets inside out. They were empty. "See? Nothin'. I ain't got nothin'. This is harassment, don't ya know!"

The second officer ignored the protest, and his tone grew impatient. "Turn around and hold your arms away from your body." With a grunt of dissatisfaction, the man complied. The officer patted down the hip pockets of his new-looking blue jeans, then fished a plastic card out of one of them. "What's this?" he asked, holding up the card for the man to see.

"That's my credit card," the mugger explained. "I keep it for emergencies."

"Uh-huh." The policeman studied the card before showing it to his partner, who raised his eyebrows. "Where'd you get this card?"

"I told you, I keep it for emergencies."

"So then, what's your name?" the officer asked him.

The man had to think for a second. "Pete . . . Holloway. Yeah, Pete Holloway." Hearing his name sent a shiver down Pete's back.

"*You're* Pete Holloway?" the second officer asked, eyeing the suspect with skepticism.

"Yeah, and that's my card. Why would I be carrying somebody else's?"

The two officers exchanged glances. "Well then, Mr. Holloway, would you mind turning around and placing your hands on top of your head for me? You're under arrest!"

The man scowled and vehemently voiced his objections. "You can't do this. You got no right!" The officer ignored the outburst and put him in handcuffs. "So what am I bein' arrested for?" he demanded sullenly.

"You've got two outstanding warrants, Mr. Holloway. We've been tracking your purchases on this card," the second officer replied, waving Pete's credit card in the suspect's face.

The man suddenly changed his story. "All right, all right, I'll tell ya the truth. So I ain't Pete Holloway, and that ain't my card. Somebody musta dropped it. I just saw it lyin' on the ground and I picked it up. Sure, I used it to buy this stuff, but I was gonna turn it in. I just needed somethin' to eat, that's all."

"Where's your ID?" the first officer asked.

"Musta left it at home," the man muttered under his breath.

"Then you'll have to come with us. We'll sort it out at the precinct."

Complaining about the raw deal he was getting, Pete's attacker was placed in the back seat of the cruiser and the officers drove out of the parking lot with their prisoner.

Pete stood at the corner of the grocery store in shock and disbelief. Then the irony of the situation struck him, and he burst out laughing until his side hurt too much to continue. Regaining his composure, he approached the spot of the arrest.

Now that was what he called justice! *Thank You, Lord, for fighting for me. I didn't get my card back, but at least You kept me from doing something I might have regretted.*

After stealing a peek at the contents of the two sacks still sitting on the bench, he hesitated, then glanced around to make sure no one was watching.

"Why not?" he said out loud to no one in particular. "After all, I paid for them, didn't I?" He snatched the groceries and started back to his shelter, where he planned to enjoy his unexpected bounty.

His sumptuous late-afternoon banquet finished, Pete relaxed on his mattress and watched the shadow of the adjacent overpass creep across the vacant lot. He was content with having both food and shelter. He felt a bit like the Apostle Paul, who'd experienced the extremes of wealth and want. He'd written to the Philippian believers, *"I have learned the secret of facing plenty and hunger, abundance and need. I can do all things through Him who strengthens me."* Perhaps the Lord was trying to teach him the same thing. This difficult journey of his might be one of those life lessons that couldn't be learned through blessings alone. But the more Pete thought about it, the more he realized it had nothing to do with food or shelter, or anything related to his physical needs for that matter. It was all about self-reliance versus total dependency on Christ. If he could finally grasp that, maybe then the Lord would open the door for him to return home.

Following a good night's rest, Pete awoke to a rare sight: overcast skies. They promised welcome relief from the usual burdensome July heat. He consumed a fruit pie and a bottle of water from one of the grocery sacks before turning his attention to the day ahead. By now the police would have questioned his attacker at the precinct and learned his true identity and discovered that the credit card belonged to the real Pete Holloway, who was likely still in the vicinity. Now they would focus their search on a radius around the store where his card had been used. Suddenly, he didn't feel quite as safe and secure as he had the previous evening. It was definitely time to leave the area. But how?

Pete rose and retrieved the heavy-duty black plastic trash bag he'd stashed inside the dryer, and began loading his belongings into it. Then he scrambled down the sloping, overgrown lot and squeezed through the loose chain link fence. After one final glance, he turned his back on his home and walked to the nearest LA Metro stop, wary of any black-and-white's prowling about.

It wasn't until he'd stepped aboard the first Metro bus that came along, paid the dollar seventy-five fare, and taken a seat, that he let his guard down. He had no idea which direction the bus was taking him, and he didn't care, so long as it took him far from East Central LA. He closed his eyes and did some simple math. The fare left him with just shy of four dollars in his pocket. That, along with the remaining food from his attacker's shopping spree, would hold him in good stead for almost a week.

Forty-five minutes later, a city park came into view. It was a welcome sight after all the crumbling brick facades that seemed to endlessly pass by his window. At the next stop, Pete exited the bus and walked back to the park. The trees were sparse and the lawn more dirt than grass, but it was still a nice change from the claustrophobic crush of multi-storied buildings. As in the other park where he'd met the two young evangelists, many homeless people occupied much of the space, but he found an empty bench and laid claim to it. From the contents of his bag, he selected some peanut butter crackers and a soda, and began to enjoy his lunch.

As he ate, Pete watched the others in the park. He'd always enjoyed studying people. His observations over the years had not only provided insights into basic human behavior but had confirmed what the Scriptures say about the universal human condition. A man sat reading a newspaper several benches away, ignoring those around him, and a young lady in a bright blue jogging suit was tossing a yellow tennis ball for her collie to retrieve. Several dozen homeless people occupied the remaining benches and sparse shade. A woman in her middle twenties wandered into the park with her three young children in tow. He watched as she headed straight for the nearest waste receptacle and began rummaging through the trash looking for something to eat. Her clothes were worn and the children dirty and ragged, their hair tangled and wild. The whole family appeared too thin to be healthy.

As the mother moved from receptacle to receptacle, he felt a twinge of guilt. He stopped nibbling his crackers and stared at the trash bag beside him. Inside was enough food to last him for more than a week, if he ate sparingly. It was certainly enough to feed a family of four for several days.

Lord, You've provided for me in the wilderness and here on the streets. I have more than enough, but here is a mother who doesn't seem to be able to provide even one meal for her children. Help me to show her compassion, just as You showed compassion to those who were in need. Bless this food and multiply it in a way that only You can.

He got off the bench and approached the young mother and her children. "Excuse me, but could I share what I have with you?" He held up the bag. "There's several days' worth of food in here, and I'd like for you and your children to have it."

The woman stared at him, then at the bag. "Why would you do that?" she asked suspiciously.

"God has given me more than I need, and you don't seem to have enough. Please take it," he insisted, offering her the bag. "No strings attached."

The young mother visibly relaxed and accepted his gracious gift. "Thank you, sir, thank you! I was afraid the kids were going to have to go hungry again today."

"Again?" Pete queried. "Have they gone hungry before?"

Embarrassed, the woman averted her eyes. "We usually have enough for one meal a day. But Darnell just turned five, and he's got an appetite like a teenager." Her son grinned broadly at the mention of his name. "Sometimes I give him mine just so he doesn't cry at night."

Pete's heart went out to the little family. "I wish I had more to give you, but this is all the food I have." He remembered something the two teenagers had given him. Pulling a wrinkled gospel tract from his jacket pocket, he handed it to the young mother. "I'd like you to have this, too. It tells you what God has done for you. Did you know He loves you so much that He sent His Son, Jesus, to die on the cross for your sins? It shows you how you can have forgiveness and eternal life by repenting and trusting Him. That's the biggest need each one of us has."

"Thank you," the woman replied, stuffing the tract into the bag with the food.

"That food will feed you and your kids for a few days," Pete said, looking down at the beaming five-year-old. "Well, at least for *one* day anyway," he added. The mother managed a crooked smile. "But those words will feed your soul for a lot longer than that. They're God's promises to you. They are truth and they are life."

"I'll read it tonight when the kids are asleep," the mother promised him. "Thank you so much for your kindness."

Pete started to walk away but stopped. He dug in his pocket and fished out three crumpled one-dollar bills and some change. After counting the money again, he turned and walked back to her. "I almost forgot. Please take this. It's not much, but it's all I have. Maybe you can get something for yourself."

For several days Pete wandered South Central LA, sleeping wherever he could. At one point he found a secluded spot in an alley, but due to his brutal mugging, opted for sleeping out in the open. He returned to panhandling, but in this part of the city the donations were few and far between and barely enough each day to purchase a couple of items from a fast-food restaurant's value menu. His hair, now longer than it had been in college, was a knotted mess, as was his scraggly beard. His clothes were dirty and tattered, and a couple of toes peeked timidly out the end of one of his shoes. He was losing weight again, and with each pound seemed to go some of his resolve to stay on the run.

After all, what could be gained by it? Nothing! Hadn't Mr. Murdock warned, *"There is no benefit whatsoever in remaining at large"*? The situation hadn't improved with time. In fact, it had grown worse, and there still was no satisfactory solution anywhere on the horizon. He toyed with the idea of walking into the nearest police precinct and turning himself in. But despite his despondency, what remained of his pride would not allow him to act on the thought.

I can't let this get the best of me. I'm a fighter, not a quitter!

Tired and hungry, Pete expanded his search for a more lucrative panhandling location. As he headed into a new neighborhood, he passed a rundown little storefront diner and stopped to read the single-page menu taped to the front window. The pictures made his taste buds tingle, but he had less than two dollars in his pocket. Maybe they'd let him wash dishes in exchange for a meal. It was worth a try.

He pushed open the fingerprint-smudged door and entered the dingy, one-room restaurant. Except for the young woman in a server's uniform standing behind the counter, it was empty. Apparently, she doubled as the cashier and waitress. As he approached the register, she looked up and smiled warmly. The simple gesture filled him with hope.

"Good afternoon," she said, her voice smooth and pleasant. "What will it be today, sir? Dine in or carry out?"

Pete lowered his voice, even though there was no one else in the room. "I, um . . . I have only a dollar eighty-three. What can I get with that?"

The girl, who wore a name tag with "Marissa" on it, shook her head. "I'm sorry, sir, but the least expensive item on the menu is the soup of the day. It's two dollars and seventy-five cents for the small bowl."

Pete glanced around again and cleared his throat. "There's no way I can, um . . . work for the difference, is there? I could wash dishes or mop floors. It doesn't matter to me."

Marissa sighed and shook her head again. "We already have a boy who comes in every evening to do the dishes and clean the place." She gave him the most compassionate look he'd seen since leaving home. "I'm very sorry. I wish I could help you." He could tell she really meant it.

"That's okay, thanks anyway," Pete said, turning to leave.

"Wait a minute!" the waitress/cashier called after him. He stopped at the door and walked back to her. She dropped her voice to a whisper. "Maybe I could give you a half bowl for a buck fifty. Would that be okay?"

"Sure!" Pete replied, grateful for the offer.

Marissa walked around the end of the counter. "Right this way." She led him to a small table by the window and handed him a menu.

"I won't be needing that," he replied.

"It's for Ramon's benefit," she explained, refusing to take it back. Gesturing toward the kitchen she added, "He's reluctant to serve anyone who can't pay. You know, if word ever got out on the street . . ."

Pete nodded. "I understand." He pretended to study the menu.

"Go ahead and order any single item you see on there," she said, leaning in and keeping her voice low.

Bewildered, Pete glanced up at her. "But I don't have enough money."

"That's all right. I'll cover the difference." She smiled kindly.

"Out of your own pocket?" Pete asked, his mouth agape. Then he grew resolute. "I can't let you do that, Miss. You can't be making much as it is in a place like this."

"God will take care of my needs. Besides, haven't you heard that it's more blessed to give than to receive?" She shot him a fake scowl.

"Jesus said that!" Pete exclaimed.

"Yes, I know. And He also said, 'Give, and it will be given to you.'" She placed a hand on her hip and cocked her head. "Now, are you going to rob me of my blessing, or what?"

Pete grinned self-consciously. "All right. I'd hate to be the one who got in the way of your blessing." He looked the menu over. "Could I have the small combo? Soup of the day and a half turkey sandwich?"

"Sure, good choice," she said, taking the menu from him. "And what would you like to drink with that?"

"The drink's included?"

"It is today," Marissa replied, winking at him.

"I haven't had a glass of cold milk for a long time. That would be really nice."

"One small combo and one cold milk coming right up."

Totally floored, Pete watched her walk away. If angels ever took on human form, that was what they'd look like!

About ten minutes later, Marissa brought out Pete's meal. "Can I get you a refill on that milk?" she offered.

"Well . . . yes, thank you." When she returned, he looked up at her. "May I ask you a question?"

"Sure, what's that?"

"You sound like you're familiar with the Bible. Are you a Christian?"

Marissa gave him a knowing smile. "Yes I am. I've known the Lord for two and a half years now. What about you, sir?"

"I gave my heart to Him as a boy."

"That's wonderful!" she replied, smiling warmly. "I'm Marissa, by the way."

"I know." Pete chuckled, pointing to her tag.

"No fair!" Marissa laughed. "You don't have a name badge."

"I'm Pete." Feeling the spiritual connection, and longing for human interaction, he asked if she would mind talking with him for a while. After glancing at the kitchen, she nodded and sat opposite him.

"Ramon won't mind as long as you're the only one here," she said. "But if any other customers come in, I'll have to get up."

"Understood. Who's Ramon, the cook?"

"Cook, owner, maintenance man, you name it. It's just the two of us until Julio comes in at five. Business hasn't been too good lately." She studied him for a moment. "So, what brings you in here today?"

Something about her made him want to open up. He'd been very guarded with most people he'd met, but now here was someone who could relate to him, another fellow believer, a sister in Christ. He began sharing his story, holding nothing back. The words spilled out like water over a dam.

Marissa listened intently, nodding frequently and interjecting with "I understand" or "I know what you mean." After ten minutes of non-stop unburdening, Pete paused to catch his breath. He glanced around the empty diner, then back at the waitress. "I didn't mean to unload on you, but just finding another believer willing to listen is such an encouragement."

Marissa smiled kindly. "I know how you feel. And I fully understand what you're going through, especially when it comes to being on the state's radar. The truth is, I've been brought in for questioning too, and I even got a 'cease and desist' letter after that. But it'll take more than a piece of paper to stop me! I make it a point to share the good news with *everyone* who walks into this place. That includes talking to them about the awfulness of their sin and warning them about hell if they don't put their trust in Jesus." She rolled her eyes. "Some people don't take too kindly to that kind of thing, know what I mean? I told that to a woman of a different faith one day, and I'm pretty sure she's one of the people who reported me. Another customer I tried talking to turned out to be a self-avowed atheist." She grinned sheepishly. "He ended up tossing his drink in my face and walking out on his meal!"

Pete was amazed at her courage. "How can you still be so bold when you've already been turned in and warned several times to stop? You must know the consequences if you continue violating the law."

"Of course, I do. The state made that very clear," Marissa replied firmly. "But that doesn't change anything. Do you remember the woman who washed Jesus' feet with her tears and then wiped them with her hair? It was because she was a sinner and loved Jesus so much. When He forgave her many sins, Jesus said, '*He who is forgiven little, loves little.*' You see, I was like that woman. I used to live a very sinful life. But when I came to Jesus, He forgave all my sin and made me a new person. I love Him so much now that I can't help but share the good news with everyone I meet. Nothing can stop me!"

"Aren't you afraid of what might happen?" Pete couldn't resist asking, even though he was fairly certain of her answer.

"Of course, I don't look forward to the consequences, if that's what you mean. But no, I'm not afraid. Besides, what it costs me to follow Him can't begin to compare with what it cost Him to save me."

Just then the door opened, and two people entered the diner. Marissa quickly got to her feet. "I'd really love to talk with you more, but I can't right now. Maybe you can come back again soon."

Pete smiled and nodded. He watched her head back to the counter. She was just like Jorge. He hadn't run from the consequences either. Then the same guilt that had crashed down on him at the news of his friend's arrest returned. Only this time it was accompanied by a tidal wave of shame.

CHAPTER SEVENTEEN
ROCK BOTTOM

PETE SAT AT HIS LITTLE window table so consumed by inner conflict that he abandoned his free meal. He thought of all the people God had sent to encourage him along the way: Jim Sutherland, Tom Barrett, Big Ben and Sandy, Wes and Terence, and now Marissa. And then there was Angela. His wife was faithfully praying and pleading for him, as was his church. He was grateful that God had not abandoned him. That had been confirmed when he was used to guide Bing to Christ. But he'd let them all down. Since deciding to run from the consequences of standing up for his faith, he'd tried the resistance route, and played the waiting game, but neither had improved the situation one iota. The only thing left was to return home and face whatever awaited him there. But hadn't he already come to that conclusion? Then why hadn't the Lord provided the means to do that?

Am I so thick-headed that there are more lessons I need to learn before that can happen? If You're still trying to teach me something, Lord, I wish You'd hurry up and get through to me. I want to go home!

Pete watched as Marissa came out of the kitchen carrying two plates of food. She set them down in front of the other customers.

"Can I get you anything else?" he overheard her say to the couple.

"No, I believe we're good," the man said with a polite smile.

"Before I leave then, is there something I can pray about for you? You see, Jesus Christ transformed my life, and because of that I'd love to pray for you."

The man glanced uncomfortably at the woman sitting across from him before replying. "Uh, that's thoughtful of you, but . . . I don't think so."

"Okay, just thought I'd ask. But have you heard that God loves you both so much He sent His Son, Jesus, to die in your place? If you haven't already done it, you can have eternal life simply by repenting of your sin and asking Him to be your Savior!" She smiled warmly at the pair. "I just wanted you to know that. Enjoy your meal." With that she turned and walked back to the counter.

Pete marveled at her zeal and boldness. This young believer really *was* passionate about sharing her faith. He turned his attention to the meal in front of him. Although his appetite had fled, it would appear rude or ungrateful to leave it. Picking up the sandwich, he forced himself to take a bite.

He was finishing the last of the soup when the door opened, and two uniformed LAPD officers entered and looked around. He hadn't seen the patrol car pull up in front of the building. How'd they know he was here? Had they been tailing him? Paralyzed with fear, his spoon halfway to his mouth, Pete watched as the officers approached the counter.

"Welcome to Ramon's Diner," Marissa said in her pleasant voice. "What will it be today, dine in or carry out?"

"Are you Marissa Campbell?" one of them asked, brushing aside her question.

"Um . . . yes," she replied hesitantly, glancing back and forth between them. "Is there something I can do for you officers?"

"You can come with us, ma'am," the policeman said.

Pete's spoon slipped from his hand, hit the edge of the bowl, and fell to the floor with a loud clatter. Both officers turned toward the noise. Pete hastily bent over to retrieve the spoon.

"Am I being arrested?" Marissa didn't seem surprised or upset.

"I'm afraid so, ma'am. You're under arrest for violating your probation."

"Exactly what have I done?" she asked, as the officer walked around the end of the counter holding a pair of handcuffs.

"You have a warrant for the public dissemination of hate speech via verbal and printed means, and for repeated non-compliance with the Reparation and Elimination Act. Please turn around and put your hands on your head." Pete heard Marissa sigh as she complied with the request.

"I want you to know two things," she said, as the policeman walked her out from behind the counter. "First of all, I don't hold any of this against you officers. I know you're doing your job. And second, God loves you so much He sent His Son to die on the cross for you. Through Jesus alone you can have your sins forgiven and know you are going to heaven instead of hell when you die. Do you have that assurance?"

The officers ignored the question and advised the waitress of her Miranda rights. As they led her toward the door, something snapped inside Pete. He jumped to his feet and stepped in front of the trio.

"Just a minute," he protested, holding up both palms. "You're making a big mistake! This young lady hasn't done anything wrong."

The second policeman placed a hand on his holstered sidearm and confronted Pete. "Sir, you need to step back," he said with a very firm voice. "This is no concern of yours."

"But all she's done is share her faith with people she meets. She hasn't discriminated against anybody. You just can't arrest her for

266 FUGITIVE OF FAITH

that. What happened to free speech? She's got a right to express her views!"

The officer tightened his grip on his holster and raised his voice. "Sir, if you don't step aside right now, I'm going to arrest you for interfering with an officer!"

"It's okay, Pete," Marissa intervened, "I expected this to happen any day now." She gave him a confident smile. "Don't worry about me, my life is in God's hands."

Suddenly very uncomfortable, Pete shivered. The first officer was staring intently at him. Then the man turned to his partner. "Derek, does this guy look familiar to you?" He paused reflectively. "What was the name of that renegade preacher in the bulletin we saw last month? Wasn't *his* name Pete something-or-other?"

"You mean the guy wanted in that shooting in Sacramento? Yeah, I think it was. But this guy doesn't look much like a preacher." He scrutinized the dirty, disheveled man standing between him and the door. "Mind showing me some ID, sir?" he asked, his hand still on the butt of his holstered weapon.

A bead of perspiration escaped Pete's hairline. It trickled down his cheek before disappearing into his scraggly beard. "I . . . I don't have any on me," he replied, his voice sounding strangely unfamiliar. "My wallet was stolen recently."

"I think we'd better bring him along just in case," the first officer said. "Besides, he seems pretty sympathetic with this girl's views. Could be he's wanted for the same thing."

"Yeah, we might be killing two birds with one stone!" the second policeman suggested mockingly, reaching for the set of handcuffs on his belt.

I can't let them take me! In full-on panic, Pete took a step back and pointed to Marissa. "You think I'm like *her?*" he yelled. "I'm not one of them, I just believe in our First Amendment rights, that's all. I never saw that girl before in my life!" He began flailing his arms agitatedly. "I just came in here to get something to eat, and she started cramming that religious garbage down *my* throat, too! *I* didn't ask for that Jesus stuff she's peddling!" He spat contemptuously on the floor before cursing and taking the Lord's name in vain. "*That's* what I think of her God, and people like her!"

The two officers stared in disbelief at the raving wild man in front of them. Then they looked at each other. The second officer arched one eyebrow and laughed derisively. "He doesn't *sound* much like a preacher either, does he? I've been around religious people enough to know they'd never curse their God like that." He took a step toward Pete and became conciliatory. "Hey, listen, buddy, I understand that you're upset. Tell you what, if you step aside, I'm going to let you go, okay? Just let us get this suspect out of your hair and you can go about your business. How's that sound?"

Dazed, Pete stared at the policeman before slowly backing away from the door. As the two officers guided Marissa out of the diner, she looked back at him with tears in her eyes. Her heartbroken face ripped him to shreds and burned an indelible image into his mind.

Pete stumbled out of the dimly-lit diner into the blinding light of the California sun and bumped roughly into a man walking past on the sidewalk.

"Hey, watch where you're going!" The man cursed him loudly.

Ignoring the insult, Pete broke into a dead run. All he wanted to do was get away from the restaurant as fast and as far as he could. He ran for three blocks until the pain from his bruised ribs forced him to slow down. Out of breath, he lunged into an alley and collapsed beside a dumpster. As the pain in his body slowly diminished, the pain in his soul deepened. Shocked by his own denial of his Lord and Savior, Pete broke into uncontrollable sobs. He wept bitterly until the tears stopped flowing and his strength was spent. Then, utterly exhausted, he fell into a long, fitful sleep.

When he awoke it was dark. At first, he couldn't get his bearings. *Where am I? What am I doing here?*

Then the awful truth of what he'd done came crashing down on him like a collapsing brick wall. Slouched against the dumpster, unable to grasp anything but his despicable betrayal of the One Who had given all and done all, Pete remained locked in a dark state of mind until the early hours of the morning.

Suddenly a disembodied voice jolted him out of his troubled thoughts. "Hey, Mac, you're gonna hafta move!"

Pete blinked open his eyes. Two garbage men in gray coveralls stood over him. He glanced toward the alley entrance and saw the tail end of an idling garbage truck at the curb.

"We're here for the trash," the man explained. "You gotta move."

Pete climbed unsteadily to his feet and shuffled off without a word. When he reached the street, he looked both ways, then turned and headed down the sidewalk in the same direction he'd run from the diner. After wandering aimlessly for several hours, he came across a graffiti-covered bench and sat down to rest. Leaning forward, he grabbed his aching head with both hands. He remained motionless, completely numb and unable to think or function at all. Eventually a hunger pang broke through the haze and prodded him to go in search of some nourishment. Six blocks away he came to a main thoroughfare and followed it for a few miles. But there were no fast-food establishments or convenience stores anywhere in sight. Tired and hungry, he sat down with his back against a utility pole and tried to formulate a plan.

Digging the change out of his pants pocket, Pete counted it again. One dollar and eighty-three cents. He scowled. Even if he found another diner, it wasn't enough to buy one small bowl of soup. As he stuffed the coins back into his jeans, he felt something in his jacket. Unzipping the pocket, he pulled out a wrinkled, folded paper. It was the church flier from the "good will" bag given to him by the two boys in the park. Smoothing it out on his leg, he studied it. A photo of the church, along with the address and phone number were on the front. He flipped it over. On the back was a list of ministries as well as the times of the services. Near the bottom, something caught his attention:

FREE COMMUNITY MEAL

2nd and 4th Saturday of the month

6:00 PM

Everyone welcome!

What day was today? He had no idea. The past few days were just a blur to him. Feeling a glimmer of hope, Pete got up and went looking for the answer. A few blocks away several men were loitering outside a barber shop. He approached the nearest one, who was scrolling down his smartphone screen.

"What day is this?" he asked.

The man glanced up. "Saturday," he replied curtly, before returning to his screen.

"*Which* Saturday?" Pete pressed. "What's the date today?"

"The fourteenth," the man said, not bothering to look up from his phone.

Mumbling his thanks, Pete walked away. He pulled out the flier and studied the address again. While it was good news that the free meal would be served tonight, the church was too far away to get to on foot. Besides, it was back in the direction of East Central LA. But as he reflected on his conversation with the teenagers and their youth leader, something seemed to tug at his heart, as if drawing him toward the warm fellowship their brief encounter had afforded him. Convinced that this was his only option, he went looking for the nearest bus stop. He had just enough change for the fare.

"Six-o-clock is a long way off," he mumbled out loud, "but where else can I get a complete meal for a buck seventy-five?"

It was late afternoon when Pete finally reached New Hope Community Church. After getting off the bus, he'd walked for two miles before realizing he was going east instead of west. Four long, tiring miles later he threw himself down on the front lawn in the shade of the church sign. He'd had nothing to eat or drink since the meal Marissa had provided over twenty-four hours ago, and his lips and throat were parched.

As he lay on the ground waiting for the church doors to open, he couldn't get the brave waitress out of his head. She had not let opposition stop her from sharing the gospel with those whom God brought across her path. Her courage in the face of arrest and incarceration put him to shame. And here he'd thought he was the brave one! He'd faced danger as a soldier without flinching. He'd met cancer head on and conquered it. He'd given up a lucrative career to answer the call to the ministry. He'd always thought he was the one making personal sacrifices in order to follow God. But he'd only been deceiving himself. His stubborn pride had gotten in the way, and he'd been handling this in his own strength. He hadn't been following the Lord, he'd been fleeing from Him! And now he'd gone and denied Him, too! He'd failed miserably. *It would be better for me to die than to live!*

Broken and disheartened, Pete buried his head in his arms and began to sob, not caring what passersby might think. He cried until he had no strength left to cry. Finally, he sat up, dried his tears, and leaned against the sign with a weary sigh. A few minutes later a couple of cars pulled into the parking lot, and people began unloading boxes of food. Several cast glances his way before disappearing into the building. Shortly thereafter, two men emerged and walked across the lawn toward him.

"Hello there, are you here for the community dinner?" the older of the two asked him.

Pete looked up at him. "Um, yes I am. A couple of kids from your church were handing out food and I learned about it from the brochure that was in the bag they gave me."

"Have we met before?" the younger man asked, stepping closer and squinting at him. "Of course! I met you in the park about three weeks ago. You're Pete, aren't you?"

Pete scrambled to his feet. "You've got a good memory. I remember Wes and Terence, the two boys who were with you, but I'm afraid I've forgotten your name."

"Ted Russell." He gestured toward the man wearing glasses standing beside him. "And this is Pastor Brooks, our senior pastor." Pete shook both men's hands.

"Ted told me about the conversation he had with you. He said you're a brother in Christ. That's wonderful, Pete." Pastor Brooks smiled warmly.

"Thank you," Pete replied politely.

Ted thoughtfully rubbed his chin. "Do you remember asking me to pray that God would lead you back to where you needed to be?" Pete nodded silently. "Well, I've been praying about that like I promised. How's that going for you? Has God been answering that request?"

Pete's shoulder's sagged and his eyes grew misty. "Has He ever! He's taken the last bit of wind right out of my sails."

Pastor Brooks glanced at the church members coming and going near the front door. "Listen, Pete, the meal won't start for another forty-five minutes or so." He placed a gentle hand on Pete's shoulder. "Brother, why don't we go in and sit down where you and I can talk privately for a while. I'd love to hear what God has been doing in your life lately."

Pete's voice trembled as he replied to the pastor's invitation. "Well, all right, as long as you don't mind listening to someone who has a lot to get off his chest."

"That's part of what I do," Pastor Brooks assured him. "I'm here to help any way I can."

For the next sixty minutes, Pete poured out his heart to the man sitting across the desk from him. The pastor's office, arranged much like his own, provided a measure of safety and comfort, allowing him to speak freely. He openly shared his life story, from his salvation as a boy to his denial of Christ the previous day. The pastor listened intently, nodding frequently and asking occasional questions.

Pete paused to take a drink from the bottle of water given him at the beginning of their conversation. Then he wiped his mouth and screwed the lid back on. "As you can well imagine, I've been in a very dry place lately. My soul feels completely empty and broken. But I'm convinced God had to bring me to this point in order to expose the stubborn pride and self-reliance that still exists in my heart."

Pastor Brooks took a deep breath before responding. "Pete, I'm not talking now as one pastor to another, but as one brother to another. It's obvious that God has been doing an incredible refining work in your life, perhaps not a very pleasant one, but a necessary one to be sure." He opened the burgundy-colored, leather-bound Bible in front of him. "You say you've been in a very dry place lately. Let me read to you from Psalm 107. *'Some wandered in desert wastes, finding no way to a city to dwell in; hungry and thirsty, their soul fainted within them. Then they cried to the* LORD *in their trouble, and he delivered them from their distress. He led them by a straight way till they reached a city to dwell in. Let them thank the Lord for his steadfast love, for his wondrous works to the children of man! For he satisfies the longing soul, and the hungry soul he fills with good things.'*

The pastor looked intently at him. "Pete, by your own admission you've been wandering in a desert wasteland, hungry and thirsty in your soul. But now, if you'll cry out to the Lord in your trouble, He will hear you! He promises to deliver you and lead you straight back to where you need to be. And listen to this. Further down in that passage we read, *'He turns a desert into pools of water, a parched land into springs of water.'* That should encourage you, Brother. I truly believe your days in the desert are about over. What do you think?"

"I certainly hope so," Pete replied emphatically. "I'm ready to do whatever it takes to follow the Lord's plan for me now, whatever that is and whatever it may cost me."

"Good for you. I'm glad you've reached that conclusion," Pastor Brooks said. "He's brought you to the end of yourself and your resources and pursued you to that sweet place of full surrender." He paused. "I'm reminded of the old hymn lyrics to that affect." From a lower desk drawer, the pastor pulled out a worn hymnal and flipped through the pages, finally landing at his destination. "This song was written by Annie Johnson Flint, a woman who suffered many trials throughout her life. Listen to her words:

'When we have exhausted our store of endurance,
When our strength has failed ere the day is half-done,
When we reach the end of our hoarded resources,
Our Father's full giving is only begun.'"

He looked up from the hymnal. "This songwriter experienced firsthand the truth of those words. And now, so have you. When you finally come to the end of your hoarded resources, that is where you start to realize and appreciate all God is doing in your life. In fact, His greatest giving has just begun, and His biggest blessings are still to come."

Pete nodded thoughtfully. "Yes, I see that now, and I believe it with all my heart."

"Good for you!" The pastor smiled broadly before glancing at the clock on the wall. "I think they've already begun serving the meal, and I know you're hungry. But before you get in the food line, would you mind if we prayed together?"

"Of course not," Pete replied quickly. "Um . . . if it's all right with you, I'd like to start." With a wave of his hand Pastor Brooks deferred to him. Pete leaned forward in the chair and bowed his head. He took a deep breath. "Father, I raise the white flag of surrender to You. I've been *so* blind to the condition of my own heart. I've been proud of all that I've sacrificed for You and all that I've done for You. But my stubborn pride has kept me from truly denying myself and taking up my cross. I've let fear conquer my faith instead of the other way around. I've been avoiding the cost of following You, and I've been running from You, relying on my own strength instead of Yours. I've denied You and cursed Your name! Oh dear Father, please *forgive* me!" He choked up and began sobbing quietly. Pastor Brooks remained patiently silent as Pete fought to regain his composure. "I'm broken, and at the end of myself. I humbly yield to Your authority, Lord. You're in full control now. Take and use whatever is left of me, if You can. I'm wholly Yours now . . . *all* of me this time. In Jesus' holy and wonderful name, amen."

Pete couldn't remember the last time he'd eaten such a delicious meal. It was as if his long-dormant taste buds had suddenly sprung to life. The wonderful spread reminded him of the potluck dinners in his own church's fellowship hall, as well as the culinary masterpieces Angela served at home, and he found himself longing for both. But it was not only his taste buds that seemed to have re-awakened, it was also his hope, hope that God was not done using him, and hope that he would soon be back home where he belonged.

Pete lingered as long as he could at the table, grateful for the church's generosity. As the volunteers started packing up the leftovers, the senior pastor sought him out. "Pete, I wanted to catch you before you left," he said, sitting down in the empty chair next to him. "Didn't you say you were planning to return to San Francisco just as soon as possible?"

"That's right. I'd already come to that decision a while ago, but obviously God wasn't quite finished working on me yet." He laughed self-consciously. "But now I believe I'm finally ready to go home."

Pastor Brooks gazed intently at him over the tops of his glasses. "And you're fully convinced that's what God wants you to do, no matter what challenges face you when you get there?"

"Absolutely, beyond a shadow of a doubt," Pete replied with conviction.

"Then how soon can you be ready to leave?"

"How soon?" Pete looked puzzled. "I'd leave right now if I could."

The senior pastor grinned and placed a hand on Pete's shoulder. "That's what I wanted to hear. Then what are we waiting for? Let's go, Brother!"

"What do you mean?"

"I mean, if you're ready to go now, I'll drive you down to the station and see that you get on the first bus to San Francisco."

Pete stared at him as the import of Pastor Brook's statement sunk in. He choked back a sob. "I . . . I don't know what to say. I didn't know how I was going to get the money for a ticket." He grabbed the pastor's hand and squeezed it firmly. "Thank you so much. Thank you for everything you and your church have done for me!"

"You're quite welcome, Pete. I'm glad we were able to help you. But before we leave for the bus terminal, would you like a chance to freshen up, first? There's a shower down in the basement, and a couple of racks of second-hand clothing."

"You have no idea what this means to me," Pete said, his voice thick with gratitude. He rose and pushed in his chair. Then he hesitated. "Um, there *is* one more thing I'd like to ask of you before we leave, though," he added reluctantly.

"And what's that?"

"Well, um, if it isn't too much trouble . . . I mean, if you wouldn't mind . . . " Pete shot Pastor Brooks a sheepish grin. "Is there a spare Bible lying around here somewhere that I could take home with me?"

With the precious one-way ticket tucked safely in his pocket, Pete sat in the curved plastic chair watching the other travelers come and go through the bustling terminal. It was hard to believe, but in two short hours he'd be on the 11:30 bus to San Francisco. The moment he had long prayed for was almost here. He was going home at last! Glancing at the sack of leftovers on the seat next to him, he once again thanked the Lord for all those who had been sent to encourage him along the way. When the time arrived to begin boarding, he got in line with the other passengers.

His heart was beating rapidly, not from anxiety this time but from anticipation. As he handed the ticket to the driver he turned and glanced over his shoulder. Out of habit he let his gaze sweep across the concourse. There was no one there come to pull him off the bus. Smiling to himself, he stepped aboard and found a seat.

As the bus left the terminal, he stared absentmindedly at the streetlights gliding one by one past his window. It wasn't until the bus had merged onto Highway 5 North and the darkness had engulfed the transport that he allowed himself to fully relax. Settling back in his seat, he closed his eyes and purged the air from his lungs. His troubles seemed to slip further away with each passing mile, and before long they were nothing but a distant memory. His thoughts turned toward home, where in just over eight hours he would learn what was awaiting him there.

CHAPTER EIGHTEEN
RETURNING TO THE SCENE OF THE CRIME

PETE PUSHED OPEN THE REAR doors of the sanctuary and stepped into the large room. The Diamond Heights Baptist Church congregation was in the middle of a rousing chorus just before the morning sermon. He stood unnoticed for a while until the worship leader spotted him. Unable to take his eyes off the bearded stranger in the stained, wide-brimmed cotton hat, the song leader faltered and lost his place. Others in the audience followed his gaze, and the congregational singing slowly faded into hushed silence. Two ushers quickly confronted Pete and spoke briefly with him. Then they stepped aside and he began walking down the center aisle toward the platform, eliciting murmurs of shock and surprise from the worshipers. John Hillenbrand, the head deacon and interim pastor, left the platform and met him in front of the communion table. Suddenly the deacon took a step back, a look of total shock on his face. The audience gasped and several men rose to their feet, ready to intervene if necessary. Then John and Pete embraced warmly and began conversing in low tones. The people began talking animatedly among themselves until the deacon turned toward them and raised one hand in the air. The crowd fell silent, holding its collective breath.

"Brothers and sisters," John addressed the hushed room, placing his other hand on Pete's shoulder, "I would like for you to welcome home our beloved shepherd and friend, Pastor Pete!"

The room erupted with cries of shock and surprise. Above the din, a female voice cried out "Pete!" Climbing over several people, Angela rushed down the side aisle toward him, followed closely by a twelve-year-old girl in a ponytail. The spouses met in a head-on embrace. While the family was getting reacquainted, John stepped to one side and conferred with several other church leaders. Then he mounted the platform and strode to the pulpit.

"Could I have your attention, please?" he began. The people took their seats and quieted down. "Thank you." He took a deep breath. "Having our pastor suddenly walk in unannounced like this is a shock to us all, but I'm nevertheless grateful that God has heard our prayers and brought him back home. As you can see, he's been through a lot since leaving us, yet he tells me that God has been doing some great things in his life. He's asked if he might address the church this morning, and I've agreed." John turned toward Pete, who was standing at the base of the steps and waved him onto the platform. As he ascended, cries of "Welcome home, Pastor Pete" and "We love you, Pastor" rose from the audience. John embraced him one more time, then motioned him into the pulpit. Pete removed his hat and slowly stepped up to the microphone. Adjusting it to suit his height, he paused to look out over his congregation. The room was as hushed as the calm before a storm, with all eyes riveted on him. He spotted several people he didn't know sitting near the back, and for a brief instant wondered what they might be here for. Then he shoved the thought aside. Clearing his throat, he took a sip from the bottle of water one of the deacons had slipped him before coming on stage. He knew what he wanted to say. After all, he'd had eight hours to prepare for this moment, and he was confident God would give him the exact words.

"I want to begin by saying how wonderful it is to be back home again! I've missed every single one of you." He made eye contact with Angela before continuing. "I must apologize for disrupting the service and interrupting your worship, but what I have to say can't wait until next Sunday. By then the opportunity may be gone. I also apologize for my appearance." He glanced down at his ill-fitting second-hand clothing and flashed a subtle smile. "This is not my typical Sunday attire, nor the way I usually groom myself before stepping into this pulpit. The truth is, I arrived back in town less than two hours ago and literally walked here directly from the bus terminal.

"For the past five weeks or so I've been living on the streets of LA. That's why I look the way I do." He held up a hand. "Please, don't feel sorry for me. My own choices led me there. Prior to that I was in Sacramento, as many of you may have heard, and several points south of there. I won't share those details with you now, but I'm sure you have many questions and I plan to answer them all soon, Lord willing. This whole ordeal began when I did something I never should have done in the first place. I signed an agreement with the state to stop preaching what they call hate speech, although you all know that what I have proclaimed from this pulpit is nothing more and nothing less than the Truth of God's Word. When I became aware that a warrant had been issued for my arrest, I made the decision to leave the area, hoping to spare my family and church from the consequences associated with being at odds with the state. While my initial intentions may have been good, I now realize how wrong that decision was. What I was actually doing was avoiding the cost of following Christ. I wasn't running *for* Him as I first thought, I was actually running *from* Him!

"Many times, during this separation from my wife and children, and from you my church family, I've attempted to justify my actions, which only led to sinking deeper into the pit I'd dug for myself. But I'm reminded of the words of Betsie ten Boom who, while in a Nazi concentration camp with her sister, Corrie, uttered this truth: 'There is no pit so deep that God's love is not deeper still.' I'm ashamed to say that I dug my own pit pretty deep. So deep in fact, that I actually . . . " Pete faltered, and he fought to regain control. After taking a deep breath, he continued. "So deep in fact, that I actually denied my Lord and Savior to avoid capture! That's right, *me*, a Christian for over thirty-six years, a seminary graduate, and your pastor for the past thirteen years. I never would have believed that I could ever sink so low. But then, I didn't see what was really in my heart. Not until I reached the bottom of that pit, did I see the stubborn pride rooted there. God exposed the selfishness and self-sufficiency I didn't know existed there. But in that moment, at the bottom of that deep pit, I witnessed firsthand the depth of God's love. And let me tell you, it's true. God's love is deeper than any pit I can ever dig myself into!"

Pete paused to let the "Amens" die down. "My friends, in that moment I thought God had abandoned me. After all, I'd abandoned Him. But I discovered that I was not alone. When I cried out to Him, He reached down into my pit and pulled me out, just as He did with David, who wrote in Psalm 40, *'He drew me up from the pit of destruction, out of the miry bog, and set my feet upon a rock.'*

"On the bus last night, I couldn't sleep. I was thinking of what I was going to say here this morning if given the chance. And do you know who came to mind? Simon Peter, my namesake. Remember how he boasted that he had left all to follow Christ, and that he would never forsake the Lord? What did he do at Jesus' arrest when he was accused of being one of His followers? He denied his Lord and cursed. Dear friends, that is exactly what *I* did!" Pete's voice cracked. "And like Peter, I went out and wept bitterly. I was broken, crushed under the guilt of my betrayal. I felt sick to my stomach, totally worthless, totally useless for the Lord. But after His resurrection, what did Jesus say when He met Peter on the shore? Did He rebuke him like He did when He called Peter 'Satan', or when Peter refused to let Him wash his feet? No! He said, *'Peter, do you love Me more than these?'* And then He gave Peter this amazing command: *'Feed My sheep.'* Feed My sheep! Peter hadn't permanently blown his usefulness for the Lord. Not at all! For you see, Peter repented. And with repentance comes forgiveness, and with forgiveness comes restoration, and with restoration, usefulness. Do you realize that Peter's greatest accomplishments for the Lord came *after* his denial? It was this same Peter, now forgiven and empowered with the Holy Spirit, who preached that impassioned Pentecost sermon.

"It was this same Peter who boldly said, *'we must obey God rather than men.'* It was this same Peter whom God used to open the gospel door to the Gentiles, and whom God inspired to pen two books of the New Testament. And it was this same Peter who so boldly proclaimed the Truth that he was arrested and sent to Rome for execution."

Pete took a moment to collect his thoughts. "I think two of the saddest verses in all of Scripture are found in the book of Ezekiel and in the Gospel of Mark. In Ezekiel's day, the people of Israel had become unfaithful, turning their backs on Jehovah, Who told His prophet, *'And I sought for a man among them who should build up the wall and stand in the breach before Me for the land, that I should not destroy it, but I found none.'* Imagine, the Lord could not find even one man in the whole of Israel who was willing to stand up for Him. How tragic! And then in the garden after Jesus was arrested, we read this statement in Mark chapter fourteen and verse fifty: *'and they all forsook Him and fled.'* Not a single disciple remained faithful in that hour. Not one! Friends, I do not want to be that man, the one who refuses to stand for the Lord, the one who forsakes Him and flees. Not anymore. I've confessed and repented of my heinous sin, and He has mercifully and graciously forgiven me. I beg your forgiveness as well. I've let you down. I've failed my church, my family, and my God. But He still loves me and wants to use me. I don't know what that usefulness will look like going forward, but this much I do know: God. Is. Not. Finished. With. Me. Yet!"

Spontaneous applause broke out across the room. Pete glanced over at Angela again, who was nodding and smiling through her tears. Encouraged by her support, he continued. "I'm not going to speak much longer." He chuckled. "The truth is, I'm exhausted. But I must emphasize this point: It doesn't pay to flee from God. If you don't believe me, just take a look at Jonah. Don't run from God. Don't run from difficulties. Don't run from troubles, or trials, or persecutions. Run *to* God, and He will see you through. Noah went into the flood and he was brought through it. Daniel went into the lions' den and he was brought through it. Shadrach, Meshach, and Abednego went into the fiery furnace and they were brought through it. David went into the valley of the shadow of death, and he was delivered through it. Stephen was stoned and went into death itself, but he saw heaven opened on the other side, and he was brought safely through it. All those who have gone on before us, who have died for the Truth, faced their deaths knowing what was on the other side.

"Even Jesus, to demonstrate God's love for us, went obediently into death, willingly laying down His life. But praise God He was brought through it! He rose again victoriously, and today intercedes for us at the right hand of the Father. And soon, very soon, He is coming again in power and glory and majesty, not as the suffering Savior this time, but as the King of Kings and Lord of Lords! And every knee will bow, even those who despitefully use you and persecute you, and every tongue will confess, even those who do not obey God, and who reject Him, denying His very existence. They will all bow, and they will all confess that Jesus is Lord. And we who have overcome by the blood of the Lamb will forever sing that glorious anthem, *'Worthy is the Lamb that was slain! To Him be glory, and majesty, and power...'* Jesus said, *'In this world you will have tribulation, but fear not. I have overcome the world.'* The key is not to flee from trouble, or to fight it in our own strength, but to face it with an eternal perspective. Step out of the physical into the spiritual, then you will see the eternal, and that will make all the difference!

"Yes, we ought to obey God rather than men. Yes, we ought to earnestly contend for the faith once for all delivered to the saints. Yes, we ought to fight the good fight of faith. But we should fear God in it all, not man, for the fear of man brings a snare. John the Baptist was beheaded, Stephen stoned, James and Paul beheaded, Peter likely crucified, John exiled for life. But they all overcame. Think of the songs in our hymnbook that reflect that resolve. It's been a while since we've sung some of them, but I'm sure you recall these words: 'Stand up, stand up for Jesus, ye soldiers of the cross. Lift high his royal banner, it must not suffer loss. Stand up, stand up for Jesus, stand in his strength alone. The arm of flesh will fail you, ye dare not trust your own. Put on the gospel armor, each piece put on with prayer, where duty calls, or danger, be never wanting there.'

"Friends, my victory lies in the blood of Jesus, as does my power and my strength, my hope and my peace. Don't stop to consider the cost of following Him. It is so worthwhile. Just remember this: It will be worth it *all* when we see Jesus!"

He let his gaze sweep across the room. "Over the past several months the Lord has rather poignantly, and often painfully, reminded me that it is my responsibility to simply obey Him and proclaim His Word, and to be a faithful servant and courageous soldier for Him. That is all. The results of that, and the consequences for doing that are totally up to Him, not me. No matter what happens to me in this world, my desire is to hear Him say when we meet face to face—and we *will* meet face to face, *'Well done, good and faithful servant.'*"

Pete stepped away from the pulpit and moved toward the steps. "So, who is on the Lord's side?" he challenged his congregation. "Are you with me?"

As he walked down the steps to stand facing those he'd come to love as much as his own wife and children, he began to softly sing the old, familiar chorus: "'I have decided to follow Jesus, I have decided to follow Jesus, I have decided to follow Jesus, No turning back, no turning back!'"

At first, his solo voice echoed across the sanctuary. Then a man stood up and began singing with him. Soon others arose and joined in.

"'The world behind me, the cross before me, The world behind me, the cross before me, The world behind me, the cross before me, No turning back, no turning back!'"

By now nearly the entire congregation was on its feet. The people's voices swelled, filling the sanctuary with a cappella harmony.

"'Though none go with me, still I will follow, Though none go with me, still I will follow, Though none go with me, still I will follow, No turning back, no turning back!'"

At the conclusion of the emotionally-charged service, people flocked around Pete, sharing hugs and tears with their pastor and offering words of support and encouragement. Angela and Brienna never left his side. As the crowd began to thin out, he scanned the room and turned to his wife.

"Where's Drew? I didn't see him in the service. Is he helping with children's church today?"

Angela lowered her voice. "No, he didn't come today."

"Is he sick?"

"No, he's not sick. He just didn't want to come." There was a deep sadness in her voice.

"What's going on, Ange?"

"The longer you've been gone, the more withdrawn he's become. He won't talk to me about it, and for the last three Sundays he's even refused to come to church."

Pete stared into space. "Come to think of it, he *did* sound a little distant the last time I spoke to him on the phone. Maybe he'll be more amenable to talking with me when I get home. But first I need to ask his forgiveness . . . for a lot of things."

Angela smiled and squeezed his side with a big bear hug.

"Ow!" he recoiled, wincing painfully.

She quickly pulled away. "What's the matter, babe? Are you hurt?" Her concern was palpable.

"Just a couple of bruised ribs," he reassured her. "I'll tell you about it later."

As the people continued filing out of the sanctuary, John Hillenbrand and one of the other deacons approached him. Both had worried expressions on their faces. The head deacon leaned in and spoke furtively. "Pastor, there are two uniformed SFPD officers in the lobby. They said they'd like to speak with you."

Pete exchanged glances with his wife. Her grip tightened on his arm.

"Don't go with them, Daddy!" Brienna begged, clinging fiercely to his other arm. "Tell them to leave you alone. You haven't done anything wrong!"

Pete slipped his arms around his wife and daughter and gave them a gentle squeeze. "Don't worry, it's going to be all right. I knew this was coming. I just didn't expect it to happen so soon." He disengaged himself from them and walked up the center aisle, followed by the few still in the room. Two rather uncomfortable-looking police officers stood just inside the main entrance, surveying the people milling about.

Pete strode up to them. "I understand you're looking for me. I'm Pete Holloway."

"I'm sure you know why we're here," one of the policemen said. "I wonder if you wouldn't mind stepping outside." He glanced nervously at the crowd that had formed around them. "Let's not make this any more difficult than it has to be."

"Of course, I understand," Pete agreed. "You won't get any resistance from me or these people here." He allowed the officers to guide him out the front door and onto the stoop.

"I hate to do this," the other policeman said, removing the handcuffs from his belt, "but I have no choice. Please turn around and put your hands on your head." Pete complied. As the officer placed him into custody, he whispered in Pete's ear, "Personally, I don't agree with any of this. I'm someone who believes in free speech, too, Mr. Holloway."

Pete smiled at him. "Thanks, officer, that means a lot."

After stating the charges and reading him his rights, the two policemen led him to their patrol car parked at the curb. Pete turned and addressed his family and congregation, who had followed him out to the sidewalk.

"Please don't worry about me, I will be fine. And don't be discouraged. Whatever happens, God is in control." Angela and Brienna broke from the assembly and hugged him again. Brienna burst into tears. Pete bent over and kissed the top of her head. "It's going to be all right, pumpkin. Be courageous for me, okay?" She nodded tearfully. Then he kissed his wife and ducked into the back seat of the cruiser.

"We'll come see you as soon as they let us," Angela promised him, as the officer closed the rear door. Blowing him a kiss, she called out, "I love you, babe. Stay strong!"

With that the patrol car drove away from the church. Pete twisted around and watched his family and congregation until the cruiser turned the corner and the gathering disappeared from his sight.

Pete Holloway, pastor of Diamond Heights Baptist Church and fugitive from the law, was booked into the San Francisco County Jail at 1:15 p.m. on Sunday, July 15th. After being photographed and fingerprinted he was deloused and given a jail-issue jumpsuit. As he put it on, he couldn't help but be grateful.

It felt so good to finally be wearing clothes that were not only new but the right size again . . . even if they were orange! He used his allotted phone call to leave a message for Mr. Murdock. Then the guard led him down a long corridor and through a series of barred gates to a locked steel door. When the CO in the control room buzzed it open, the guard motioned him through.

"Can you tell me when the next meal will be served?" Pete asked politely.

The guard scowled as if he'd just been asked to help plan an escape. "Whenever they get around to it," he replied coldly.

Pete nodded silently and stepped through the doorway, involuntarily flinching when the heavy door clanged shut behind him. He surveyed his new digs. The rectangular room was fairly large, with four long rows of steel bunk beds bolted to the floor. Most of them were occupied. Ignoring the stares and glances of the other detainees, he found an empty upper bunk near the center of the room and climbed aboard, careful not to disturb the occupant of the space below him. There was no mattress, only a welded steel shelf. With a weary sigh he stretched out on his back, shielding his eyes from the florescent ceiling lights with his forearm. Between the cold, hard steel beneath him and the angry, blinding glare of the lights above him, he held out little hope of getting any sleep.

"Hey, man, what you in for?" The voice startled him. He turned and looked straight into the face of the young man who occupied the condo below him. He appeared to be in his mid-twenties.

"What you in for?" he asked again.

Pete cautiously sized him up, but there was no indication in his tone or face to suggest the question was anything other than one of curiosity. "I um . . . I'm accused of violating the hate speech law," he finally replied.

"Never heard o' that. What is it?"

Pete didn't feel like talking to anyone and prayed that the man would leave him alone. "Listen, I'm really exhausted. I haven't had any sleep for over thirty-six hours. I'll tell you about it after I get some rest, okay?"

"Whatever, man." The young man shrugged his shoulders and dropped from sight.

Pete lay on the rack for a while until the urge to use the facilities got the better of him. He leaned over the metal rail and spoke to his inquisitive neighbor. "Hey, is there a restroom in this place?"

With a toss of his head, the young man grunted, "Back there, in the corner."

"Thanks." Pete climbed down the end of the bed frame and made his way to the far corner of the room. He was greeted by a dirty, stainless steel toilet bolted to the floor, out in the open for all to see. The floor around it was wet with urine, bits of soggy toilet paper, and muddy shoe prints—or what appeared to be muddy shoe prints. A small, grimy sink was set into the wall beside it. Pete gingerly stepped closer and noticed the toilet bowl was nearly filled to the brim with more than just water.

A nauseating odor assaulted his olfactory senses and he nearly gagged. Abandoning his original intentions, he turned his back on the repugnant "restroom" and hastily retreated to the neutrality of his iron bed.

"Mr. Holloway, it's good to finally meet face to face," Walter Murdock said, shaking Pete's hand. The two sat down across the metal table from one other in the county jail's video-surveilled interview room. His lawyer clasped his hands together. "So, how are you doing?"

Pete wasn't sure how to respond to the question. "Well, I've been through quite a lot from a physical and mental standpoint, but I think I'm okay now." He grimaced. "But my guess is that's probably not true from a legal standpoint."

"I'd say that would be a fair statement," his counsel replied grimly, before rebuking Pete for not heeding his earlier warning. "But at this stage that's all water under the bridge. Nevertheless, your decision to remain at large will definitely impact what transpires from this point forward. Right now, we need to discuss your options."

"Do I even *have* any options?" Pete wondered.

"Some, although perhaps not as many as before." Mr. Murdock opened his briefcase and took out a sheath of papers. "Let me walk you through what to expect over the course of the next few weeks." He slipped on a pair of glasses as he picked up the top page. "Tomorrow you will be arraigned before the court, where you will be formally advised of the charges against you and asked to enter a plea. You will receive a copy of all charges at that time. Of course, I'll be there to guide you through the process."

"Do you know what the charges are?"

"There are several against you in San Francisco County. Initially, violating the Hate Speech Reparation and Elimination Act, as you well know. But resisting arrest has been added to that."

"But I didn't resist arrest!" Pete protested. "I simply left before the warrant could be served."

"The law allows for knowingly and willfully contributing to the *delay* of the warrant being served, and I'm afraid your decision to evade arrest and remain at large qualifies as a delay." Pete's counsel shifted in his seat. "However, those charges aren't our biggest worry at this moment. I'm more concerned with the charges in Sacramento County regarding your involvement in the police-action shooting on May nineteenth. And I expect additional charges could be forthcoming from the other jurisdictions you visited while at-large. Those we'll address later. But the fact that you have current charges pending in another jurisdiction will weigh heavily on the judge's decision whether or not to allow bail. Due to the serious nature of those charges it's entirely possible, even likely, that you will be denied bail until your extradition and second trial in Sacramento."

"So far this doesn't sound very promising," Pete bemoaned, "and we haven't even talked about possible sentences yet."

"We'll cover all that in due time," Mr. Murdock promised, "but first things first." He removed his glasses and laid them on the table beside the folder. "I'm going to advise you to plead 'not guilty' tomorrow. The arraignment is mostly a procedural formality, but how you plead will set the stage for how your case proceeds through the courts. We might not be able to get you out on bail, Mr. Holloway, but that's the least of our concerns. Right now, we need to focus on the trials. In the days ahead I'm going to need a thorough and accurate accounting of your every move and action since leaving home, but I believe we still have several viable options available to use in your defense." The barrister offered a rare smile. "There is no need to abandon hope just yet."

"Now *that's* a little more encouraging," Pete responded, feeling his spirits rise a notch.

"Will Peter Holloway please step forward," the bailiff called out in a loud voice. Pete glanced across the room at Mr. Murdock before rising from his seat among the other detainees in the back of the courtroom. He met his lawyer at the table in front of the bench. "Your Honor, the State of California versus Peter James Holloway," the bailiff announced, handing the judge a folder containing the case charges.

The Honorable Susan Crandall reviewed the papers in front of her. Then she looked at Pete over the top of her silver readers. "Mr. Holloway?"

"Yes, your Honor." Pete's heart was suddenly in his throat.

"I see here that you have been charged with violating the Hate Speech Reparations and Elimination Act. Also the Voluntary Compliance Agreement, which you signed." She continued reading. "And I see that evading arrest has been added to those two charges." She looked up at him. "Mr. Holloway, do you understand the charges as stated against you?"

"I do, your Honor."

"And how do you plead?"

Pete's voice quavered as he replied, "Not guilty."

The state's attorney stepped forward and pointed to the paper in the judge's hand. "Your Honor, due to the much more serious warrants pending in Sacramento County, and the defendant's elaborate efforts to avoid arrest, the state believes this man to be a flight risk, and therefore requests the court deny bail and remand the defendant into custody."

As Judge Crandall reviewed the other charges, Mr. Murdock quickly responded. "Your Honor, my client returned to San Francisco of his own volition. He has no criminal history other than a few minor parking tickets. He is a life-long resident of this county, an Iraqi War veteran, a Purple Heart recipient, and a college and seminary graduate. He is a family man, a pastor of a local church, and a well-respected member of this community. In addition, there are relevant extenuating circumstances accounting for his actions in Sacramento as well as his attempts to evade arrest, all of which will be presented by counsel during defense. Therefore, I respectfully request that my client be released on bail pending trial."

Judge Crandall stared at Pete while answering Mr. Murdock. "Counsel, all that may be true, but the fact remains that your upstanding client did indeed willfully and knowingly go to great lengths to avoid capture." She frowned and studied the folder again. Then she removed her readers and announced her decision. "I will concede that the alleged recent actions of your client, as specified in these charges, do not seem to be in keeping with his general character. Therefore, I will allow for the possibility of extenuating circumstances in this case. And since the defendant does not appear to be an immediate danger to the community, I will grant bail.

However, due to the serious nature of the charges pending in other jurisdictions, I'm going to set that bail at three hundred and fifty thousand dollars." She looked at her calendar. "Trial will be scheduled for . . . six months from today, February nineteenth, at ten-o-clock. That is all." With a tap of her gavel, the Honorable Susan Crandall dismissed the players in the courtroom drama and moved on to her next case.

CHAPTER NINETEEN
PAYBACKS ARE
A BLESSING

"THREE HUNDRED AND FIFTY THOUSAND dollars!" Angela blurted out in disbelief, almost dropping the receiver. "Why so high?"

Pete looked at his wide-eyed wife through the plexiglass portal and replied into his own handset. "It's because of that incident in Sacramento. Mr. Murdock was totally shocked that the judge granted bail at all, but by setting it so high, it's not much different than denying bail outright. We'd have to come up with ten percent of that if I expect to get out of here before the trial. You know we don't have that kind of money, Ange."

Angela appeared unfazed. "I know we don't, but I'm not going to leave you sitting there for six whole months. There's got to be something we can do. Our retirement savings would cover some of that, and maybe we could get a loan or take out a second mortgage for the balance."

Pete shook his head vehemently. "Listen to me, sweetheart, we can't dig ourselves into a financial hole like that. I've already lost the car, and we still have nearly two years of payments left on it. Besides, we need money for court costs and lawyer fees and whatever fines the state is going to levy against me."

"I could talk to my parents, or Uncle Tony," Angela suggested, continuing her line of thinking. "And I'm sure there are those in the church who would be more than willing to help."

"No!" Pete insisted. "I'm not going to have our relatives and our church take on a burden I've brought on myself. This is *my* problem, and I'm the one who has to take responsibility for it."

The quiet strength that Pete found so attractive in his wife manifest itself in her response. "Babe, this is not just your problem. It's *our* problem. I vowed to take you for better or worse, remember? Granted, this isn't one of our better moments, but we're in this together. I want you home. I need you home!"

A lump rose in Pete's throat. He placed a palm against the glass and Angela met it with hers. "I know, Ange, I want to be with you, too."

"Besides," she added, "after the trial you may have to spend even more time away from us."

"That's a real possibility. But if I have to do time, I'll be credited for the days I've already served in here. It adds up to the same thing. Only this way we wouldn't need to put up thirty-five-thousand dollars we don't have."

Angela made short work of her husband's argument. "Pete, you've got to think of your children. Brie is sad and misses you terribly. She really needs you now. But she's not the one I'm worried about. It's Drew. He's becoming colder and more distant every day, and I fear we're on the verge of losing him. Aren't the spiritual and emotional needs of your family more important than our finances?"

The worry on his wife's face, and the weight of her words struck conviction in Pete's heart. His shoulders sagged in surrender. "You're right, Ange. Our family comes before our finances. It always has. Tell you what, let's ask the Lord to show us what we need to do before we make a decision of this magnitude."

Angela smiled and blew him a kiss. "Now you're beginning to sound like the Pete Holloway I married!"

The next day Pete was transferred from the temporary "holding pen" to a different wing of the county jail. Here he would live among the inmates who were awaiting trial or who were already serving sentences. Before, he'd shared a room with men who'd been picked up for relatively minor offenses such as disorderly conduct, public intoxication, and petty theft. But here he would be incarcerated with more serious offenders, and he didn't relish that fact at all.

He tried to look on the bright side. At least he had a bunk with a mattress, a pillow, and a blanket. The guard led him up the open staircase and along the mezzanine to his cell. To his immense relief, his new cell mate did not appear to be threatening at all. In fact, the middle-aged man seemed just as relieved the new arrival was no more intimidating than he was. The guard informed Pete that lock down was between ten and six every night. The rest of the time, the men could congregate in the lower area, which housed metal picnic tables and a large TV on the wall or go outside to the recreation courtyard.

When the guard left, Pete got acquainted with his cell mate, and then decided to get some sleep. After spending the previous three nights on the torturous steel rack, the thin mattress was a welcome luxury, and the pillow simply heavenly. He slept most of the afternoon away, and then went out into the yard for some fresh air. At one end of the asphalt-paved area, a testosterone-charged game of basketball was in progress. Several groups of men hung out around the tables, loudly bragging and occasionally arguing, while others kept to themselves along the perimeter fence.

To avoid any unnecessary confrontation with some of the rougher-looking inmates, many of whom sported prominent gang tattoos, Pete skirted the clusters and sat down with his back against the chain link fence. He relaxed and allowed the warming rays of the sun to soak into his body. Soon his thoughts turned to his family and he began to pray for them.

Suddenly, a shadow fell across him. Squinting up into the sun, he made out the silhouette of an inmate looming over him. His heart skipped a beat. Then he heard a familiar voice.

"Pastor Pete? What are you doing here?"

Pete scrambled to his feet. "Jorge?" He grabbed his close friend and embraced him warmly. "Mi amigo, is it ever good to see you!" Holding him at arm's length, Pete looked the fellow pastor in the eye. "Are you *still* in here? I thought for sure you'd be out by now."

"What do you mean 'still'?" Jorge replied, laughing. "This is my third visit to the Riviera Maya. I even heard they were installing a revolving door at the intake center on account of me."

Pete chuckled, and then grew serious. "They've arrested you two more times? For what?"

"What do you think? The same as before. For continuing to preach the Truth and refusing to sign the Compliance Agreement."

Pete felt a familiar twinge of guilt knock on his heart's door, but he denied it access. "What penalties has the state thrown at you?"

"The first time I was arrested, they said I must complete their reeducation program as a condition of my release. The second time

I was fined two thousand dollars, but you know I do not have that kind of money. The state was willing to work out a payment plan, but before that could be arranged, I was arrested a third time for violating the hate speech law again." He rolled his eyes. "I do not know what the consequence will be this time."

Pete looked at Jorge with open admiration. "You are strong and courageous, amigo." He let out a sigh. "I used to think I was, too, but God showed me otherwise."

"It is not me who is the strong one, Pastor Pete," Jorge replied quickly, "it is my Savior! Jesus said, *'Apart from Me you can do nothing,'* and the Apostle Paul said, *'I can do all things through Him who strengthens me.'* My heart is often weak and fearful, but I am able to remain strong only because I walk in His strength."

"That goes for me, too!" Pete attested adamantly, patting his friend on the back. "'*Not by might, nor by power, but by my Spirit, says the Lord of hosts.'* Right, Jorge?"

Jorge nodded and smiled. "Right, amigo, that is the truth!" Then his face grew somber. "So, you are here for the same reason as me, then?"

"Well, yes and no. I did a foolish thing by signing the Compliance Agreement, Jorge. I thought that would get the state off my back and out of my church. However, things quickly went downhill from there." Pete shared the details of his months-long journey as a fugitive. When he finished, Jorge put a hand on his shoulder.

"We all have a different path to travel," the fellow pastor sympathized, "but praise God He brought you back to where you need to be. You have experienced much, amigo, but you have also learned much. *'And to whom much is given, much shall be required.'*" He cocked his head to one side. "What do you plan to do with the lessons you have learned?"

Pete gave his friend a wry look. "Well, it appears my immediate future, like yours, is in the hands of the state. But I plan to follow the rules as much as I can from now on."

Jorge raised an eyebrow. "Even if the rules are bad ones like the Hate Speech Reparations and Elimination Act?"

Pete noticed the gleam in his friend's eye and grinned broadly. "Okay, the *higher* rules, then. When there's a conflict, you and I are still obligated to obey God rather than men."

"I thought you were bringing Drew," Pete asked through the receiver, as he looked around the empty visitor's room. "Did he refuse to come with you?"

"Well, not exactly," Angela replied, "When I asked if he was coming, he became emotional."

"In what way? Was he angry? Belligerent?"

"No, he actually got tears in his eyes and ran back to his room and wouldn't come out." A look of pain crossed her face. "Pete, I don't know what to think. He's struggling to hold in his feelings, whatever they are. It's not healthy for him to remain bottled up like this. And I can't get him to open up to me. That's why you need to come home as soon as possible."

"I've been praying earnestly about that like we agreed," Pete replied, absentmindedly twisting the steel cord on the receiver. "I learned from Mr. Murdock yesterday that the prosecution may ask for a trial date extension in order to buy more time to gather evidence against me from the other jurisdictions I was in. So if we don't post bail now, there's no telling how long I'm going to remain here before trial. Ange, I think you should go ahead with the loan option we talked about."

His wife's face lit up. "One step ahead of you. I've already talked with the loan officer at the bank, and he's agreed to start the application process, just in case we made the decision to go that route. He said the approval shouldn't take more than five to seven business days."

"Fantastic! As soon as the money's deposited in our account you can post bail and I'll be out of here and home the same day, or the next at the latest. I can't wait, sweetheart! This blowing kisses to you through half-inch glass is getting old mighty fast."

Angela smiled warmly. "I can't wait either, babe. Oh, by the way, I heard from Maria that Jorge was arrested again."

"Yeah, so I heard."

"How'd you find out? Who told you?" Angela looked surprised.

Pete allowed himself a slight grin. "Jorge himself. We ran into each other the day I was transferred here, and he told me all about it. I tell you, he's a gift from God, Ange, just when I needed the encouragement."

"Then did he tell you what Maria and I have been up to the past month?"

"No, what?"

"After I lost contact with you and Jorge was arrested the second time, Maria and I started a petition asking the governor to either repeal the hate speech law or modify it to exempt churches from being penalized. We've collected over twelve thousand signatures so far."

"That's wonderful! Thanks, hon, I hope it makes a difference. But you know the governor's behind the law one hundred percent."

"I know, but I had to do something. I wasn't about to just sit here and do nothing while you were gone. However, you'll be pleased to know that Maria is going to present our concerns before a legislative sub-committee next week."

Pete's jaw dropped. "She's going to do *what*? Somehow, I can't picture Maria speaking before a room full of politicians. That's so out of character for her. She's one of the most timid people I know."

"I thought the same thing, so I asked her how she could be so bold. Know what she said?" Pete shook his head. "She said, *'I can do all things through Him who strengthens me.'*"

Pete pursed his lips. "I've recently heard that verse somewhere," he mused.

The guard stopped at the open cell door and looked in on Pete, who was resting in the upper bunk. "Grab your things, Holloway," he announced. "Time to go!"

Pete opened his eyes and sat up. "Go where? What's going on?"

"This is your lucky day, my man. You're gettin' outta here."

Pete scrambled out of the bunk. "I'm being released?"

"Yup. Somebody just posted your bail." Pete stood rooted to the floor—his mind awhirl. "Well, hurry up, I don't have all day," the guard added impatiently.

Pete hastily gathered the few items allowed each inmate and followed the guard along the mezzanine and down the steel staircase to the locked door of the unit. The CO unlocked the door and the two stepped through. This time, the sound of the door clanging shut behind him evoked immense relief instead of the intense trepidation he'd experienced the first time he passed through this portal going the other direction. The two walked down the long corridor toward the outtake room.

"Good luck, Mr. Holloway," the guard said, holding open the door. "Try and stay outta trouble now, you hear?" he advised with a devilish grin.

"Thanks," Pete replied, "I will." As the door closed behind him, he approached one of the teller-like windows. After he had signed the release paperwork, the clerk pressed a button and the door buzzed open. Pete stepped through into the waiting room.

"Daddy!" Brienna cried, rushing forward and throwing her arms around her father.

Pete bear-hugged his preteen daughter, lifting her off her feet and twirling her in a circle. "Pumpkin! I'm so glad to see you. I've missed you terribly." Kissing her on the cheek, he set her down and embraced his wife. Not caring if anyone witnessed their joyous reunion, he planted a very real kiss on her lips. "Sweetheart, it's so good to be able to hold you again!"

"And me you! The best part is, now you're finally coming home." She gazed lovingly into his eyes while still clinging tightly to him.

"At last," he smiled, placing an arm around both of them. "I don't think I could have stood another day without you guys." He started guiding them toward the front door and freedom. "It was definitely the right decision to get that loan, Ange. Thanks for posting bail for me."

Angela hesitated. "Um . . . Pete, we didn't need the loan after all."

Pete stopped and stared at her. "Then where did you get the money for my bail?"

"I didn't post your bail," she replied, fighting to keep a smile at bay. "I didn't have to."

He frowned. "Ange, I thought we agreed not to ask our family and friends to help with this."

"I didn't ask anyone to help," she promised, allowing the smile to slip from its moorings. "The money came from a totally unexpected source." She gently took him by the arm and pointed him toward the far end of the room. "*He* insisted on putting up your bail money."

For the first time, Pete noticed the tall, lanky man clutching a Stetson hat standing quietly near the window. The elderly gentleman was smartly dressed in a crisp, plaid shirt and khaki trousers, and sported a bolo tie and shiny new cowboy boots. His short, white hair was neatly trimmed, his clean-shaven face deeply tanned. Confused, Pete took a step toward the stranger. The old man broke into a broad grin, revealing several missing teeth.

"Betcha never thought you'd see me again, did ya Preacher?"

Pete was flabbergasted. "Bing? Bing, is that you?" He walked over to the man and stared into the eyes of his homeless friend. "What in the world are you doing here? I didn't recognize you at all! You look totally different." He glanced at his beaming wife and daughter, then back at Bing. "I don't understand," he said, shaking his head in confusion.

"Better let me explain then, Preacher," Bing said. "Back in LA, you showed great kindness to me. You not only cared enough to sell your watch so I could go visit my estranged family, you cared enough about my soul to tell me about Jesus. After we went our separate ways, I couldn't stop thinkin' about what you'd done for me. I wanted to do somethin' in return, but I had no idea where to begin. Then I remembered you said your plan was to return to San Francisco, so I decided to look you up. I lost that scrap of paper you gave me with your home phone and address, but it wasn't hard to find the information on the internet." The old man chuckled. "In fact, I think it was easier for me to locate you than it was for the police all this time!"

"That's because I'm staying in one place now," Pete replied sheepishly, pulling up his pant leg to reveal the black monitoring bracelet around his ankle. "I'm not allowed to leave the county before the trial."

"Well, anyway, I'm glad I was able to find you," the old man said. "I gave your lovely wife here a call, and that's when I learned you were bein' held in the county jail until you could raise the bail money."

"But where did you get thirty-five-thousand dollars, Bing?" Pete wondered. "You were . . . I thought you were broke."

Bing crinkled up his nose and squinted at him. "I let on I was broke! I lived like I was broke. The truth is, I had a pension waitin' for me if I ever wanted it. Two pensions, actually, just sittin' there accruing in the bank. But I didn't care about money, or anything else for that matter. I'd pretty much given up on life itself. You see, when I lost my family and my job, I just drifted from place to place before landin' on the streets of LA. I didn't much care what happened to me. I lived that way for over a decade, until you came along and introduced me to Jesus." He broke into a broad smile. "And that changed everything, Preacher!"

A lump rose in Pete's throat and he found it difficult to speak. He grabbed Bing's hand and held it in his. He fought to find the words. "Bing, I'm overjoyed that you found the Lord. And I can't begin to thank you for what you've done. This is a total shock, believe me! I only wish there were some way to pay you back for this."

Pete's surprise benefactor held up a hand in protest. "Whoa, Preacher, you can't pay back a payback! The way I look at it, we're even now. It's the least I could do. Besides, you did a greater thing for me when you led me to Jesus. Now I have a real purpose in my life . . . what's left of it, anyway." Pete started to speak but choked up. Instead, he gave the old man a warm hug. Bing accepted it awkwardly and grinned sheepishly. "But come to think of it, there *is* one small thing you can do for me, though . . . if you wouldn't mind."

"You name it, Bing, whatever you need," Pete agreed fervently.

Bing's eyes sparkled with mischief. "Please just promise me you won't jump bail, Preacher. I'd hate to think that I contributed in any way, shape, or form to your delinquency!" He glanced at Angela and winked.

Both Pete and Angela laughed heartily. "Believe me, my running days are over, my friend," Pete affirmed. "You have my word on that. From now on I face things head on, with both eyes wide open!"

"That's good to know," Bing replied. "And so will I."

"Did you ever locate your family?" Angela asked, stepping forward.

"As a matter of fact, I did," Bing said. "I made contact with my oldest daughter and her children in Tucson. It's gonna take some time, of course, but they said they're willin' to give me a chance to prove that I've changed." He gave Pete a grateful nod. "You were right after all, Preacher, about it bein' worth the effort to reach out to them. I'd like to tell you folks more about it sometime." He turned to Angela again. "But right now, don't you think you need to get this husband of yours home, Mrs. Holloway?"

"Yes, of course," Angela agreed. "But Mr. Cherry, we'd love to hear all about it and get to know you better. Perhaps you could come over for supper some night," she suggested, glancing at Pete, who nodded his approval.

Bing gave her a broad, gap-toothed smile. "I'd like that very much, Mrs. Holloway, but your husband has just been returned to you. You folks need this time to be alone as a family. Someday, perhaps. Anyway, I'm flyin' back to Tucson tomorrow." His face lit up like a child's on Christmas morning. "Guess what! I'm gonna meet two of my great grandchildren for the very first time!"

CHAPTER TWENTY
IT'S ALL MY FAULT!

PETE HOLLOWAY STOOD IN THE doorway of his home and surveyed the living room. His eyes landed on his favorite chair. Smiling to himself, he hurried over and sat down in it. Wiggling deeper into the overstuffed cushions, he let out a happy little sigh. "It still fits!" he announced to his wife.

Angela laughed lightly. "It should. You're the last person to sit in it." She walked behind the chair and began massaging her husband's shoulders.

Pete closed his eyes and let out another sigh. "Ahhh, that feels so good, Ange. You don't know how much I've missed your massages . . . among other things."

Angela laughed again and sat down across his lap with her legs dangling over one arm of the chair. She leaned her head on his shoulder and gave him a loving squeeze. "It's been too long, babe. Tomorrow will mark twelve weeks exactly since you left. Let's make sure we're never apart that long again, shall we?"

The thought of spending time in prison crossed Pete's mind, but he wisely let it pass. "Never, sweetheart! We'll face whatever comes our way together from now on, I promise."

Brienna entered the room carrying a large, round cake. "Daddy, I baked a 'Welcome Home' cake for you. We're going to have a big celebration tonight at dinner."

"Let me see that thing," Pete said eagerly. He looked at the labor of love in his daughter's hands. "Wow, that's beautiful, pumpkin. You did a great job with the decorating. Thank you so much. I can't wait to eat it." He waved her toward him. "Set that work of art down on the table and come here a minute." She obeyed and he grabbed her arm, pulling her into the chair on top of them. The chair protested loudly as the three of them laughed together.

"I don't think this chair was built to accommodate our entire family," Pete joked.

"You mean *most* of our family, don't you?" Angela corrected him.

Pete sobered quickly and gave a nod toward the stairway. "Is he still up there?"

A worried look appeared on his wife's face. "Well, I hope so. I don't know." She motioned for Brienna to get off her lap. "I'd better go see if I can get him to come down and welcome you home." She got up and started toward the doorway, but Pete stopped her.

"Ange, let me go up to him. Maybe if I talk to him in the comfort of his own room it'll be easier for him to open up about his feelings. I need to ask his forgiveness, and the sooner the better. I've waited too long as it is."

Angela slipped her arm around her daughter's waist. "Okay, we'll be down here praying for you."

Pete nodded and went upstairs to Drew's bedroom. He paused outside the closed door to gather himself. He'd gone over what needed to be said a hundred times in his mind, but now standing here, he suddenly wasn't at all sure what to say.

Father, help me! This is my son, and I need Your wisdom how to seek his forgiveness and mend our broken relationship. I'm at a loss here. I know it might take a while, but if Bing can do it, so can I. Give me the right words, Lord. Then he knocked on his son's door.

"Drew? I'm home . . . finally! May I come in?" Silence greeted him. He knocked again. "Drew? I know you're upset with me, and I don't blame you one bit, but I've really missed you, Son. Could we talk for just a minute?" He paused, listening. No sound came from the room. "Drew?" He turned the knob and opened the door.

No Drew.

After a quick glance around the room, Pete gently closed the door and went back downstairs.

"What is it?" Angela asked anxiously, noticing the tight-lipped expression on her husband's face.

"He's not in his room," Pete replied, avoiding her gaze.

"He's gone? But he was there when we left. He said he didn't want to come." She caught the sadness in her husband's eyes. "Pete, I think he's just not ready to face you yet," she offered, hoping to lift his crestfallen spirits.

Pete sank into his chair again. "I had no idea he was this angry with me, Ange. I know he was upset about our choice of schools before, but this seems much more serious. What should we do?"

"Give him time," she suggested gently. "Let him get used to you being home again. He'll come around once you've been here a few days, I'm sure of it."

"Where do you suppose he's gone off to?" Pete frowned.

"He's been spending a lot of time at Jeremy Thatcher's house lately," Brienna chimed in.

"The guard on his basketball team?" Pete asked, turning to his daughter. "I didn't know Drew and Jeremy were that close off the court."

"They're not," Brienna replied, rolling her eyes. "He's only interested in Jeremy's sister."

"I'll call around and see if he's over at any of his friends' or teammates' houses," Angela volunteered. She noted the lines on her husband's face. "Don't worry, babe, we'll find him. He'll probably come back later this evening anyway. I've never known him to miss a meal."

Drew did not come home that night. Or the next. On the third day following his disappearance, after exhausting all leads, Pete and Angela were forced to do what no parent ever wishes to do: file a missing person report on their own child. The officer who took their statements promised the department would do everything in its power to locate their son, but that did not offer much in the way of reassurance to the anxious couple.

"There must be hundreds if not thousands of missing persons in a city this size," Angela bemoaned, as they lay in bed that night, "lost children, runaways, abductees, not to mention those with dementia or mental illnesses who simply wander away from home. The police can't possibly have enough resources to adequately investigate every single case. Drew is nothing more than a statistic to them!" She began to cry softly.

Pete gathered her in his arms. "I know what you're saying, sweetheart, but Drew's got one thing going for him that's far more important than any search effort. He's a child of God, Ange. He belongs to the Lord."

"I know, and that's comforting," she replied, wiping away the tears and forcing a smile. She touched Pete's face. "But would you mind praying for his safe return once more before I turn out the light?"

Two more days passed without any word on Drew. They searched everywhere they thought their son might have gone, and Pete called the station daily to check the progress of the investigation. But there was no good news. After the last call, he slumped wearily into his recliner, well aware that statistically the chances of a runaway's safe return diminish with each passing day. Angela began massaging his neck muscles to relieve the tension.

"It's all my fault," he finally blurted out.

"What's your fault? Drew running off like this?"

"Yes. I should never have left in the first place. Even if I'd come home earlier like I should have he might not have run away. He's really upset with me for putting him and the family through this."

"You don't know that for sure," Angela replied, squeezing his shoulders until they hurt. "And you can't go beating yourself up like this. Hindsight may be twenty-twenty, but the guilt can blind you if you let it."

"I planned on asking him to forgive me for going on the run to avoid the consequences of my actions. Now I think he's gone and done the same thing to avoid me. What kind of an example am I? What kind of a father does that?"

"The very best kind," Angela said firmly, evoking a yelp out of her husband. "The kind of father who admits his weaknesses and failures, and who humbly confesses and learns from his mistakes."

She walked around the chair and sat down in his lap. "Aren't you forgetting something, Pete?"

"What's that?"

"You've got one thing going for you." She pulled his face close to hers and whispered in his ear. "*You're* a child of God, too, babe!"

The ring tone of the phone jarred Pete out of a troubled sleep. He groped the nightstand, and after locating the device sat up in bed and placed it against his ear. "Hello?"

"Mr. Holloway?"

"Yes?" he responded, not recognizing the caller's voice.

"This is Sergeant Collins with SFPD. Sorry if I woke you, but you'll be pleased to know that we've located your missing son."

Fully awake now, Pete threw back the covers and swung his feet over the edge of the bed. "You found Drew? Thank you, God!"

Angela crawled over and grabbed Pete's arm. "They found Drew? Is he all right?"

"Is he all right?" Pete relayed her question to the officer.

"He's fine, sir, just fine. One of our night shift patrols spotted him near the Glen Canyon Park Rec Center, asleep in the baseball dugout. He's here at the Ingleside Station now, if you'd like to come pick him up."

"We'll be there within half an hour." Relief flooded through Pete as he uttered the promise. "Just don't let him out of your sight."

"I don't plan to do that, Mr. Holloway," the sergeant replied with a laugh. "He'll be here waiting for you."

An hour later, Pete drove the family van into the garage and shut off the engine. Drew had been strangely detached and non-communicative on the ride home. Angela turned to her silent son in the back seat. "You must be starved, honey. Can I fix you something to eat?"

"I'm fine," Drew responded flatly. "I just wanna go to bed."

Angela turned to Pete with a look of desperation. Picking up her non-verbal cue, he put his hand on her arm. "Ange, Drew's right. It's two-thirty in the morning, and we're all tired. We can discuss this later." He gently squeezed her arm.

"All right," she acquiesced, "but in the morning I'm fixing everyone's favorite breakfast."

Pete awoke late the next morning to the smell of bacon wafting up from the kitchen. He took a quick, hot shower, dressed, and went downstairs. Angela and Brienna were already seated at the table.

"Good morning, Daddy," Brienna greeted her father with her usual morning cheerfulness.

"Good morning, pumpkin," Pete replied, giving his daughter's ponytail its usual morning yank. He took his seat and looked across the table at Angela. "Is Drew still asleep?"

"He came down while you were showering and loaded up a plate of bacon and eggs and took them and a big glass of orange juice back upstairs," she explained, her eyes reflecting the sadness in her heart. "I wasn't sure what to do so I just let him go to his room."

"That's fine," Pete agreed, "for now, anyway." He glanced at his daughter before continuing. "But we can't go on like this indefinitely, Ange. I'll give him twenty-four hours to adjust to me being home. Then I'm going to have a talk with him."

"Drew, may I come in?"

His son had remained in his room since being brought home from the precinct, emerging long enough only to use the bathroom or to grab something from the refrigerator. Pete opened the door and stepped into the room.

Drew was sitting on his bed, propped against the headboard, playing a video game on his laptop. He ignored his father's presence. Pete walked across the room to the desk and wheeled the chair over to the bed. He sat down and took a deep breath.

"Son, our family can't go on living this way, and you can't continue ignoring us as though we don't exist." Pete fought for the right words. "You and I have always had a good relationship, haven't we? We've been able to talk through almost anything, no matter how difficult the subject. But that doesn't seem to be the case lately. Would you be willing to tell me why that is, from your point of view?" He waited patiently, praying his son would break his self-imposed silence.

Drew remained tight-lipped. Pete searched for any hint of expression in his son's face but found none.

"Well then, if you're not willing to talk to me, I have some things I need to say to you. Would you at least be willing to listen to me?" Drew nodded without looking up from his game. "All right, I appreciate that. Son, since leaving home I've spent a lot of time thinking about what's happened, about my decisions, my choices, my actions. Do you recall the conversation we had after your championship game? The one where you told me I'd compromised my faith by signing the Compliance Agreement?" He paused, hoping for a reply. He got a slight nod instead. "Drew, I've been wanting to tell you that you were right all along. I never should have signed that document, especially since I never meant to abide by its terms."

Pete caught the quick glance his son threw at him. Encouraged, he continued. "I *was* afraid of losing my church, and everything I've labored so long to achieve. But none of that belongs to me, like you tried to tell me. It's all God's. And because I couldn't see that at the time, I made another wrong decision, and that was to run away from the consequences rather than to stay and face them like a man." Pete shifted uneasily in his chair. "Drew, listen to me carefully. Because of my own stubbornness and pride, I've caused a lot of hurt and heartache for a lot of people. I've been a bad example as a father and a Christian. Would you forgive me for what I've done? And for hurting you? I know you're terribly upset with me for running away like I did, and I don't blame you at all. I'm so sorry!"

Drew stared at his father before breaking his silence. "You think I've been avoiding you because I'm upset that you ran away?"

"Well, aren't you?"

Drew hesitated, wrestling with his answer. "I was at first. But not now."

"Go on, I'm listening," Pete said, encouraged that his son was communicating once again.

Drew looked away. "You wouldn't understand," he mumbled.

"Try me, son. I'm ready to face the truth, however difficult that may be. Whatever you're feeling right now, it's all because of me."

"It's not because of you," Drew countered, his voice quavering.

"Sure it is," Pete persisted. "I'm the one who hurt you. It was my decision to run. I've taken full responsibility for that. Drew, you had nothing to do with any of this. It's all my fault."

"It's *not* all your fault!" Drew exploded, the tears welling up. He quickly averted his eyes. "It's all *my* fault!"

Pete stared at his distraught son. "What do you mean?"

Drew buried his face in his hands. "None of this would've happened if it wasn't for me. I'm the reason you're in trouble!" he cried, his body beginning to shake. "It's all my fault because *I'm* the one who turned you in!"

Pete gasped loudly, as if all the oxygen had suddenly been sucked out of the room. He sat stunned in the desk chair as Drew buried his head in his pillow, sobs racking his body. In open-mouthed disbelief, Pete grabbed the back of his neck with both hands and stared unseeing at the ceiling, unable to catch a breath or a thought. His racing mind seemed to be stuck in neutral. For the longest time, the only sound in the room was Drew's muffled crying. As the air slowly returned, Pete stirred, stretching his taut body. Every joint ached as if in an advanced state of arthritis. His mind finally slipped into gear, and he rediscovered his voice.

"Son, are you saying that you're responsible for turning me in *both* times?"

Drew fought to regain control of himself. He shook his head. "No, I don't know who did that the first time," he said in a muffled voice, his face still in the pillow. "But I reported you the second time. *I'm* the reason why they issued the warrant for your arrest!"

Pete stood up and silently paced back and forth across the bedroom for a few minutes. Then he returned to the chair and drew a long breath. After slowly exhaling through pursed lips he spoke. "Why, Drew?" he asked softly.

His son drew a sleeve across his face and looked up at him through watery eyes. "I was angry that you were willing to compromise to keep your own dream alive but not mine. I stewed about that for a long time. Finally, I got so mad that I wanted to punish you for it." He turned away again, unable to face his father. "But I thought you'd only have to pay a fine, or do community service, or something minor like that. I never meant for it to go this far!" He choked up and began crying again.

Pete looked at his guilt-ridden son lying face down on the bed. In that moment his own heart broke, and he felt the ache that only a parent can feel for a hurting child. He got out of the chair and sat down on the edge of the bed and began to gently rub his son's back, just as he'd done every night when Drew was younger.

"Son, it's okay," he told him in a gentle voice, "I understand why you did what you did. I'm not upset or angry about it. I forgive you."

Drew pulled his head out of the pillow and looked at his father with red, swollen eyes. "How can you even say that? I've ruined everything!"

"You mean because you turned me in?" Pete wondered. Drew nodded. "No, you didn't ruin everything. If you hadn't reported me, someone else would have, maybe the same person who reported me in the first place. It was only a matter of time."

"I still don't deserve your forgiveness!"

Pete smiled at him. "And I don't deserve yours. But we're told to forgive one another even as God for Christ's sake has forgiven us. Neither of us deserves God's forgiveness, but He does it because of His love for His Son. Drew, no matter what you do, you will always be *my* son. Nothing can ever change that. For that reason alone, I'll always love you. I've already asked God to forgive me for failing Him, and for failing you, and your mom, and your sister, and our church family. Now I'm asking *you* to forgive me. Can you do that?"

Too overcome to speak, Drew nodded. He threw his arms around Pete and the two clung tightly to each other. As they wept together, Pete felt the pent-up emotions evaporate from his son's body. After a while, they disengaged and sat quietly on the bed, side by side.

Then they prayed together. When they were finished, Pete looked at his son and smiled. "So then, are we tight again?"

Drew looked at his father and a faint smile creased the lines on his face. "Yeah, Dad, we're tight." They fist-bumped each other. The air escaped from Drew's lungs in a long, low *whoosh* as the weight of the world lifted from his shoulders.

Pete rose and replaced the chair under the desk. "Why don't I go see if your mom has started lunch yet," he suggested as he headed for the door.

"Dad, what's going to happen to you?"

"You mean at the trial?" Pete turned around in the doorway. "I don't know for sure. After this one's over I'll have to stand trial in Sacramento, too." He smiled at Drew. "But let's not worry about that now, okay?"

"What about our church? Are you still going to be the pastor?"

Pete walked back to where Drew was sitting on the edge of the bed. "I don't know that either, son. The truth is, I'm not sure *what* the future holds." He placed a gentle hand on his son's shoulder. "But whatever it is, we'll face it together like we've always done, as a family, and as children of our heavenly Father." His smile morphed into a mischievous grin. "Hey, why don't you and I go downstairs and see if we can each snag us a piece of Brie's cake before lunch?"

322 FUGITIVE OF FAITH

"I'm glad everything's good between you and Drew again," Angela said, as she squeezed a dab of mint-flavored toothpaste onto her toothbrush.

Standing in front of his side of the double vanity, Pete attempted to talk and floss at the same time. "So am I. It's good to . . . have him back as an active . . . part of this family. I can only imagine how heavy his burden of guilt must have been." He turned his head toward her. "Ange, you should have seen how relieved he was when we forgave each other. You could almost see the weights lift off his shoulders."

"I knew he was deeply troubled about something," Angela acknowledged, "and I could tell he was carrying a heavy burden of some sort, but I just couldn't get him to talk to me about it!" Her face brightened. "Anyway, I'm thankful that now we're a whole family again." She ran her toothbrush under the stream of water.

"Yes, we have so much to be grateful for," Pete added. "Even with the uncertainty of what lies ahead, we're truly blessed. God is so good!"

After completing their nightly ritual, they climbed into bed. For several minutes they lay quiet before Pete asked, "Ange, are you at all anxious about what the future might hold for us?"

She turned her head and looked at him. "Well, I'm not thrilled with the idea of you having to go away again for a while, or that we may have to leave the ministry. But no, I'm not anxious. In fact, I have real peace about it."

"So do I!" Pete replied, propping himself up on one elbow, "and it's a peace unlike anything I've ever experienced before. In a way, it's even deeper and richer than the peace I found when I gave my life to Christ back in the fifth grade."

"Perhaps that's because you've had to go through some deep valleys and face some difficult trials throughout your Christian walk," Angela offered, "and in every one of them He's been right there with you." She smiled warmly and placed a hand on his arm. "He's never left your side, Pete. And because of that, your relationship with Him has grown deeper and stronger and closer than ever before."

"You're right, it hasn't always been an easy road. It's taken some hard twists and turns I hadn't planned on, and I never could have expected." Pete flopped back onto the bed and stared at the ceiling. "I've failed Him so many times, Ange," he admitted wistfully, "but I'm so grateful He's never failed me. From now on, I'm determined to live joyfully in His presence and walk daily in His strength, come what may!"

"You're beginning to sound a lot like King David again," she replied with a laugh. "He said, 'You make known to me the path of life; in your presence there is fullness of joy; at your right hand are pleasures forevermore.' Even with all we've been through and with all we're facing, we can live in total joy and peace knowing that God is in control and with us every step of the way."

Pete grabbed his wife's hand and held it. "Sweetheart, I'm so blessed to have such a strong, godly woman like you alongside me on this journey. But I can't understand one thing. Why would you still want this imperfect, inconsistent, and often inconsiderate husband of yours?" He gazed tenderly at the 'messenger from God' lying beside him. "Ange, how can you still love such an insignificant flea like me?"

With a twinkle in her eye Angela replied, "That's easy, babe. Because you're *my* flea!" She smiled and gave him a knowing wink before turning out the light. In the darkness she snuggled closer to him. He felt her lips brush his cheek. "And because in my book," she whispered softly in his ear, "you're still the *hottest* flea on that dog!"

The End

For more information about
David Mathews
and
Fugitive of Faith
please visit:

www.davidjmathews.com
www.facebook.com/davidmathews.author
davidmathews.author@yahoo.com
@davidmathewsau1

For more information about
AMBASSADOR INTERNATIONAL
please visit:

www.ambassador-international.com
@AmbassadorIntl
www.facebook.com/AmbassadorIntl

Thank you for reading this book. Please consider leaving us a review on your social media, favorite retailer's website, Goodreads or Bookbub, or our website.

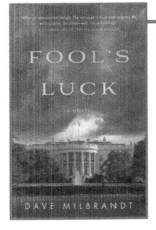

When high school teacher Myles Bradford wins the Powerball lottery, he decides to do something truly unexpected: he runs for president. Myles has to decide how much he is willing to lose in order to win . . .

Five years ago, Braelyn's daughter died. Her marriage imploded, and Forest Hill became Braelyn's sanctuary. Five years ago, Drake became lost in overwhelming grief, and he lost his heart to divorce. After serving in the army, Drake is looking for a new life, and he stumbles upon Forest Hill.

Can Braelyn find forgiveness or will she allow bitterness to ruin her sanctuary? And can Drake reclaim his heart?

Kate Sullivan will stop at nothing to find the man she holds responsible for her sister's death, and movie director Chris Johnston has information she needs. To get the answers she seeks, Kate joins his new production company, but when revenge and love collide, both Kate and Chris get more than they bargained for.